MINE

SARA FIELDS

Published by Stormy Night Publications and Design, LLC.
www.StormyNightPublications.com

Fields, Sara
Mine

Cover Design by Korey Mae Johnson

*For all of the booksluts out there who love to take it like a good
girl. Open wide. Wider.*

Good girl.

CHAPTER 1

ew Hope, Pennsylvania

Maci Williams

"I triple dog dare you."

I met Ryan's gaze and smirked in his direction. The music pumped over the speakers, and I leaned back in my chair, appraising him with a cold, defiant look. The fire crackled, each snap and pop of the burning wood loud to my ears. The flickering flames danced with a warm, amber glow, casting playful shadows on the ground as his dare hung in the air between us.

I could never turn away from a dare... *Never.*

"Do it. You won't," he pushed, and I shook my head, looking down at the very full shot glass right in front of me.

It was honey whiskey.

I wasn't usually a party girl. In fact, this was the first party I'd ever been invited to, and it was at my own house. The cool kids didn't usually like hanging out with the nerdy kids, and I was definitely one of the latter. I'd always been a straight A student in all my AP classes and the first one to volunteer for extra credit. Most of my nights, at least before our graduation, had been spent doing mountains of homework, instead of smoking weed and drinking until all hours of the night, and that definitely didn't make a girl a part of the 'in' crowd.

Right now, though, all of the smart kids were off starting their freshman year of college, and here I was, finally invited into the cool kid fold because they thought it was awesome that I already had my own place, and that I was taking a gap year. That decision had earned me somewhat of a rebel reputation, and with that came cool status.

Honestly, I wasn't really sure what it was. I was still trying to figure that out.

Tonight wasn't the time for that though.

Tonight, I was making a whole new group of friends.

I wrapped my fingers around the shot glass, threw it back like it definitely wasn't the first shot I'd ever taken, and tried my best to hide the face I made as the whiskey burned its way down the back of my throat, all the way down to the pit of my stomach.

Gross.

Why did people like this stuff?

Instead of showing just how much of a noob I was though, I smiled, swallowed back my look of disgust, and held the empty glass up like I'd just won an Olympic medal.

"Won't I though?" I grinned.

All at once, the rest of the group roared in support, which made me feel like a badass despite the horrible taste still burning my tongue.

"Fuck, Maci. I didn't think you could do it," Ryan grinned. Our eyes met for a moment, his bold and mine shy before I finally looked away.

"Give her another," Kendra barked. Her own eyes were glassy as she stared back at me. She's always been the most popular girl at school. Head of the cheerleading squad. Homecoming queen. First picked at every school dance and in every group project, except she'd gotten caught with a shit ton of weed in her locker a month before graduation and that had literally fucked up her whole life.

Turns out, her boyfriend Tucker had been dealing and he'd used her locker to store it, only the jackass let her go down for it without even saying a word. The school had expelled her, she'd gotten arrested, and her parents had made her get her GED, just so she could go to the local community college instead of some ritzy school out in California.

Honestly, I felt a little bad for her. I wasn't sure I wanted to go to college yet, but at least I still had the choice, unlike her.

"Not so straight laced then, huh?" Carmen smirked, and Ryan winked in my direction.

"Seems not," he declared, and he quickly poured me another shot of honey whiskey. I took it down like a champ, the burn still sizzling just as much on the way down as the first.

Was whiskey always this *bad*?

I shook it off with a huff and the group laughed.

"Fuck, this place is nice, Maci. No parents. No rules. Just us," Kendra murmured, and the rest of the group agreed, nods circling all around the fire.

I smiled, feeling seen for the first time in my life.

My house was out in the boonies, but it was home to me. A two-story colonial with a ton of acreage all around it gave us enough privacy to have a campfire out in the backyard without worry of being disturbed. Even if we made a ton of noise, the nearest neighbor was half a mile away, so the chances of anyone knowing we were back here drinking was slim to none.

I kind of felt like a bad girl for breaking the law. I wasn't old enough to be drinking, yet here I was.

Whatever. I'm nineteen. I'll do what I want.

"Thanks. It was my grandma's place, but it's mine now," I answered quietly, trying to not let my sorrow show and shrug it off. I must have done a good enough job because Kendra downed another shot, and everybody began egging her on to take another.

With a grateful sigh, I took the moment for myself.

I missed her.

My grandma had mainly raised me as best as she could, but she'd been diagnosed with pancreatic cancer and was gone now, so I was on my own. She'd left me her house, which gave me a nice place to live. I wasn't too worried about money because I had a job and a reasonable allowance to live off of from my godfather. It was enough to live comfortably and pay the bills, plus a little extra for some fun. I wasn't rich by any means, but I was at least taken care of.

Ryan met my gaze, his bright green eyes looking at me with a hint of open curiosity. He poured several fingers of alcohol for himself before downing it too. Playfully, he winked in my direction and my breath hitched in the back of my throat.

I'd had a crush on Ryan for as long as I could remember.

I'd known him most of my life because he lived right down the street from my grandma's house. His parents had known mine, at least before they died when I was little, and they'd always checked up on me over the years to make sure things were going okay for my grandmother and I. He'd been around more since she'd passed, which had been a nice distraction from my grief. In that time, it felt like we'd grown closer.

His smile grew as wide as the Cheshire cat's.

"What do you say, Maci? Want to blow this popsicle stand and go for a drive with me? I've got someplace special I want to show you," he offered, and the group quieted, watching us closely. I could practically feel them all holding their breath.

His emerald irises glimmered in the soft glow of my back porch lights. He ran his fingers through his shoulder length blonde hair, sweeping it to the side effortlessly, making my heart skip a beat in my chest.

I'd always thought he just saw me as some poor orphan, but in the last few months I'd started to think that was silly. Maybe, just maybe, he actually liked me too.

"Maci?" Ryan pressed.

"I'd like that," I said softly and a round of hoots and whistles sounded all around us.

"Fucking *finally*!" Kendra declared and the rest of the group stood up and actually cheered with their excitement.

I blushed as bright red as a cherry tomato.

Honestly, I'd never even been on a date with a boy before, because that's what this was right? He was taking me out for the night, just me and him. Maybe he'd even kiss me.

A first kiss would certainly round off the night and make it the best night you've ever had...

I knew I shouldn't get my hopes up or let myself get carried away. Ryan was the bad boy of the group, and he'd dated only the popular attractive girls, nothing like plain Jane red-headed me. I had a smattering of freckles on my nose and these weird, blue-green eyes, none of which met the classical standards of the pretty models plastered all over Cosmopolitan magazine, or literally anywhere else.

"Come on, Maci," Ryan urged, and I stood up from my chair. My stomach fluttered with a mix of excitement and nervousness and maybe a bit from the whiskey as he took my hand and tugged me into the front yard towards his car, a bright blue Mercedes Benz that his parents bought for him the year he turned sixteen. Like the perfect gentleman, he opened the passenger side door for me and bowed his head while I climbed inside and slid onto the soft beige leather seat.

"After you," he winked, and I giggled softly.

He closed the door behind me and strode over to the driver's side, stumbling a little along the way. Had he drunk too much already? I shook my head. That couldn't be it. Ryan could hold his liquor. He bragged about it all the time, so I shouldn't have anything to worry about.

With a nervous swallow, I smiled as he climbed in the car with me. After he turned the key in the ignition, the engine purred to life just like a kitten. With a wry grin, he backed up out of my driveway and drove off into the night towards the center of town, the soft rumble of the engine the only noise disrupting the quiet between us.

"Where are we going?" I finally asked, wanting to break the silence.

"It's a *sssurprise*," he replied, his voice light and only a tiny bit slurred. I told myself that he was fine. He had to be fine. Sure, I'd never been around him when he was drunk before, but he's always kind of looked out for me in a way no one else did, kind of like the big brother I'd never had in a way.

Maybe he pitied me because I was an orphan after all, or maybe he'd liked me all along. Either way, I didn't question it because I really didn't want to find out it was the first.

"Come on, spill the beans, Ryan. Where are we headed?" I teased, the corners of my lips curling into a playful smile despite my never-ending frayed nerves trembling in the octaves of my voice.

He chuckled, his eyes glinting with a mischievous spark. "Ah, Maci, where's the fun in knowing everything?"

I shot him a mock glare, but I broke out in a smile a second later.

He winked, his playfulness catching. "Maybe I'm feeling a bit unpredictable tonight."

"You can say that again," I quipped, and he laughed a bit harder.

"You know, that's what I like about you. You can roll with the punches and still have fun," he quipped, and I looked down at my hands in my lap, smiling to myself. I didn't really know what to say, so I stayed quiet.

Suddenly, Ryan's laughter subsided, and he muttered, "Uh-oh, looks like we're running on fumes." He gestured to the fuel gauge, and I glanced at the dial, seeing that it was clearly past empty.

Like the kind of empty that meant we probably wouldn't make it the rest of the way down the street, let alone wherever he was taking me.

A flicker of concern crossed my face. "Do we have enough to make it to the next gas station?"

Ryan grinned, a hint of mischief in his eyes. "We're living on the edge tonight, Maci. Hold on tight."

He pressed on the gas and fishtailed around a turn before speeding off down the road like a bat out of hell. I gripped the hand rest on the car door, giggling in delight as we raced through the night. In the distance, about a mile away, I saw a gas station and Ryan only seemed to speed up more.

It wasn't far. We should make it, hopefully.

Instead of slowing down, Ryan pressed harder on the gas pedal, the engine roaring to life like an angry lion. My giggles turned into a mixture of nervous laughter and excitement, and I started to get a really bad feeling in the pit of my stomach.

"Ryan, slow down!" I exclaimed, gripping the hand rest even harder, but he only seemed more determined to embrace his reckless speeding like he was a Nascar driver on the last lap. I swallowed hard, telling myself everything was going to be alright. He was just showing off for my sake. That's all this was.

Until it wasn't.

As we hurtled towards the gas station, the world outside morphed into a dizzying blur. The bright lights of the station smeared across the windshield, streaking the night with elongated lines of white and yellow.

Slow down!

My heart thundered in my chest. A knot of dread coiled tightly in the pit of my stomach, growing with each fleeting second that brought us closer to what felt like the inevitable.

My fingers gripped the handrest with a vice-like intensity, my knuckles whitening under the strain.

Too close.

Fuck. He isn't slowing down.

If anything, he was still accelerating, the car's engine emitting a high-pitched whine that screamed in my head.

Panic surged through me. My breathing became shallow, rapid bursts of air that did little to quench the growing hysteria spiraling inside of me. I could feel the car's tires lose their tenuous grip on the pavement, skidding with a treacherous squeal that seemed like a harbinger of doom.

With a sudden, violent jolt, the car careened into the gas station. It was going too fast to navigate the turn properly, the back end fishtailing wildly out of control.

A sickening crunch shattered the air as the car collided with a pump, the sound a grotesque symphony of breaking glass, rending metal, and the tortured screech of twisting steel.

A burst of flames engulfed the pump, the air thick with the acrid scent of burning fuel. I could feel the heat radiating from the fire, and the world quickly became a blur of orange and red.

I acted quickly, my instincts kicking in. I shoved the car door open and stumbled out of the car, only to look back and see that Ryan had done the same thing.

The flames greedily licked at the car, the once sleek vehicle now a blazing inferno. Panic surged through me as I ran to Ryan's side, the heat intensifying with every step.

"Ryan, we need to get further away! It could blow!" I shouted, my voice barely audible over the roar of the flames.

He nodded, his expression set firmly with determination and abject fear. We sprinted further from the erupting chaos, the air quickly growing thick with smoke. Behind us, the car, now completely engulfed in flames, seemed to pulsate with an ominous energy. As we reached what felt like a safe distance, a deafening explosion shattered the night.

The force of the blast sent shockwaves through the air, rattling everything around us. I instinctively threw myself to the ground, shielding my head. The explosion echoed in my ears, leaving them ringing and my eyes burning from the smoke.

When I finally dared to glance back, a plume of blazing smoke billowed into the sky where the car once stood. The remnants of Ryan's car were now scattered across the gas station, each fragment still burning brightly in the dark of the night.

It was like waking up from a nightmare only to find out it was real.

The fire had voraciously consumed not only the car but had also spread to the nearby pumps and structures. Yellow, orange, and red tongues of fire danced wildly, casting an eerie glow on the whole place, making it seem like something out of a horror movie.

Fuck. Fuck. Fuck!

The heat emanating from the blaze distorted the air, creating shimmering waves of intensity. The fuel pumps hissed and crackled as the flames eagerly devoured them. The acrid scent of burning fuel hung thick in the air, adding a sinister note to the already tumultuous scene.

I stared, not believing what I was seeing even though deep in my heart, I knew it was real.

Sparks and embers spiraled up into the air, carried away by the heated currents, creating a mesmerizing yet terrifying display. I watched them for what felt like forever, trying to convince myself that this was nothing more than a bad dream, but I never woke up.

It took only minutes, but soon sirens wailed in the distance.

Fuck. This is bad, really fucking bad.

Raw panic etched across Ryan's face as he muttered something unintelligible, his voice growing desperately urgent. "I can't get caught, Maci. One more strike and they'll put me behind bars. Meet me at your house later, okay?" Without another word, he darted away, disappearing into the shadows of the night and leaving me to fend for myself all on my own.

What the fuck? One more strike?

Left standing amidst the chaos, a sinking feeling settled in the pit of my stomach. Before I could process what had just transpired, the distant wail of sirens grew closer. Then all of a sudden, I was surrounded. Emergency responders and police cars careened all around me, their flashing lights painting the scene with a stark intensity.

Oh my god… I needed to get out of here.

Even as I turned to flee, my heart pounding in my chest, my feet froze in place. I didn't move. I closed my eyes. I couldn't run. That would only make things worse.

You're already fucked.

"Hands up!" one of the police officers bellowed as he barreled out of his car, gun drawn in the air and pointing straight at me. There were a handful of others that did the same thing and my panic slowly closed in on a breaking point. I blinked away tears.

This was bad.

This was going to ruin my life. There would be no going to college after this. My life would be even more fucked than Kendra's, and that was saying something. What kind of jail time was I going to face? What would they even charge me with? Underage drinking? Felony destruction of property? Something worse?

A single tear rolled down my right cheek, dripping down to my chin and falling to the ground beneath my feet.

I was nineteen, *plenty* old enough to be tried as an adult…

I slowly raised my hands, fully surrendering as the officers closed in. Nervously chewing the inside of my cheek, I didn't move as the sounds of approaching footsteps came closer, even though I wanted desperately to be anywhere but here.

This isn't real. This is just a bad dream.

The officer who had shouted at me read me my rights in a firm, measured tone. "You have the right to remain silent. Anything you say can and will be used against you in a court of law. You have the right to an attorney. If you cannot afford one, one will be provided for you. Do you understand these rights as I have read them to you?"

Wake up!

I nodded, the weight of his words settling heavily on my shoulders. Someone grabbed my wrists and pinned them behind my back. The cold metal of handcuffs clicked around my wrists. My eyes watered with more tears, but I quickly blinked them away. As they escorted me to a waiting police car, the gravity of the situation became more pronounced with my every step.

This is the real fucked up kind of bad. The kind of bad that will follow me for the rest of my life...

I am so fucked.

Once inside the police car, the officer continued to explain the legal process. "You're under arrest for destruction of property and reckless endangerment. We'll be taking you to the station for booking, and from there, you'll be processed according to *fullest* extent of the law."

I hated that he put so much emphasis on that single word. That made things even worse for me.

Fuck.

As the police car drove away from the chaotic scene, my shoulders bowed forward and I closed my eyes, trying to grapple with how the night could have been going so well and then gone so wrong just in a matter of seconds.

The police radio crackled to life, breaking the heavy silence within the car. "Dispatch to Unit 14, we have confirmation on the apprehension of the other suspect. Both suspects are now in custody."

I couldn't help but glance towards the front seat, where the officers exchanged a nod of acknowledgment. I knew what that meant. They'd caught Ryan too, and a terrible part of me thought that at least I wouldn't be going into this alone. I shifted in the backseat, the handcuffs cutting into my wrists uncomfortably.

I hated myself for even thinking that.

The police car continued driving through the night, the radio intermittently updating the officers on the ongoing situation. The whole fire department had been called in to combat the flames, but there was a growing worry that the entire gas station might blow. I hoped it wouldn't.

I hoped no one had gotten hurt either...

As we approached the police station, I couldn't shake the sense of inevitable doom that awaited me there. The drive was only about five minutes, but it was the worst five minutes of my life. I sank down in the backseat, not wanting anyone to see me.

Fuck!

I'd never even gotten detention at school, let alone anything like this. Now, I was getting arrested and the possibility of going to jail for the rest of my life felt very real.

I was panicking, even more than before.

Unlike Ryan, my parents weren't going to come bail me out. There wasn't anyone for me here. I was alone. I had no one.

I had to deal with this *all on my own*.

I wanted to cry.

I didn't know what to do. When was I supposed to call a lawyer? How did I even find one? How did I know if I had a good one? Could I even afford one? Questions spiraled through my mind on overdrive, and I bit my lower lip hard enough to taste blood.

When we pulled up, they opened the door and one of the officers wrapped his hand around my arm and roughly yanked me out of the car. I knew better than to complain as they led me inside the station, the harsh fluorescent lights blinding at first in contrast to the dark autumn night.

What happened next must have been completely routine for them, but entirely too terrifying to me.

They led me into the back, where the booking process began. The station's sterile air, laced with the harsh scent of disinfectant, heightened my nervous panic. An officer instructed me to stand against a faded gray wall after they collected my fingerprints, and I had to blink away tears for what felt like the thousandth time that night.

The clatter of the camera shutter echoed terribly loud as my mugshot was taken. The harsh flash briefly illuminated the entire room, casting elongated shadows that frolicked across the cinderblock walls like monsters creeping through

16

the night. Each click of the camera seemed to echo like the slamming of a door.

It was hard not to cry the whole time.

The formal documentation of charges followed. The officer's pen scratched against the paper as they listed all of them. My mouth dried with each offense until my tongue felt like it was made of cotton. I didn't dare say a word for fear that my voice would quiver before I burst into tears right there in front of them.

Keep it together, Maci.

Finally, they led me down a dimly lit corridor, and I quickly found myself shoved into a holding cell. The heavy door slammed shut so loudly it rung in my ears, leaving me in a small, dimly lit space. The hard, narrow bench offered meager comfort, and I sank onto it, the cold metal seeping through my clothes.

As I sat there in the stifling silence, I finally lost control. Tears leaked out from the corners of my eyes, and I burst into sobs. I tried to be as quiet as I could, but my whole life had taken a turn for the worst in the matter of a single night.

Before, there had been hope for my future. Right now, I had *none*. This kind of mistake would follow me for the rest of my life. Every time someone did a background check, they'd see this. It would show up when I applied for an apartment or even a job.

It would be a black stain on my record forever.

I looked up at the ceiling, trying to force myself to wake up from this nightmare and hoping I'd find myself safe in my bed. I tried pinching myself and grimaced from the pain.

This isn't a dream.

This was absolutely, one hundred fucking percent real.

Eventually, I cried myself to sleep.

* * *

Abruptly, the metallic clank of the cell door being unlocked jolted me awake. A uniformed officer stood at the entrance, his stern expression illuminated by the muted glow of the overhead light. "You've got one phone call," he stated, his tone brusque.

I blinked, totally disoriented by the sudden awakening along with my surroundings.

Where am I?

Then it all hit me in a rush. The shots of whiskey. The gas station. The car crash. The fact that I'd been arrested and booked on felony charges.

Rising from the bench, I followed the officer through the labyrinth of corridors to the police station in a haze of fear and panic. The distant sounds of clattering keyboards and hushed conversations over donuts and coffee echoed from somewhere out of sight, nothing more than background noise for the march of my doom.

We reached a small room with a single phone mounted on the wall. The officer gestured towards it in silence, and I nodded in acknowledgment, saying nothing in return. I stepped over to the phone and stared at it for a long moment.

Who could I call?

I chewed my lip. My parents were dead, and so was my grandmother. Ryan's parents might help me, but the chances were slim. I hardly knew them and even though they'd checked in on me over the years, I doubted they'd lend me enough money for bail. I had no other family to speak of. No aunts or uncles or cousins.

There was literally only one person that came to mind.

My godfather.

I hardly knew anything about the man besides his name, Nikolaos Kaligaris. I'd met him once when I was a little girl, but I didn't really remember anything about him. He lived overseas in Athens, Greece, I think, but I wasn't certain. I'd spoken to him on the phone on a handful of occasions, mainly a couple of times on my birthdays as I was growing up and more around the time that my grandmother had passed away.

With his help, I'd been able to make the arrangements for her funeral and burial. He'd ensured that the liens against her house were squared away, paid off the mortgage for me, as well as all the bills that came with owning a home. He hadn't been too excited over the idea that I wanted to take a year off instead of going to college right away, but he'd made sure I had more than enough to live comfortably. He'd always been kind, but I didn't know about something like this.

Maybe if I explained what happened last night, he'd help me.

I didn't have any other choice. There was no one else.

I reached for the phone and pressed it to my ear. The dial tone buzzed, and I paused, holding my fingertips over the keys.

What was his number?

For a moment, my mind went blank, but then I took a deep breath and tried to calm myself. I recited a few facts about Greece to myself, which was something I did sometimes to slow my mind down, and then it finally came to me. I sighed in relief and dialed his number with trembling fingers.

After a few rings, a rumbling voice answered on the other end. "Hello?"

His voice caused the hair on the back of my neck to rise, just like it always did. It reverberated through me like a summer storm, rolling down my spine and settling in the pit of my belly with a finality that left me breathless.

The relief in my voice was palpable as I replied, "It's Maci. I... *Ummm*... I'm in trouble, and I was hoping that you maybe would help me."

A heavy sigh on the other end conveyed a mix of concern and disappointment, which made my heart pound even faster in my chest.

The silence stretched on until he finally asked, "What have you done?"

I took a deep breath, struggling to find the right words. My heart hammered in my chest, and I opened my mouth, only to close it again before I could figure out what to say.

"I made a *really* big mistake…"

A lengthy pause followed before my godfather's voice softened. "Where are you?"

"At the police station," I answered softly, my voice breaking a little bit. I didn't want to cry again. I'd already cried for much of the night. For a long moment, the other end of the phone was silent, and I worried that he'd hung up on me. Then he cleared his throat.

"I didn't know who else to call," I added quietly.

"What happened?" he asked, his voice a tad bit weary, and I chewed on my lip. I swallowed heavily and recounted the events of the night to him, not leaving a single detail out. He listened quietly, and by the time I finished, he sighed.

"Okay, take a deep breath, Maci. We'll get through this. I'll get you the best lawyers that money can buy, and we'll sort this out. I'll be there as soon as I can."

"Thank you," I whispered.

"Hold tight. As soon as I'm able, I'll get your bail settled away, and then I'll get you out of there. Don't worry. Do you understand me? I will handle this," he instructed, his voice so firm that it rattled the very marrow in my bones.

"I understand," I whispered.

"Good. Now be a good girl and do everything the officer says for you to do. If he says sit, you sit. If he wants you to jump, you jump. Get the picture?" he added sternly.

"I will," I professed quickly. My words hitched in the back of my throat, and I tried to swallow back a tear-filled cry. I blinked several times, trying to keep a hold of myself while I felt like I was breaking apart on the inside.

"Listen to me, Maci-girl. Everything is going to be okay. Trust me. I've always seen to it that you were cared for before, haven't I?" he asked, his voice softening a little.

"Yes," I whispered.

The truth was that he had. Ever since my parents' death, he had watched over me from afar. He'd made sure that my grandmother and I led comfortable enough lives. He'd even set up a small trust fund for me to use once I turned twenty-five or graduated from college, whichever came first. I'd lived a normal, happy life, at least until now.

"I'll be there soon. Take care of yourself until I get there," he added.

"Thank you, godfather," I answered.

"You're welcome, Maci-girl."

I hung up the phone and turned back to the officer, who led me back to my holding cell in silence.

CHAPTER 2

 *thens, Greece*

Nikolaos Kaligaris

Jesus Christ.

I didn't need this today.

I hung up the phone with a sigh. My goddaughter was generally a good girl. She got good grades, was in the most advanced classes, and had good prospects for a ton of college scholarships when she finally got her ass in gear and applied herself after taking this ridiculous gap year she'd insisted on.

If she were my daughter, college was exactly where she'd be.

With a firm shake of my head, I brushed my fingers against my brow. This was a headache I didn't need right now. I was in the middle of a very expensive acquisitions deal for a vineyard in Santorini and the negotiations were growing increasingly tense. The Kostopoulos family wanted more money, and I was already offering a very generous amount. I hadn't reached my cap yet, but it was time to play hardball.

They were going to learn that my family name meant something, and they were going to learn that very quickly.

I leaned back in my chair and glanced at the clock. It was only three in the afternoon, which meant it was eight in the morning back in Pennsylvania. As soon as I chartered my private jet, the trip would be a solid ten-to-eleven-hour flight, but it was one I was familiar with since I'd made it time and time again. Philadelphia had a massive port, and there were plenty of times I was needed there to personally handle several high value cargo deliveries to the right buyer.

I sighed again, shaking my head with frustrated annoyance. I didn't want to go to the United States today. The timing was particularly bad, and there was business that needed to be tended to.

I should just let her deal with the consequences of her actions. She was nineteen now, a fully grown, highly intelligent adult that should know better than to get into cars with drunk boys, but I knew that I couldn't ignore the whole thing because this wasn't going to go away on its own.

I had the power to change things for her and make sure she still had a good life. I would need to do nothing more than make a few phone calls, sign a few checks, and bring in the right people to make this disappear for her.

With a heavy sigh, I knew I couldn't leave her to handle this on her own.

She'd made a mistake. She didn't deserve to suffer the rest of her life for it, not when she had the potential to truly become something great, plus I'd made a vow to her father years ago that if anything ever happened to him and his wife, I'd look out for her as best as I could.

Years ago, I'd flown to the States when she'd been born to visit my old college buddy, Michael. It had been just like old times. I smiled fondly just thinking about them. I still remembered the way she'd smiled up at me with those pretty blue-green eyes of hers. Michael had chosen me as her godfather right then and there, and I'd taken the honor to heart.

I hadn't expected him and his wife to die only a few years later.

I wished things had been different. I wished there had been some way I'd been able to save them from that drunk driver that night, but even with the best doctors and medical care in the world flown in to help them, they'd passed away within hours, leaving their three-year-old little girl alone with nothing more than me and her grandmother.

I'd taken care of her, but in a way that wouldn't bring her into my world. I'd made sure her grandmother's mortgage was paid every month, that her water, electricity, and everything else was taken care of. I'd given her a normal life and helped steer her in the right direction from time to time when she needed advice, but those moments were few and far between over the years.

I hadn't seen her since she'd been a toddler, not since her parents' funeral.

I picked my cell up off of the wooden surface of my desk and dialed my secondhand man, Andreas Dounas.

As soon as he picked up, I launched in. "Come into my office. Something urgent has come up, and I need you to help me handle it as quickly as possible."

"Coming right up, boss," he answered quickly. I hung up the phone and waited, hearing his footsteps on the stairs and then down the hallway before he was knocking at my door. He didn't wait for me to call him in, he just entered the room and took a seat in the leather armchair in front of my desk, the old leather squeaking loudly as he settled into place.

Behind his polished spectacles, his keen hazel eyes appraised me expectantly. He cocked his head and crossed one leg over the other. He painted the picture of a distinguished gentleman, with his silver-gray hair meticulously combed back and his grey tweed tailored suit perfectly pressed and fitted to his powerful frame.

"Maci needs my help. I need to book the jet to the States, immediately," I dictated, and he nodded. He didn't need any further explanation. He'd learned a long time ago not to ask questions.

Andreas had been at my family's side for years. He'd known of Maci's existence when no one else did. If anyone else found out about her, her life would be in danger, and I couldn't live with myself if that happened. My world was treacherous, and she didn't belong in it. I wanted her to lead a normal life, and mine wasn't that.

As the heir to the formidable Kaligaris shipping dynasty, my family's maritime legacy extended across a vast expanse of international waters. My world consisted of immense power and influence, a never-ending realm of legal and illegal business dealings, as well as a massive amount of cutthroat competition.

The Kaligaris name commanded respect and fear, with our shipping empire being among one of the largest in Greece. We'd built our fortune over generations, but the international shipping business was not a safe place.

As much as it was controlled by my father and a number of others, much of it was tangled up with the secretive motives of the Greek and Italian mafias. My father needed a sharp mind to navigate such dangerous waters, and he was grooming me to take his place when the time was right. I would take over his position when he finally passed, but that wouldn't be for a while yet.

For the time being, he ran the family. Right now, I was simply helping us to grow even bigger, or at least that was my goal. I was trying to diversify our business dealings, and I didn't have time to deal with wayward girls that needed their asses thoroughly welted by a belt to set them straight.

"I can start planning right away, boss. Should we say that you're just checking on a special shipment coming into the Philadelphia port?" Andreas offered thoughtfully.

"Yes. Her existence needs to remain secret. I can't have the Pappas family finding out about her or anyone else," I confirmed, and he nodded quickly.

"Understood, boss. I'll handle the arrangements and keep it tight. Your secret will remain safe. I promise."

* * *

I worked quickly.

In less than an hour, I was on my private jet. By the time I touched down, I had called in several favors from the local and state judges in Pennsylvania. At first, they didn't want to post her bail because she had already proven to be a bit of a flight risk, but after several very expensive payoffs, I saw to it that she would be released first thing in the morning on bail. I'd already arraigned several top lawyers and built her a formidable team. I would make sure that she got nothing more than a slap on the wrist and community service by the time this inevitably blew over. Best case scenario, I'd get it thrown out on a technicality and this would disappear for her entirely.

First thing the next morning, I was standing inside of the police station, waiting for her to be processed and let out. The aroma of stale coffee lingered, and I wrinkled my nose in disgust. I checked my watch and saw that it was five past nine.

Typical. They would be on time if I ran this place.

That, or they would be fired on the spot.

Finally, the heavy doors at the end of the hall swung open, revealing a small petite form no more than five feet two inches tall. A telltale flash of rich auburn waves covered her face, hiding her from me at first glance, until she looked up and her pale bluish-green eyes gazed at me for the first time since she was a little girl.

Maci Williams *wasn't* a toddler anymore.

Her glossy tresses caught the light just so, shining like strands of polished copper and framing her pale complexion as they fell down several inches past her shoulders. A smattering of freckles dotted her nose and flushed cheeks. Her features were like that of a doll, soft and dainty and entirely too beautiful for a nineteen-year-old girl. Her lips were the color of a blooming rose and her tongue darted out to lick them.

That little pink tongue would look awfully nice sucking your cock...

I watched the tip of that tongue with a building sense of shame, knowing I shouldn't be looking at her like that but doing it anyway simply because I could.

Once her tongue was safely back in between those pretty lips, I let my gaze travel down further still. Time seemed to pause as my eyes traced down the contours of her slender form. The subtle curves of her waist and hips were absolutely divine. Her breasts were the perfect size, just enough to fill the seat of my palm and no more.

I wondered if her nipples were a dusky pink to match her lips.

Fuck.

It had been far too long since I'd been with a woman. She was my fucking goddaughter for Christ's sake. If Michael knew that I was thinking about his child like this, he'd probably smite me dead from the grave.

I swallowed hard, but my eyes still wandered. Her long lean legs were accentuated by the sway of her hips as she walked, which bespoke of a quiet confidence and a hint of mystery, at least until our eyes met and her steps faltered.

Her eyes were such a mesmerizing color, a bluish green that was like the depths of a tranquil lagoon bathed in the moonlight. There was a subtle shift in color between sage green and pale blue and when the light hit them just right, they radiated with an ethereal luminosity.

I couldn't look away.

I shouldn't be looking at her like that, like I wanted to tear her clothes off and fuck her right on the floor of the station.

Held captive by the secluded oasis of her eyes, I didn't look away until the burly bored-looking man at the counter annoyingly cleared his throat. Immediately, I wanted to punch him.

"Maci Williams?"

"That's me," she said quietly, the musical cadence of her voice enough to send a jolt of desire straight down my cock. I lifted my chin higher, appraising her coldly and doing anything I possibly could to hide the direction of my thoughts.

She couldn't know that I wanted nothing more than to push her down on her knees and fuck that pretty mouth with my cock.

"You're free to go. Your bail has been posted. I just need you to sign here," he said as he glanced down at a clipboard. After a moment, he handed it over to her and the pen scratched against the paper as she signed it.

It was loud in the ensuing silence.

"Here's your things," he said blandly, handing over a plastic bag with her phone. The officer's gaze bored into her as if assessing the gravity of her choices, and I found myself aggravated on her behalf.

He didn't get to look at her like that.

I did.

"Anything you need to declare missing or stolen?" he said coldly, and she shook her head.

"No, just this," she answered. Her gaze flittered nervously to mine, and I softened my face. She'd probably had a long night, and I wanted to get her out of here before I said anything about how foolish she had been. Right now, she just needed someone to take care of her and I would be that man for her.

I could be more than enough man for her...

The man at the counter turned away, and I strode forward with a gentle smile when my thoughts were anything but that. She turned to face me and flinched a little.

Maybe she expected me to yell at her, but I wasn't the kind of man who wore his emotions on his sleeve.

No. You're just the kind of man that wants to do very shameful things to her far too young body whether she likes it or not.

"How're you holding up, Maci?" I asked gently, and her expression turned weary, like she had finally allowed herself a moment to relax.

"It's been hard," she admitted, and I smiled softly.

"Let's get you out of here," I offered, guiding her gently out the door to my black Range Rover just outside. Like a gentleman, I opened the passenger side for her to climb inside before I hopped into the driver's seat.

A heavy silence reigned between us before the audible sound of her nervous swallow stole away the quiet.

"Thank you for what you did for me," she murmured, and I cleared my own throat.

"The legal team I put together for you are some of the very best in the country. At worst, you'll be offered a plea deal, and at best, they'll be able to expunge it off your record for good. Maybe get you some community service. Either way, everything will be alright," I explained, my tone carrying with it the weight of reassurance, and she nodded beside me.

Her fingers flexed and curled together in her lap, and I had trouble not imagining them wrapping around my cock.

With a weary sigh at the direction of my thoughts, I turned over the engine and the low rumble reverberated as I pulled away from the station. As the countryside passed by, I found myself compelled to dive into her decision to get into this mess in the first place. I wanted to know why.

So, you can punish her as you see fit.

I shook my head. I needed to get ahold of myself. I was better than this.

Soon, I couldn't hold myself back any longer.

"Now, care to share why you decided to take a moonlit drive with a drunk boy in the first place?" I inquired, my tone firm and completely devoid of any playful undertones.

Immediately, her whole body tensed with defensiveness. From the slight stiffening in her shoulders to the rigid set of her jaw, everything about her told me that she didn't want to be scolded, but I wasn't about to give her that choice.

It was either that, or I was going to pull this car right over and...

Stop. Stop right fucking there.

"He seemed fine when we left," she declared, her fingers clenching against her thigh. Her chin jutted out with her sudden defiance, and all I could think of was grabbing that chin and fucking that beautiful little mouth.

"Seemed fine? You should know better than that, Maci," I rebuked, and her hands tensed a bit tighter.

With a quiet huff, she lifted her chin, and I wanted nothing more than to pull the car over and put her over my knee for the kind of punishment she deserved.

It was stupid getting into a car with a drunk driver. Honestly, if she had been my daughter and not Michael's, I would have taken her home and given her a strict dose of my hand and then my belt.

She's not yours.

My cock hardened uncomfortably, and I shifted in the seat. She was looking defiantly out the window, so she hadn't noticed, but I tried to get control of myself anyway. I shouldn't be thinking these things about her. She was my goddaughter for Christ's sake, and she was an adult now. She needed to understand that her decisions had consequences, that she wasn't a kid anymore, and that things like these were really hard to sweep under the rug, no matter what I told her.

"I didn't know it would turn out like that," she muttered, rolling her eyes towards the window in the sort of sneaky way that told me that she hoped I wouldn't notice.

Naughty. Fucking. Girl.

"Use your head, Maci. You're a smart girl. If you're going to hang out with your friends and drink together, you stay put," I continued, and her lower lip protruded in the tiniest little pout I'd ever seen.

"You're not my dad," she replied, clearly annoyed, and I gripped the steering wheel tighter.

If I was, you'd be sitting on a bright red bottom right now, you naughty little girl.

My cock surged with desire, damning me once again. I gritted my teeth and stared at the road for a long moment before taking a deep, calming breath.

She's not yours. You can't do things like that.

"You may not see me as your dad, but I do care about you," I retorted, my voice holding an edge of sternness.

She huffed audibly, the atmosphere growing increasingly tense between us. "I can take care of myself. I don't need a babysitter."

My grip on the steering wheel tightened further, my frustration showing even though I tried my best to hide it. "This isn't about that, Maci. It's about making responsible choices. You can't afford to be reckless."

She shot me a defiant look, her eyes narrowing slightly. "I'm not reckless. I just wanted to have some fun."

"The kind of fun that landed you arrested and locked in a police station," I countered sharply.

Maci crossed her arms, a clear sign of resistance. "You're overreacting. It was just a stupid mistake."

"Just a stupid mistake that could have had serious repercussions," I insisted, my tone unwavering. "You're capable of more than this, Maci. Don't undermine your potential with impulsive decisions."

She pouted, her annoyance evident. "You act like I ruined my life or something."

"If not for me, you certainly could have," I countered, and she opened her mouth but then wisely thought to close it.

Good girl.

The car moved in silence for a long moment, the tension hanging thick in the air between us.

Maci glanced out the window, her thoughts momentarily distant. "I appreciate your help. I really do."

"I know it's hard on your own, but you're a smart girl. Use that head of yours before doing something like getting in cars with drunk boys."

"I didn't mean for it to happen like that," she finally relented.

"I know, Maci-girl. Just don't let it happen again," I added softly.

Or else I'll take my belt off and show you what happens to naughty little girls who need a lesson in what's acceptable and what's not.

"I won't," she answered, her tone only a touch haughty now.

For a while, I drove in silence, the weight of our conversation lingering on my conscience. She still seemed a bit pouty and defiant, but less so than before, which made me feel a little better too.

I started to feel really fucking warm.

"I'm going to take you home and you're going to get some sleep. Tonight, you and I will go out to dinner together. I want to hear about how your year is going and what your plans are for the next," my voice was still firm, but with a hint of warmth now.

"You'd want that after everything that happened?"

"I would. I could use some good company after that long flight," I offered, and she looked guiltily down at her lap.

She really did need a spanking, the kind of spanking that made pretty little tears drip down her cheeks while she begged to be a very good girl and take your *co...*

No. Stop right there. You can't have her like that.

Gritting my teeth once more, I turned forward and stared at the road. We were closing in on her grandmother's house, a small two-story home that had been in the family for more than fifty years. I pulled into the driveway and sighed, happy to see that it at least looked to be very well cared for.

The house stood proudly at the end of a quiet cul-de-sac, its exterior clad in weathered bricks. A well-maintained front yard, dotted with traditional flora like rhododendrons and azaleas, hinted at a gardener's touch. The porch, adorned with a wooden rocking chair and a hanging basket of vibrant petunias, added a touch of rustic to the home.

"Do you take care of the flowers?" I asked, nodding towards the blossoms that ornamented the front yard. I didn't remember any bills coming across my desk for a gardener, so I was curious.

Maci smiled, a genuine warmth in her eyes. "Yeah, they've always been Grandma's thing, and I picked it up from her. There's something about tending to plants that just soothes the soul, you know?"

There was a sparkle in her eye that caught my attention. The way her face lit up as she spoke was adorable.

She was really quite beautiful.

I slowly nodded. "Tell me, what's your favorite flower?"

She paused, contemplating the question with a thoughtful expression. "I'd have to say sunflowers. They're so vibrant and uplifting. I remember Grandma used to grow them in the backyard when I was a kid."

"Sunflowers are a really good choice. They brighten up any space," I remarked, my face softening a bit. Immediately, I was reminded of her age, her young joy written all over her face, which made my sordid thoughts that much worse.

She's nineteen. You're twice her age.

"Yeah, exactly. And they're sturdy too, resilient even when the weather gets tough. Kind of like people," she added with a smile. The genuine passion she had for caring for the gardens shone through, and I found myself holding on to the edge of every word as if I wanted to get to know her better.

I didn't know what to make of it, so I pushed it far away. I didn't want to get to know her better. I couldn't. My life was too dangerous for her, and every part of me knew it.

Every part of me except for *my cock*.

"I can see that," I replied thoughtfully. I glanced at the house and so did she. The time had come for us to part, and strangely, I sort of didn't want her to go.

"Thank you again for taking care of things for me," she offered quietly, the earlier defiance in her tone melting away.

"You're welcome, Maci. Now go get some rest, and I'll be here to pick you up at six o-clock. Dress nicely," I replied.

"Okay." She blushed and hopped out of the car. I watched her stride up to the house with far too much interest. Her jeans were too tight, cupping her young round butt far too well for my liking.

I should follow her inside. I should show her what happens to naughty girls who need…

No. You can't. You won't.

She fumbled with her keys at the door for a moment as though she was a little bit nervous before she got the right one and turned it in the lock. There was a wistful expression on her face as she opened the door and looked over her shoulder, and for a moment, our eyes connected.

And for a fraction of a second, my heart stopped.

Desire, forbidden yet undeniable, surged through me. I shouldn't want her. Yet in that stolen moment, I found myself drawn to her in a way that defied explanation. In that moment, the lines between us blurred.

I forced myself to turn away first because I fucking *had* to.

I turned the key over and pulled out of the driveway in such a rush that the tires squealed against the pavement. I took off down the road and finally pulled in a breath.

I didn't look back.

I couldn't.

CHAPTER 3

 aci

As I fumbled with my keys at the door, my nerves tightened with uncertainty in my chest. Finally finding the right key and turning it in the lock, I couldn't help myself. I turned back and locked eyes with him.

In that moment, time seemed to stand still. His gaze, intense and probing, had caught me entirely off guard. His eyes held a depth of feeling that went far beyond what a godfather and goddaughter should be, and that shared glance made my heart flutter in a way I couldn't understand.

My cheeks heated, and my eyes, wide with both surprise and yearning, held his for a moment that seemed far too long.

My heartbeat stuttered when he was the one to break it off first.

Closing the door behind me, I pressed my back against the wall, my hand to my chest as I drew in a shaky breath.

What was that?

For a second time that day, I questioned the direction of my own mind. I leaned my head back against the wall, looking at the ceiling with a heavy sigh. My skin prickled with heat, and I swallowed heavily.

What was wrong with me?

I hadn't seen my godfather since I was a little girl. I was too young to remember him, but I'd seen a few grainy pictures of him in the crowd at my parents' funeral. I hadn't looked at those in years though.

Seeing him in the police station for the first time was enough to make my heart seize in my chest.

His stormy grey eyes had met mine with a firm intensity. His well-trimmed beard framed an overly tense jawline, and his tousled dark brown waves hinted at a subtle disarray, like he'd run his fingers through his hair just a few moments before he'd walked in the door.

Dressed in a tailored suit, he looked nothing short of supremely powerful. The fabric clung to his form in a way that accentuated his muscular features, his strong shoulders, and his chiseled physique more than enough to capture my full attention. The stern expression etched on his face had made my stomach flutter with a sudden vat of nerves, and I'd had swallowed them back. His every feature, from his olive skin to his sculpted nose, screamed sophistication, authority, and control. His Greek heritage was written all over his face.

Yet in that moment, I hadn't been able to help but feel myself drawn to him in a way that I shouldn't have been. My gaze had lingered for far longer than it should have. In no world should I be having such thoughts. He was my godfather, a mentor figure at most, but my core had squeezed tight almost in open defiance of that.

It isn't right...

Trying to ignore the direction of my thoughts, I turned and locked the door behind me.

Shaking off the distracting image of my godfather, I decided to retreat to my bedroom in an attempt to regain my composure. The warm glow of the familiar space provided a comforting contrast to the chaos that I'd gone through the last two nights.

I sniffed the air, realizing that the scent of stale coffee and sweat still lingered, and I slowly grasped that it had stuck to my clothing. Wanting to wash away not just the residue of the police station but also the confusing emotions that lingered, I decided to take a shower. I peeled my shirt over my head and tossed it in the hamper, along with my underwear and my jeans. Padding into the bathroom, I turned on the water and waited until steam was rising before I climbed inside.

I loved showers. They always felt so good, whether it was to start off the day or to bring it to a close.

The water flowed over me and worked its magic. The soothing warmth eased the tension in my muscles and offered a momentary escape from the whirlwind of my own mind. As the water droplets traced a gentle path down my skin, I let myself relax as much as I could, but thoughts of last night and Nikolaos Kaligaris kept creeping back in before I could stop them.

Shaking my head, I reached for the shampoo and pumped a bit into my hand. I wasted no time massaging it into my scalp, letting the heat of the shower pulse away the soreness that lingered from trying to sleep on a metal bench for two nights in a row. I scrubbed my skin until it was a rosy pink, wanting to wash away every bit of that police station from my body. When I was finally satisfied, I combed conditioner through my hair and finally rinsed off after a while longer. Then I climbed out.

Drying off with a towel, I walked out of the bathroom and into my closet to exchange it for the comfort of a soft nightshirt.

It had been so difficult to sleep in the holding cell. The bench had been too hard, and someone down the hall had been snoring loud enough to wake the dead, plus there hadn't been a pillow or even a blanket to huddle beneath. The station had been quiet otherwise, but I hadn't been able to get comfortable, not when I was scared and unsure of what was going to happen to me.

I glanced at my bed, yearning for the soft covers, and I gave into the urge. Climbing into bed, I pulled up the covers to my ears and snuggled within their warmth.

I closed my eyes, but I didn't fall asleep. For a while, I just lay there, and I tried to count sheep and think sleeping thoughts, but instead my mind kept turning back to my godfather time and time again, and I couldn't make it stop.

His stern, stormy grey eyes lingered in my mind, their intensity seared into my consciousness.

The way he'd clenched his jaw when he'd scolded me... The sternness etched into his expression echoed throughout my memory like a haunting storm passing through the middle of the night.

A disconcerting awareness began to unfurl within me—a part of me, unbidden and unsettling, wanted him. The realization brought a flush to my skin, a prickling heat that swept over me in waves.

I *shouldn't* be feeling this.

I had a crush on *Ryan*. He was the one I should be thinking about. He was my age. We'd been in the same graduating class, and even though last night had happened, he was the more reasonable option for me, especially considering the other one in question was my godfather. I forced my mind back to Ryan, but it didn't stay there. It refused.

Instead, it kept turning back to Nikolaos and my body grew hotter still.

I laid there for a long time, grappling with the way my nipples were hardening beneath my nightshirt and how my legs felt antsy, like I could go and run a mile right now even though I was physically exhausted. My fingers clutched at the bed as I warred with myself.

I shouldn't be thinking about him this way.

I shouldn't.

But I am.

And I couldn't make myself *stop.*

Tentatively, I unclenched my hands and pressed them against my belly. Heat spiraled up and down my limbs, tingling in the tips of my fingers and the ends of my toes. A soft whimper escaped me as the sensitive bundle of nerves in between my thighs started to pulse.

Pulling in one heated breath after another, I tried to think about anything other than him, but it was useless.

I'd never felt anything like this before, at least not as intensely. Sure, I'd slipped my hand between my thighs late at night on rare occasions, but not like this, never thinking about my godfather. Before, I'd thought about Ryan kissing me. Sometimes he liked to brag about how good he was at going down on a woman, and I'd simply sat there and blushed and imagined him doing that to me.

Something about Nikolaos, though, made me think that he would do it far, *far* better.

Maybe it was because Ryan was a *boy* and Nikolaos was a *man.*

"Just don't let it happen again."

His words played over and over again in my mind, and I remembered how that single sentence had petered off, like he was going to say something else, and the words had died on his tongue.

Or else...

Or else what?

My mind whirled with possibilities. Would he scold me? Would he take away his financial help, or worse... would he *punish* me?

I gulped at the heavy meaning in that single word. My fingers twitched against my stomach, and I bit my lip, squirming against the bed a little at the sheer heat raging inside of me.

If he was going to punish me, how would he do it?

Instinctively, a part of me knew. I'd seen his broad hands clench around the wheel and the image of those same hands smacking my bottom flashed before my eyes.

Oh my God! What is wrong with you?"

The last thing I wanted was for him to put me over his knee like he was my daddy giving me a spanking for being a bad little girl who'd been so naughty that she needed to be put over his knee.

My body definitely didn't agree with my head though. Instead of deciding that my mind was certifiably insane, the rest of me thought that was a grand idea and pulsed with another sharp surge of heat.

I licked my lips and opened my eyes, staring at the ceiling as I tried to reign in the naughty thoughts spiraling in my head, but it was quickly becoming more and more useless.

What would it feel like if he took me over his knee? Would he spank me over my jeans or would he take them down?

My sharp intake of breath was audible when I thought about something even more shameful.

What if he pulled my panties to my knees, bent me over his knee, and spanked my *bare* bottom?

My clit throbbed and I shifted in the bed, spreading my thighs apart to try to make things better but that only seemed to make things worse.

My right hand slid down a bit further to my lower belly and traced the line of my hip bone, back and forth, back and forth, until the sensation between my legs became too much.

I wasn't going to be able to sleep until I made myself come.

With a building amount of trepidation, I pulled my night-shirt up a little, just so I exposed the hem of my panties. Pressing my lips together with a quiet hum of nerves, I hesitated for a long moment before I finally relented and slipped my fingers beneath the waistband. I pushed on until my fingertips grazed the folds of my pussy.

I wasn't just wet.

I was *soaked.*

When my fingers brushed against my clit, a surge of pleasure radiated through me, and I yelped out loud in surprise.

I shouldn't be feeling like this. I shouldn't want to touch my pussy while thinking about my godfather, but here I was, and that was exactly what I was doing.

Would he think it was naughty if he found out?

I closed my eyes and moved exceedingly slowly, sliding the flats of my fingers over my clit in smooth, small circles, losing myself in a fantasy that I would never admit to anyone else *ever*.

My mind jumped to later that day, after dinner when he'd dropped me back home, only, he wouldn't leave. He would stay here to punish me instead, just like I needed to be punished...

He turned the key in the ignition, and a heavy silence fell between us. I held my breath, not knowing what he wanted or what he was going to say.

"Now, naughty girl, I think it's time we had a discussion about how bad of a decision it was to get into a car with the drunk boy you had a crush on," he began, and I looked at him, indignant and defiant.

"A discussion?" I asked, my heart hammering in my chest with increasing frequency.

"Yes. Head inside, Maci. Wait for me in your bedroom, and I'll be inside to deal with you in just a moment," he instructed and some-where deep down, something compelled me to obey him.

"Deal with me?" I muttered, the question hanging on to the edge of my voice.

"Yes, naughty girl. I'm going to deal with you the way you deserve to be dealt with," he answered, his voice firm and no nonsense.

"And how's that?" I asked haughtily.

"With your bottom bare over my knee," he answered, and I stopped short.

"I'm nineteen. I'm not going to let you spank me like a child," I countered, and he just leveled me with a look that said he was going to do exactly that whether I liked it or not.

"You will go inside and wait for me in your bedroom, Maci," he scolded, and I crossed my arms in a huff.

"Whatever," I proclaimed, but I was already opening the door and heading inside before I knew what I was doing. I stomped through the front door, all the way to my room, before I sat down on the bed with a nervous shudder.

Wait.

This was real. This was really happening. My godfather had just picked me up from the police station after I got arrested, and now I was about to get my bottom spanked for being naughty enough to get myself into such a mess in the first place.

I closed my eyes as something else hit me.

I wasn't just about to get a spanking on my bottom with my panties up. He'd specifically said my bare bottom, and that was almost too shameful to think about.

He was going to see my ass. Every single naked inch of it.

As he bared me.

I squeezed my eyes tighter, knowing that was probably not all he was going to see.

In all likelihood, I wasn't going to take this gracefully. I'd never been spanked before, and from every modern-day exposure I'd

49

had of such a thing, I knew it would sting. I'd kick and he'd probably see in between my legs.

Or worse...

What if he made me stand in front of him when he pulled my panties down? If he did that, he'd have a direct line of sight to my pussy, and I was terrified that he'd see how puffy and wet I was right now just thinking about it.

A quiet cry slipped from my lips as I heard the distant sound of the front door opening and closing. The heavy cadence of his footsteps carried to my bedroom, and he was at my door before I knew it.

"Alright, little girl, stand up. It's time for your spanking."

My fingers moved faster on my clit, and all of a sudden, my entire body seized. My thighs trembled, and my eyes fluttered as they rolled back in my head. White hot euphoria raced through my veins. Fierce, powerful pleasure pushed my head up into the clouds, and then all of a sudden, I was falling into the abyss with no end in sight. I keened, my shrill cry echoing throughout the room, and then I just came harder.

It was the hardest orgasm I'd ever had in my life.

When it was finally over, I pulled my hand from my panties, feeling naughtier than ever.

If I'd ever needed a spanking, it would be right now.

Honestly, I *deserved* it.

CHAPTER 4

 ikolaos

I drove back to my hotel in a rush. The moment I walked inside my suite, I unbuttoned my blazer, shrugged it off, and threw it on the couch like the fabric had singed my fingers.

For some reason, the heat was stifling in here even though it was late October, and the beginnings of fall were showing all over the state. Any other time, I might have appreciated the changing leaf colors in this part of the world, but today was *not* that day.

Today, my mind was on a naughty little girl who needed to know there were *very real* consequences for her actions.

I should have fucking stayed.

I should have bent her over the back of her fucking couch, pulled those far too tight jeans down, and belted her bare ass for getting herself into as much trouble as she had.

She fucking deserved it.

Fuck that.

She *needed* it.

It had taken everything I had in me to stay in that car and drive away. Even now, my body was vibrating with tension, and I couldn't stand it.

The heat was still too much to bear, so my fingers flicked open the top buttons of my white shirt. Now that the collar wasn't as tight, I felt a bit better, but it was still too hot. I ratcheted the air conditioning down as low as it would go and yanked open the fridge to take out a bottle of water. Twisting the cap open, I took a long sip, but that didn't help either, so I switched it for the bottle of Jack Daniels on the bar instead.

I took a swig, and the delicious burn of the cheap alcohol didn't help the situation like I was hoping it would.

My cock was so hard that it hurt. My balls fucking ached too. And it was all *her* fucking fault.

Fuck me. Why was I like this? She was my goddamn goddaughter for Christ's sake. Not only that, but she was only fucking nineteen. I could be her real father, and she was practically still a kid.

She certainly didn't look like a kid though. She looked like a grown woman in need of a real punishment, not just with my belt, but with my cock inside that tight little bottom while she screamed for mercy right before she came long and hard for me like the good fucking girl I knew she could be.

Fuck!

I pushed myself up out of the chair and made my way into the bedroom. I felt like a dirty old man, thinking about her like that. I'd never been like this with any other woman. I didn't understand why it was like this with her.

She was forbidden. Not only was she too young, but her innocence didn't belong in my world. She needed to be kept far from it, it was far too dangerous, but my cock was getting a different message, and I couldn't make it stop. I sat down and took another swig of whiskey. It was cheap stuff, but the burn of the alcohol was still the same.

I downed the rest of my drink, slammed the glass down on the side table, and undid several more buttons down the line of my shirt, but nothing fucking changed the fact that I wanted to drive right back to Maci's house, rip her fucking jeans down, and paddle her bare ass before I fucked that sweet little pussy until she screamed for mercy, and then I'd fuck her some more.

Dear God. I was fucking hopeless.

Reaching down, I unbuckled my belt and ripped it out of my slacks. The delightful swishing sound reminded me of the sound a belt made right before it welted disobedient flesh, and I gritted my teeth and tossed it on the bed.

Not knowing what else to do with myself, I strode into the bathroom and started taking the rest of my clothes off. As each stitch of cloth pulled away from my skin, I breathed easier and easier.

I turned the shower on and waited until the steam was drifting up towards the ceiling before I climbed inside.

Stepping into the shower, the hot water beating against my skin, I tried to let the steam wash away the persistent thoughts of her pert little ass and her beautiful, perky young tits. My shoulders tensed, and I punched a fist into the solid marble wall, but it didn't help.

Not even a little bit.

Every drop of water against my skin seemed to echo the pulse of my frustration.

As the steam enveloped me, I clenched my jaw, the tension radiating through my muscles. I massaged shampoo into my scalp and tried to rid my head of any thought of her, but the image of her bent over the couch with her ass bare was almost too much for me to handle.

Almost.

My cock throbbed and I leaned forward, letting the water beat down on my back.

I wasn't a good man. Not when I had thoughts like this.

Maybe I just needed to get it out of my system, or maybe I just needed to go back home and fuck the first woman that fell into my bed.

My hand wound around my cock, and I let my mind wander to my last good fuck. I remembered her pretty blonde hair, her full tits, and her tight ass like it was yesterday. With everything in me, I focused on her, but it wasn't enough.

Eventually, my thoughts turned right back to Maci, and I literally growled out loud. My snarl echoed off the tiles, and I punched the wall again, but my cock just jerked in my hand, and I knew I was too far gone to ignore it anymore.

I couldn't go to dinner with her in this condition. Not like this...

Fuck me.

Whatever this was, it needed to stop. I needed to put an end to it. Clenching my jaw, I tightened my grip around my cock and gave in.

I *wasn't* happy about it.

To be honest, I was pretty fucking angry about what I was doing and why I was doing it.

Fuck it.

I would stroke my cock and think about exactly what I wanted to happen this afternoon, and I'd never tell anyone about it. It would be my dirty little secret.

She'd never find out. No one would.

.   .   .

I burst through her front door, only to find her sitting on her ass in the middle of her living room watching television. Not only had she ignored my directive to sleep off the night, but willfully so.

"Godfather," she breathed, almost like she couldn't believe I'd just walked in on her. She must have taken her bra off after I left because her hard nips showed right through her shirt like two fucking delicious little headlights. I wanted to rip that shirt right off and take those nipples in my mouth and punish them with my teeth.

"Naughty girl, you've failed to do as you were told," I said, an air of weary disappointment in my tone.

She stiffened on the couch, a guilty look painted all over her face, the kind of look that told me she knew she was in trouble, and she probably wasn't going to like what happened next.

Good.

That's what was making my cock so goddamn hard right now.

I strode over to her and wrapped my hand around her upper arm, yanking her up and off the couch a bit more roughly than she'd expected. She tried to pull away from me, but I didn't let go.

"What are you doing?" she squeaked.

I didn't let go of her arm. Instead, I marched her straight around to the back of the couch and roughly bent her over it. She tried to stand back up, but I pressed a hand firmly down on her lower back and pinned her in place.

She was small, dainty even. She didn't stand a chance against a man like me. I was so much bigger and stronger, and in that moment, she realized it too. I loomed over her and stood directly behind her, not caring that she could probably feel how hard my cock was for her through her jeans.

"Nikolaos!" she yipped, but I grabbed the back of her neck and lifted her roughly up against me so she could feel exactly how much her fear was turning me on.

I didn't care that she was scared. It fucking made my cock harder.

"You and I are going to discuss what happens to bad girls who get in trouble with the law, and when we're done, you're going to thank me properly for saving you from rotting in prison with that pretty little mouth," I warned her, and she visibly shivered right in front of me like a fucking cat in heat.

It was absolutely delightful.

With the back of her neck firmly in my fist, I reached around her waist with my other arm and undid the button of her jeans. Without a word, I yanked her zipper down and then her pants came next. I didn't care that her panties went down with her jeans.

I just wanted her ass fully bare for what came next.

Clenching my jaw, I pushed her back over the couch and pinned her in place. She struggled, but I easily subdued her. It was too easy, even. Almost like she knew what was coming and tentatively accepted it, which was absolutely fucking delicious.

With one hand, I unbuckled my belt and ripped it out of my slacks firmly enough for the strap to cut through the air and make such a delicious sound that she jumped a little bit.

She was nervous.

She fucking should be.

I folded the belt over in my fist, letting it hang by my side before I finally took one look down and nearly came right there in my pants like a young man who'd found his father's porn stash and just seen tits for the first time in his life.

Her ass was fucking incredible. So fucking bitable and perfect. Shaped like an upside-down heart, her curves were full in all the right places. Right at the cusp of her lower back, she had these two little dimples that begged to be licked and kissed and utterly fucking worshipped.

I traced my fingers around one and then the other, making her tremble before me.

My power over her was fucking incredible. Like a fucking drug that was surging through my veins, an addictive euphoria that I knew I'd never be able to get enough of no matter how many times I had her.

And I would have her.

Again and again, with her screaming my name in surrender each and every night...

"You know what's going to happen next, don't you?"

"Yes," she whimpered.

"You know you deserve it too," I continued.

"I know," she wailed. "But I've never..."

My cock was so hard that it ached, and my balls felt like they were about to burst. With my pelvis pressed against the side of her hip, there was no way she wouldn't feel it either.

I grinned. The thought of her knowing pleased me.

I didn't give her any warning before I whipped the belt across her naughty flesh. The gasp of air that burst free from her lips was fucking music to my ears, and the flinch that followed was absolutely perfect, but what I really loved was watching the white line from the belt rise on her flesh. Then it turned a rosy pink, and then a brilliant red as the welt from my strap marked her skin.

I didn't waste any time. I whipped her a second time, and she cried out. I watched the resulting welt rise with just as much enthusiasm, and then I painted her ass with a third and a fourth and a fifth before she tried to reach back and block the belt.

Easily, I redirected the belt in midair so that I didn't strike her fingers. I wanted her ass sore, but I didn't really want to hurt her.

This was all about teaching her a lesson and that was it.

I grabbed her wrists, one after the other, and pinned them safely behind her back before I renewed her belting with much more fervor than before.

I didn't stop until every inch of her ass was bright red and welted and there were pretty tears streaming down her cheeks as she begged me for forgiveness.

Honestly, every moment of that belting was perfect.

When I was finally satisfied that she had been spanked hard enough, I threw the belt aside and appraised my work like an art collector looking at his finest piece.

Her sobbing echoed throughout the room, which made my cock hard as an iron rod, but I ignored it for the moment because I noticed something else, something far more important.

Her wetness was stringing between her thighs. It was practically dripping down her pretty flesh, and I took a deep breath.

I had planned to punish her mouth, but maybe I needed to deal with her pussy first.

Slowly, her sobbing quieted as I grazed my fingers over her beautiful welts.

My welts.

My girl.

Mine.

Fucking all mine.

I didn't ask to take her. I didn't ask to plunge my cock into her soaking wet pussy, and I didn't ask her if she wanted to come for me.

I just took her because she belonged to me, and she fucking needed it.

The tight glove of her pussy squeezed around my cock, and then she was coming so hard that she felt like she was vibrating around my dick.

"That's it, princess. Come hard for me with your ass welted and your pussy full of my cock."

My fingers squeezed tight around my cock, working my hand up and down my turgid length until my balls were full. I imagined sinking deep into her pussy, over and over again until she screamed my name, and then suddenly, I was roaring as my seed spurted out all over my hand and dripped down into the shower basin.

Utter rapture erupted up from the base of my spine as one surge of come after another burst out of me. I stroked myself faster, harder, almost as if I was punishing myself for thinking about fucking my goddaughter, but it didn't matter.

When my orgasm was over, I expected to feel better, but my disappointment rained over me like a fallen snow on a cold winter's day. Ice dripped down my spine at the realization of what I'd just done. Instead of relief, I just wanted her more.

Mostly, I wanted my seed not to be wasted in the shower.

I wanted it to be deep in her pussy, or her tight little ass, or splattered all over her face.

As it should be.

After it was finally over, I leaned forward and realized something else.

My cock was still fucking hard.

And it wasn't inside her.

* * *

Things took a fucking nosedive from there. An hour after I got out of the shower, my phone rang, and my entire world turned upside down.

I grabbed the phone, its shrill ring cutting through the heavy air in the room.

"You need to come home."

The voice on the other end belonged to Andreas. His usually steady voice trembled as he spoke, and I tensed, alarm bells immediately ringing in my head.

"What the hell is going on?" I demanded, a knot of unease tightening in my chest.

"Nikolas, I'm sorry to be the bearer of bad news, but your father... he's gone. He died five minutes ago, and they couldn't revive him."

The words hung in the air, the weight of their meaning settling over me like a suffocating blanket.

I clenched my jaw, struggling to process the unexpected blow. "What do you mean, gone?"

"A sudden heart attack, Nikolas. We rushed him to the hospital, but he didn't make it." Andreas' voice, normally unshakable, wavered with a vulnerability that mirrored my own shock.

My mind raced, grappling with the enormity of what I'd just been told. The patriarch of the Kaligaris family was gone in the blink of an eye.

I knew what this meant.

The weight of responsibility, the mantle of leadership, and all the things that came with that suddenly fell upon *me*. I felt the room spinning, the ground beneath me shifting as I tried to come to terms with the sudden turn of events.

I am the patriarch now.

"Andreas, I... I need to come home," I finally managed to say, the gravity of the situation settling over me like a hazy shroud.

"Yes, Nikolas. You need to come back. The family needs you now more than ever. The shipping business, the legacy your father built, it's now yours to control."

"Is the jet ready?" I asked, my tone clipped.

"It's on the tarmac waiting for you," he answered quickly.

"Good."

CHAPTER 5

 *ix months later*

Maci

We didn't have dinner that night. In fact, the only word he'd sent was a note delivered on his behalf that had detailed that urgent business had come up, and he needed to leave immediately to return to Greece. A little part of me had been disappointed, but another part of me was relieved that I wouldn't have to see him after what I'd done.

After I touched my pussy while thinking about him punishing me...

I shook my head and plunged my hands back into the dirt, digging another hole. When I was done, I leaned back and lifted my head, letting the sun's rays beat down on me like they could burn away the wicked thoughts bouncing around in my head.

I focused on being grateful that I was free and had the sun beating down on my head in the first place.

My godfather's team of lawyers had been an absolute godsend. Not only had they navigated the confusing labyrinth of the legal system for me, but they'd unearthed a simple technicality that got my entire case thrown out of court. I didn't have to serve any time or even do any community service at all. It was as if the night had never even happened.

However, the same couldn't be said for Ryan. The legal fallout hit him hard, and he bore the brunt of the consequences for our reckless night out. The judge slapped him with a considerable amount of jail time. I couldn't do anything to help him. Even when I asked my lawyers for advice for him, they refused, and I realized that Nikolaos had probably forbidden them from doing anything to help the boy that had gotten me into all this trouble in the first place.

I sighed.

I needed to focus on things I could change rather than those I couldn't. For instance, right now I was planting a row of sunflowers in hopes that the seeds would take root and bloom into beautiful blossoms in the coming months.

I'd gotten a job as a waitress at a local restaurant in town and was saving money to potentially go to college sometime in the future. I had decided that I did want to go, I just didn't know when. A part of me wanted to take another year off and see the world, but I hadn't done anything yet to actually take a step in that direction.

Maybe I'd visit Greece.

A familiar pair of dark, stormy grey eyes flashed before mine, and I flinched, thinking about touching myself with thoughts of him in my head again before bed tonight.

No. That had been a one-time thing, I lied to myself, even though I knew full well that it hadn't. It had been several times, more than I could count on two hands and two feet number of times, and a rush of fiery heat flushed my face.

It was my dirty little secret.

I was lucky he lived overseas. I didn't know if I could face him now, after everything I had done in the privacy of my very own bedroom.

I wiped the back of my hand across my brow, the sun hot overheard. With a determined resolve, I crouched down, feeling the cool soil against my fingertips. The vibrant yellow packets of sunflower seeds lay beside me, promising a burst of sunshine in the weeks to come. I couldn't wait to watch them bloom, knowing I had planted them myself.

Dipping my fingers into the soil, I created small, welcoming pockets in the earth, each one a potential home for a sunflower to take root. The sun warmed my skin as I carefully placed the seeds into their designated spots. With each gentle press, I imagined the vibrant petals and the towering stems that would soon grace my backyard.

My grandmother would be proud.

I missed her. Most days, I enjoyed my time alone. The majority of girls my age didn't own a home like I did, and I was grateful for that, but there were a few times that I wished she was still here beside me, making her famous apple pies just for funsies in the middle of the summer because she knew it was my favorite. Sometimes, I watched our favorite show *Gilmore Girls* just because it reminded me of her when I was feeling lonely without her, like she was there with me even though she wasn't.

As more time had gone on, it had become easier, but I never really stopped missing her. My phone alarm buzzed, reminding me that the pie I'd made was done in the oven. I tossed a few more seeds into place before I pushed myself up off the ground and made my way back into the house.

The aroma of baked apples and cinnamon greeted me as I opened the oven door. The pie looked good, its golden crust hinting at the delectable deliciousness within. However, as I pulled it out and set it on the kitchen counter, a subtle pang of nostalgia swept over me. It was a good pie, undoubtedly, but it wasn't quite like my grandmother's—something about the way she effortlessly worked her magic always added that extra touch of something special, and I hadn't been able to get it quite right yet.

That didn't mean that I wouldn't keep trying.

Then a weird sound reached my ears, almost like a boot scuffing against the floor, and I put the pie down on the counter before I stilled, listening intently. My heart skipped a beat.

What if someone had found out I was here alone? I'd taken a few self-defense classes in the past, but I'd never thought I'd need to use them. Not out here in the middle of nowhere Pennsylvania.

I told myself that I was being crazy. It was probably just the house settling or some animal in the yard, which wasn't outside the realm of strange things that had happened to me since my grandmother passed. Just a few months ago, a racoon had taken residence in the attic, and that had been wicked fun trying to get him out of there without losing an eye in the process.

As I stood there, trying to dismiss the unease creeping over me, another sound pierced through the air. A soft shuffle, like footsteps. My breath caught in my throat as I strained to listen. The creak of a floorboard followed, and a chill ran down my spine.

That wasn't an animal. Someone was in the house.

I moved cautiously, pulling off my oven mitts and tiptoeing away from the sound, my eyes scanning the room for any signs of movement. Fear gripped me as my mind raced through scenarios of how to escape. I knew the layout of the house like the back of my hand, and I aimed for the back door.

Silently, I navigated through the hallway, my senses heightened to every creak and groan of the old floorboards. The adrenaline surged through my veins as I neared the back door, my footsteps quickening with each step. But just as I reached for the doorknob, a tall figure in a suit emerged just outside the door, blocking my path and my avenue of escape.

Shit.

This wasn't good. Panic tightened my chest as I stumbled backwards. Maybe I could make it to the front door before he grabbed me, but even I knew the possibility of getting out of here without getting caught was quickly getting slimmer by the second.

His gaze met mine, a mix of authority and inscrutability, and I turned to run. The hope of escape fueled my sprint, my feet pounding against the creaky floor. I heard the back door squeak as it opened, and his footsteps behind me as he followed, his steps calm while my frantic ones echoed throughout the house.

As I neared the front door, my eyes widened in horror. Another man, equally imposing in a dark suit, stood waiting, blocking my path to freedom.

Desperation set in as I skidded to a stop, trapped between the two looming figures. The front door swung open with an eerie creak, revealing the ominous silhouette of several more men gathered on the threshold. In a heartbeat, half a dozen dark-suited figures streamed into the house, their presence filling the once-familiar space with an air of foreboding.

I felt a surge of helplessness, my breath catching in my throat, and I tried to remain brave.

"Who are you?" I exclaimed, taking a step back right into the man that had chased me through the house. In an instant, I tried to pull away, but his hands closed around my upper arms and held me in place. Several others moved towards me, and my breath hitched with my panicked nerves.

A wave of adrenaline surged through me, and I lashed out, kicking and punching with all the strength I could muster, but the sheer number of men rapidly overwhelmed me. Strong hands grabbed my limbs, quickly restraining my futile attempts to break free. The struggle intensified, my heart pounding in my ears as I tried to squirm free, but nothing I did granted me even an inch of freedom. It was a nightmare.

"Maci Williams." One of them stepped forward, and I visibly flinched.

"What do you want?" I asked, my desperation quickly becoming clear. Were these men going to kill me? Rape me?

A wicked grin broke out all over his face as he appraised me like I was some treasure he'd just come across at an auction.

"You're going to be very useful, I think," he declared, and my blood ran cold. "Allow me to introduce myself. I'm Alexander Pappas, the heir to the Pappas crime family."

I started, certainly not expecting something like that. For a moment, I was silent, trying to figure out if he was serious or not.

"What? Like something out of the movies?" I finally blurted out, my disbelief more than a little obvious.

"You're Nikolaos Kaligaris' goddaughter, aren't you?"

I opened and closed my mouth, not knowing if I should answer, and I eventually settled on denial. I didn't know why, it just felt right.

"I don't know who you're talking about," I finally replied, and his grin grew at least two times its previous size.

"Take her, boys," Alexander demanded, and all of a sudden, the hands gripping me tightened, and before I could do anything to stop it, one of them slipped a black hood over my head. Another one of them wrenched my arms behind my back and metal cuffs clicked into place.

Fuck, that hurt.

I started to scream.

"No one is going to save you, Miss Williams. Not from the likes of us," Alexander added, and I screamed that much louder.

He was right though.

No one came to save me.

CHAPTER 6

 *ikolaos*

I wished my father were here. He'd have known exactly what to do and say to make sure this meeting between families tipped in our favor, but I was still learning the ropes. Since his death, I'd been thrust into the role of family patriarch, and I needed to prove myself as capable a leader as my father.

The stakes were too high to play any games. I needed to make all the right choices at all the right times to make sure my family name stayed at the top where we belonged.

I hadn't been expecting to take the Kaligaris family reigns for another decade or two. I'd spent the past years building my own empire, diversifying the family business to make us that much more stable.

I needed to think beyond shipping, like investments in other businesses, legit ones that wouldn't draw unnecessary attention. The game had changed, and I needed to evolve with it. It wasn't just about being on top; it was about staying there, and I planned on doing just that.

I couldn't be foolish about it, either. It was my firm belief that diversification was key to holding power, and that putting all my chips in one basket was a surefire way to sink the ship. Power can sometimes be a fleeting thing, and I had to remember that.

I took a deep breath, preparing myself for the battle to come before I took a step and entered the lavishly adorned meeting room. The rich scent of mahogany and lingering cigar smoke surrounded me as I strode inside with my chin held high.

It had taken weeks to set up this meeting between families, and it had to go perfectly.

There was only one man waiting for me. Seated at the grand mahogany table was Antonios Stefanidis, patriarch of one of the other dominant shipping families here in Greece. He had an air of stoic authority that commanded respect. His salt-and-pepper hair, meticulously groomed beard, and penetrating hazel eyes spoke of both wisdom and a calculating business acumen honed through decades of navigating the turbulent seas of commerce and organized crime.

He'd been at this for far longer than me, and right now, I wanted him to be my ally. This meeting depended on it.

"Good to see you, Nikolaos," Antonios greeted, his voice resonating with power.

"I trust business has been favorable for the Stefanidis fleet, Antonios," I remarked, my words carrying a polite, but cunning, edge.

Antonios nodded, pride glinting in his gray eyes. "Indeed, but the waters are unpredictable. That's why I'm here, isn't it, Nikolaos?"

Antonios was a shrewd man. I'd give him that.

I leaned forward, fixing my piercing gaze on Antonios. "Let's get to the heart of the matter. The routes through the Eastern Mediterranean are becoming more challenging. I propose a strategic alliance to strengthen our positions."

Steepling his fingers, Antonios considered my proposal with a thoughtful expression. "An alliance, you say? What terms do you propose, Nikolaos?"

With a steadying breath, I started to outline a plan involving joint ventures, shared intelligence, and mutual support during crises. The negotiation wove through maritime law intricacies, the dynamics of rival factions, and the delicate balance of power that shaped our world.

"Together, we could create a formidable force," I continued, my voice carrying conviction. "Our combined fleets would be a power to be reckoned with, ensuring the prosperity of both our families for a long time to come."

Antonios leaned back, calculating. "And what guarantees do I have that this alliance won't be a Trojan horse? Loyalties can change in a moment. You know this as well as I do. Alliances shift in our world just like the tides."

I chuckled, amusement glinting in my eyes. "Trust is earned, Antonios. Let our history speak for itself. Our families have coexisted for generations. An alliance between us is not just about profit but about securing our legacy."

Antonios leaned forward, his eyes narrowing slightly. "Nikolaos, you've always been a shrewd businessman. What's in it for the Stefanidis family beyond mere assurances?"

I smiled and nodded, acknowledging the astuteness of his question. "Our combined strength would open doors previously inaccessible. Access to new trade routes, shared intelligence on potential threats, and a unified front against common adversaries. It's not just a partnership; it would be a strategic leap forward for both our families."

He considered my words carefully before responding, "But alliances come with a great many risks. What safeguards would we put in place to prevent betrayal?"

"Mutual oversight," I suggested. "A joint council comprised of representatives from both families, ensuring transparency and accountability. We'll be partners in decision-making, Dimitrios, not mere allies."

Antonios nodded thoughtfully. "I can see the merit in such an arrangement. However, my concern lies with the delicate matter of territories. How do we navigate potential conflicts of interest?"

I leaned back, tapping my fingers on the polished surface of the table. "A defined territorial agreement, clearly outlining the spheres of influence for each family. We'll establish boundaries that respect the strengths and specialties of our respective fleets, minimizing the potential for friction."

Antonios mulled over the proposal, his fingers drumming lightly on the armrest of his chair. "And what about our rivals, Nikolaos? The Arvanitis family, for instance. How will they perceive this alliance?"

"Our unity will be a testament to our strength," I asserted. "It sends a clear message to rivals that we stand united against any external threats. Besides, the Arvanitis family won't risk antagonizing both of our powerful alliances simultaneously."

A wry smile played on his lips. "Very well, Nikolaos. Let's draft the terms of this alliance. But remember, any betrayal will not be taken lightly. I will make you rue the day you betray me until your very last breath."

"Agreed," I affirmed, extending my hand for a final handshake.

For the next several hours, we delved into the specifics of the agreement. We decided that over the next few days, a contract would be devised and signed, solidifying the terms of our agreement in writing.

We ended the meeting with another firm handshake, and I took my leave, flying high on the feeling of victory. With the Stefanidis family at my side, my position in the shipping world would be even stronger.

And I needed it.

I didn't want to rock the boat, but I didn't plan to continue dealing in business with the mafia. It was my full intention to crack down on any and all illegal activities in my organization. It was time to clean house, and I needed to be the one holding the broom.

I was going to make the Kaligaris family name fully legitimate.

As I stepped out of the opulent meeting room, Andreas was waiting for me just outside the door, his expression a mask of concern.

"There's something you're going to want to see, boss," he began, his voice tinged with urgency.

"What is it?" I pressed.

"We need to head down to the piers right away. We found something that's for your eyes only," he answered cryptically.

Whatever he found needed to be out of range of potentially dangerous ears, and I nodded, understanding at once.

Pulling my shoulders back, I followed Andreas out of my office building and into a waiting car. The drive down to the docks was very short. He led me onto a massive tanker cargo ship in silence, and I didn't ask any questions because there was a look on his face that told me he didn't know what to say.

We descended through the labyrinthine corridors of the ship, passing dimly lit storage spaces until we reached a nondescript cargo area. The hum of the ship's machinery surrounded us, creating an eerie backdrop to whatever this was.

Andreas gestured towards a large shipping crate, his eyes reflecting a mixture of grim determination and obvious unease.

"This is where it gets ugly, boss."

With a turn of a latch, the container doors creaked open, revealing a scene that froze me in my tracks. I stared, my eyes wide, disbelief tightening inside of me like a vice.

Fuck.

It was my goddaughter.

There was a dirty gag stuffed in her mouth. Rope bound her ankles together and her arms were cuffed behind her back. Her once vibrant auburn waves were ratty and disheveled, tangled all around her face. Her cheeks were stained with dirt and what looked like trails of tears. Her beautiful blue-green eyes reflected a mix of terror and relief upon seeing me. It broke my heart to see that the spark of defiance that had danced within those pretty eyes had been dimmed by whatever she'd endured.

Someone was going to pay for this. *Dearly.*

"What the hell is this?" I seethed, my eyes narrowing as my heartbeat pounded in my chest. Blood rushed through my head, and I fisted my hands at my sides. Rage boiled within me as I took in the gravity of the situation.

I had worked so fucking hard to keep her out of my world, and here she was, right in the goddamn middle of it.

"The Pappas family had their eyes on her. They're the ones that took her. They aimed to use her against you. We intercepted them before they could get her to a secure place." Andreas answered quickly.

"How the fuck did they find out about her?" I roared.

Andreas hesitated for a moment, his eyes flickering with a hint of uneasy remorse. "When you were last in the States bailing Maci out of jail, something happened that we didn't catch. I think you might've been followed. We traced it back, and it seems they got wind of her existence during that trip."

My jaw clenched, the weight of guilt settling heavy in my stomach. The realization that my meticulous efforts to keep Maci hidden had faltered left me boiling with anger and frustration.

"Followed? How the hell did that happen?" I snarled.

Andreas shifted uncomfortably before continuing, "We think one of your fake names might've led them to your real one."

What the actual fuck?

"Let's fucking deal with this later," I grumbled, striding towards her. As gently as I could, I untied the gag and tossed it aside. The knots holding her legs together were loose, and I grimaced at the red marks on her ankles where the rough rope had rubbed at her skin. I traced my thumb across one of them, and she flinched.

"It's alright, Maci-girl. I've got you," I said softly, and her eyes watered a little, but she blinked her tears away.

Such a strong little thing. She needed to be taken care of and right now. I was going to put my anger aside and comfort her in exactly the way she needed.

She twisted her body, showing me the metal cuffs behind her back. I dug into my pocket and pulled out the tiny key I kept on me in case of emergencies.

I would say now counted as one of those.

Carefully, I slipped the key into the slot and turned it, unlocking one side of the cuffs and then the other. As soon as the pressure gave way on her arms, she cried out in real pain, and I quickly started massaging her shoulders, hoping that I could rub a little bit of it away.

How long had she been like this?

"Call in a doctor. Make sure she's paid enough to keep her lips sealed shut," I barked, and Andreas nodded quickly. I turned to Maci, knowing she needed me the most right now. I'd handle the breach of information later.

"I'm going to take you to my home now, Maci. I'm going to pick you up and carry you out of here," I offered quietly, and she nodded in silence. She bit her lower lip, as I wrapped my arms under her knees and around her waist. With hardly any effort at all, I lifted her up off the metal floor and shrugged her up against my chest. She wrapped her arms around my neck and held on.

I didn't miss the fact that her body molded perfectly against mine, like she had been made for me and only me.

Swallowing gruffly, I pushed my wayward thoughts aside and carried her through the tanker up to my car waiting outside. I kept her firmly against me, and she didn't fight, even as I held her in my lap for the drive back to my home in Vouliagmeni, a beautiful suburban area just outside of Athens.

I gritted my teeth, my anger returning in spades. If I hadn't taken that trip to bail her out of jail, my enemies would have never found out about her.

After all this time, all that I'd done to protect her and to keep her out of my world, she was a part of it now.

And she'd never be able to leave.

CHAPTER 7

 *aci*

Every part of my body hurt. My shoulders ached, my joints burned, and the skin around my wrists and ankles stung, but sitting in Nikolaos' lap was slowly simmering away all my pain. His warmth was comforting, and I took the opportunity to snuggle in closer against him as though he could take away everything that had happened to me over the past several days.

I didn't know how much time had passed since I had been taken. It had all started to run together. I had been kept hooded and bound most of the time, but even when the men had taken them off, there were enough guards surrounding me that escaping or fighting back wasn't even a remotely viable option.

I couldn't take on a dozen mafia soldiers. I wasn't a battle-hardened Viking. I was just a simple girl from New Hope, Pennsylvania whose biggest worry had been whether or not I was going to college next year and when my sunflowers were going to bloom in the spring.

The men had been cruel, but as long as I went along willingly with whatever they wanted, they didn't hurt me all that much. It had only taken one very painful backhand to the face to convince me to be obedient.

From what I could tell, at least to the best of my ability, they'd loaded me on a plane, then into a car and then onto a cargo ship. I'd woken up in the darkness, and it wasn't until the older man that had initially found me had opened the door that I'd even realized I was in a massive metal shipping crate in the first place.

I wasn't even really certain of where I was now. I guessed I was in Greece, solely because of my godfather, but I wasn't sure. He lived in Athens somewhere, or that's what I'd thought.

My godfather.

What was he doing here? Was he a part of the Pappas family too? Was I in danger? Had all this been his idea?

I stiffened and his arms tightened around me.

"You're alright, Maci-girl. You're safe now," he whispered, and for some reason his words comforted me. I didn't really know why, but they did. I curled against him even closer and peeked out of the window to look around. Having never been overseas, I didn't recognize anything.

"Where are we?" I asked quietly. My voice was hoarse, and I swallowed past my thirst. My stomach panged with hunger, and I realized I couldn't remember the last time I'd eaten. He reached into a compartment in the car, pulled out a bottle of water and handed it to me.

"Drink," he commanded.

I drank nearly half when he cleared his throat and curled his arms around me, holding me tighter.

"We're just outside of Athens. I'm bringing you to my home in Vouliagmeni," he explained gently.

As the driver glided the car through the winding roads, I couldn't help but curl into his lap. Eventually, the car slowed to a stop, and my gaze fixated on a sight that left me breathless—a colossal mansion that stood like a regal sentinel overlooking the brilliant blue waters of the Mediterranean Sea.

The sheer magnitude of the residence was staggering. It sprawled elegantly across the landscape. Towering pillars adorned the entrance, and the expansive grounds seemed to extend endlessly, utterly surrounded with manicured gardens and statues that whispered of wealth and sophistication. The architecture exuded grandeur, each facet of the mansion a testament to opulence that surpassed anything I'd ever seen in my life.

Gazing up, my eyes traced the intricate detailing of the structure, from the balconies that overlooked the sea, to the windows that seemed to frame a world of extravagance within, to the wrought iron gate that framed the entryway.

The mansion wore its wealth unabashedly, and I couldn't help but feel a sense of awe at the sheer scale of it.

Who the fuck was my godfather that he could own a home like this?

"This is your home?" I asked, my disbelief shining through with every syllable.

"Yes," he answered simply, but he said nothing more to explain how he could afford something like that.

"How?" I finally whispered.

"I'll explain everything after we get you cleaned up and medically cleared to make sure you're alright," he replied, deflecting my inquiry for the moment.

I chewed the inside of my cheek, uncertainty gnawing at my insides.

"Will you tell me if I'm safe with *you*? That you're not like Alexander Pappas?" I pressed.

"You're safe with me, Maci-girl," he replied, but he said nothing to answer my other question. I was just about to open my mouth and press a bit further, but the car door opened, and the older gentleman that had initially found me smiled warmly.

"My name is Andreas Dounas. Should you need anything at all, please don't hesitate to ask," he said, nodding his head politely.

"Thank you," I responded.

"A doctor is already waiting inside for her," he added, looking directly at my godfather now with the sort of deference someone would give a king, and alarm bells sounded in the back of my head in spades now. I felt more and more uneasy as the seconds ticked by, but I tried to remember how he'd taken care of me over the years and how he'd made sure that my grandmother and I had wanted for nothing all our lives.

I *tried* to give him the benefit of the doubt.

Andreas offered me a hand, but Nikolaos tightened his arms around me and carried me out of the car himself.

"I can manage," I insisted, wanting to at least have a little bit of autonomy. With a gentle nod, he lowered me to my feet, his touch almost reluctant, as if uncertain about releasing me from the cocoon of his arms. One foot touched the ground and then the other, my legs unsteady at first and his fingers didn't release me until I was standing up all on my own.

I took a step forward, and when I staggered, his hand was quick to reach out and catch me before I fell. Without another word, he swept me off my feet and carried me inside.

I didn't say anything else because I was too busy taking in everything around me.

The interior of the mansion mirrored the luxury displayed outside. Intricate chandeliers spread a warm, golden glow across the space, illuminating the polished marble floors in a soft light. The furniture was beautiful, all hand-carved out of the best materials money could buy. It was just another piece of evidence that my godfather wasn't who I thought he was, and that there was far more to the story than I'd ever thought.

"I can walk, really," I tried once more, but Nikolaos ignored me this time and hefted me a bit higher in his arms, almost to emphasize his point in silence.

There was a pretty blonde woman in a white coat waiting for us in the foyer. I guessed that she must be the doctor Andreas had mentioned, and when she began speaking, I was sure of it.

"Where would be the best place for me to examine her?" she asked, her voice clipped and professional.

"The sitting room. Right this way," Nikolaos led the way, striding straight into a room off the foyer. The room exuded a refined elegance, with tasteful furnishings arranged around a low wooden table.

The doctor motioned for me to sit on a plush chair, and Nikolaos reluctantly set me down, his expression revealing a complexity of emotions that I couldn't quite get a read on. He moved to the side of the room, hovering at the periphery almost as if he didn't want to leave me before he made sure I was alright.

"Ms. Williams, can you tell me if you're experiencing any pain or discomfort?" the woman questioned, and I took stock of my body before shaking my head.

The doctor immediately took charge, her skilled hands conducting a thorough check of my body as she delved into her exam. She checked my wrists and my ankles the most thoroughly, and I was pleased to see the marks from the cuffs and the rope had already begun to fade. Before, they were an angry red. Now they were a rosy pink.

"Just aches and pains, I guess. Nothing too bad," I finally offered, attempting to downplay the lingering soreness.

Her examination continued as she listened to my heartbeat and then poked and prodded my stomach to make sure I didn't have any injuries beneath my clothing. Honestly, it was little more than my yearly physical.

This all seemed like a bit much, but I knew if I just cooperated, it would be over sooner rather than later, so I just went along with it.

The doctor pressed further, "Any specific areas of concern?"

"No, just kind of sore all over," I admitted.

"Have you noticed any dizziness or headaches?" she probed further.

"No, not really. Just thirsty and hungry, to be honest," I replied, feeling a bit like a specimen under blatant scrutiny.

"Alright. We'll make sure you get something to eat and drink. Anything else you want to mention?" the doctor asked.

"There isn't really anything else," I answered quickly.

"Can you stand up for me?" she asked, cocking her head to the side.

Quickly, I stood up and was relieved to find that my legs no longer wobbled from misuse.

"Good, good. I find nothing of note, Mr. Kaligaris. She needs a good meal and plenty of water, but she's perfectly healthy otherwise, if a bit worse for wear," the doctor proclaimed.

"I'll see to it that she's taken care of. I trust that Andreas noted that this visit is of the utmost discretion?" Nikolaos asked, and she nodded quickly.

"Yes, sir. He did indeed," she replied.

"Thank you, doctor." He bowed his head, and she took her leave. I watched her go and swiveled my gaze back to my godfather, catching what appeared to be a predatory look on his face for a fraction of a second before it disappeared.

He took several steps towards me and swept me off my feet again.

"I really can walk, you know," I tried again.

"I know, but you don't have to," he answered, his gravelly voice making my abs squeeze tight. It felt odd to be cared for so thoroughly like this, so much so that I didn't really know how to handle it.

He carried me through the house up to a guest room, which was easily big enough to be the master bedroom. A king-sized bed, draped in luxurious dark blue linens, dominated the center, inviting sleep with its plush pillows and sumptuous duvet. Large windows framed by heavy, ornate curtains offered a view of the meticulously manicured grounds surrounding the mansion.

A writing desk stood against one wall, accompanied by a velvet-upholstered chair. The room was bathed in soft, natural lighting shining in from the window.

In one corner, a sitting area featured plush armchairs and a small coffee table. A discreet door hinted at an attached en-suite bathroom, undoubtedly as lavishly appointed as the rest of the space.

"I imagine you'd like to shower?"

"Yes, that would be lovely, but you're going to have to let me stand on my own two feet for that," I answered.

With a soft, reluctant sigh, he put me down. "Is there anything that you'd like to eat? I can have my chef prepare whatever you want," he offered.

"Surprise me," I replied, my voice quiet. I watched him with cautious ease.

"Come downstairs and find the kitchen when you're ready," he replied, then nodded curtly and headed out of the room, closing the door behind him.

For the first time in days, I sighed in relief. I hugged my arms around my chest.

I couldn't ignore the persistent fear in my head about my godfather. It was obvious that he was someone important and that he was far richer than I had initially thought him to be.

I told myself that didn't mean that he was someone danger-ous. Maybe he was a stockbroker, or some rich CEO of a tech company, or just a run of the mill billionaire like they featured in Business Weekly.

Or maybe he's a mafia boss himself.

I shook my head, trying to get my thoughts into a better place, and decided that a shower was exactly what I needed.

I ventured into the master bath and turned on the shower, letting the stall swirl with steam before I stripped out of the dirty clothing that I'd been wearing for days on end. The water pelted down on me as I arched my head back and wet my hair with a groan.

I'd almost forgotten what it felt like to be clean.

Under the soothing cascade of water, I let the warmth wash away the grime of the past few days. The steam enveloped me, and I luxuriated in the simple pleasure of getting clean again. My fingers massaged shampoo into my hair, the lather carrying away the residue of stress and fear. I scrubbed my skin until it tinged a bright pink, reveling in the sensation, and then I combed conditioner into my hair, running my fingers through it and feeling how soft it got almost immediately.

The hot water seemed to wash away not only the physical dirt but also the lingering traces of torment from my encounter with the Pappas family. I shivered as I remembered how it felt to be kidnapped by them, to feel completely fucking powerless in their hands. Then I immediately pushed thoughts of that away.

For a moment, I closed my eyes, allowing the water to cascade over me, the rhythmic sound almost echoing a soothing lullaby.

I was safe. Everything was going to be alright. Nikolaos had told me I was safe, and I needed to believe him.

Sooner or later, my godfather would send me home and this would all be over before I knew it, a distant nightmare to file away in the deepest recesses of my mind. I wouldn't have to think about how those grimy fingers felt on my skin or the sordid threats they'd made along the way.

I shivered.

With a deep breath, I shut the water off and strode out of the shower. I wrapped myself in a fluffy towel, ecstatic to find it warm. Even the tiles were heated beneath my feet. Every toiletry from the shampoo in the shower to the moisturizer on the bathroom counter was luxury and probably cost more than I made in a year. I combed my hair, brushed my teeth, and spoiled myself with everything there was at my disposal, including one of those fancy Korean face masks that made my skin super soft.

It was like my own personal spa.

In the closet I found a host of clothing for women, from dresses to pantsuits, to t-shirts and jeans, and everything in between. After some digging, I found a stretchy pair of black yoga pants, a long sage green sweater and some fluffy socks.

As I descended the stairs, the tantalizing aroma of grilling meat enveloped me, drawing me to the kitchen with eager anticipation. When I entered, my eyes widened at the sight of a table covered with what looked like a feast of traditional Greek dishes.

There were succulent skewers of marinated and grilled meat, their enticing aroma mingling with the fragrances of fresh herbs and citrus. There was also a colorfully vibrant Greek salad, a medley of crisp cucumbers, juicy tomatoes, briny olives, and crumbled feta cheese.

My mouth watered and I sat down. There was a plate awaiting me, and I waited a little while for Nikolaos, but my hunger got the best of me, and I started piling on the food. I covered the delicious grilled meats with Tzatziki sauce and ate to my heart's content. Every bite seemed more flavorful than anything I'd had back in the states.

By the time I finished my meal, Nikolaos hadn't come to join me, and I figured maybe he was in an important business meeting or something. Eventually, I washed my dish and headed back upstairs to my room.

I slipped into the bed and closed my eyes, falling asleep at once, absolutely exhausted.

I'd ask him all my questions tomorrow.

 ikolaos

I didn't join her for dinner that night. Mainly, I didn't want to get into it with her when I was angry, and I was fucking livid right now. I didn't trust myself around her.

If she had never gotten into that car with her dumb drunk friend, none of this would have happened. The Pappas would never have found out about her existence. She'd still be safe at home with nothing more to worry about other than what she was going to do with the rest of her life like a fucking normal young adult.

"There aren't many options, boss," Andreas stated. "I've made sure those involved were taken care of, but Alexander Pappas is a bigger issue. The mobsters involved in the kidnapping have been eliminated, but he's still at large."

"They know she exists. They'll kill her just to get to me," I snapped.

He didn't reply to my anger. He knew better than that.

My mind spiraled through possible ways to safely take her away from my world, but even as I said them, I knew they were pointless.

"We could fake her death and give her a new identity," I suggested, frustration evident in my voice.

"And risk the Pappas family discovering the truth? They have connections everywhere. Faking a death is no guarantee they won't find her," Andreas replied, his tone measured.

"Then we get her into another country. Far away. Somewhere they won't think to look," I proposed, steepling my fingers, my tone hopeful.

"That could work, but they have ways of finding people. She won't be truly safe, and you know it," Andreas countered.

I slammed my fist on the table in frustration, knowing he was right. "Dammit, there has to be something we can do. I won't let her be a pawn in their game."

Andreas leaned back in his chair, studying me carefully. "There's one more option, but it's extreme."

"Tell me," I demanded.

"We eliminate the Pappas family entirely," he suggested, his expression dead serious.

I scoffed at the idea. "That's a war I'm not ready to start. The consequences would be catastrophic. We can't afford to escalate things to that level."

"Then we need to find another way to keep her safe, boss," Andreas replied, his gaze unwavering.

I sighed. I knew I was fighting against myself. I knew there was only one option left. With a sigh, I finally said what I'd known all along to be the inevitable.

"She'll need to stay here. With me. Permanently."

CHAPTER 9

$\mathcal{M}$ aci

When I finally opened my eyes the next morning, it was well past noon. Honestly, it felt really good to sleep for so long. It had been days since I'd gotten a good night's rest, and it had been fucking awesome to sleep in a bed rather than on a cold metal floor. I stretched my arms high over my head and groaned. There was still a slight residual ache in my shoulders, but I felt mostly fine otherwise, like the last few days hadn't happened at all.

But it hadn't been a dream, not when I woke up in a room like this.

With a yawn, I climbed out of bed and padded into the bathroom. After splashing some water on my face, I brushed my teeth and my hair. When I was ready, I raided the closet for a new comfortable pair of leggings, as well as a pretty long sleeve wrap dress. Then I headed downstairs to the kitchen, where despite the late hour, there was still the aroma of bacon wafting through the house.

Tentatively, I turned the corner into the kitchen to see that my godfather was there already, waiting for me. He was sipping a cup of black coffee as his eyes flicked up to meet mine, and I found myself, once again, entranced by the tumultuous depths of his stormy gaze.

My pussy clenched when it shouldn't have, but before I could give my wayward body any credence, he cleared his throat.

"Maci, come sit," he said, his voice warm, and I moved to take a seat across from him at the polished wooden table.

The silence between us was heavy, and I couldn't help but feel the tension in the room, nor could I tell what he was thinking. I cleared my throat, trying to dispel some of the unease.

"Thank you for everything, Nikolaos," I said softly.

He nodded, his expression remaining unreadable. "I think it's time for the two of us to talk."

"There's so much I don't understand," I began, my voice shaky. "Why did they want me? Why did you bring me here? Who are you?"

He sighed, placing his coffee cup down and leaning forward, his hands clasped together. "Maci, there are things I haven't told you, things I've kept hidden to protect you so you could have a safe, normal life."

I furrowed my brow, feeling a growing sense of frustration rise within me. "Protect me from what? What's going on?"

He hesitated for a moment, as if debating how much to reveal. "I'm the patriarch to a major shipping family here in Greece, one of the biggest ones in the world."

"So, you're like the mafia," I answered, raising an eyebrow and pulling back just a little bit.

What if he was dangerous too?

"No. I'm not a mob boss, but I do oversee a massive empire. There is certainly legitimate business that we do every day that brings in a great deal of money, but there's a darker side to my world that involves very dangerous people who would use you against me, who would kill you to get to me. Those people are part of the mafia."

I blinked, trying to process his words. "You mean like the Pappas family?"

He nodded gravely, "Yes, like the Pappas family. They're not just my enemy, Maci. They're part of a world I've tried to shield you from all this time."

My mind was spinning. I had thought my godfather was just a successful businessman, but I had no idea the sheer scale of it, and now it seemed he was involved in something much more complicated and dangerous then I could have ever imagined.

"What do we do now?" I asked, my voice trembling with uncertainty.

He reached across the table, his grip on my hand firm and reassuring. "For now, you stay here with me. I'll do everything in my power to keep you safe, Maci. I promise."

"For how long?" I asked.

"Indefinitely," he answered, and I started, not really believing what I'd just heard with my own ears.

He couldn't be serious. He was asking me to give up my life, to move away from everything I held dear based on what? Some gut feeling that I was still in danger?

My anger flared, and I stood up abruptly, facing him. "I can't just abandon my life, Nikolaos. I want to go back home."

He rose from his seat along with me, his expression a mix of concern and determination. "Maci, you don't understand the danger you're in. My enemies won't stop until they find you. I've seen firsthand what they're capable of. They're vicious, and they'll use any means to get to me, even if it means hurting you or even worse, killing you in cold blood."

I could feel my emotions spiraling out of control, frustration warring with the fearful fury that had settled in my chest.

"You're involved in all this illegal stuff, and you expect me to just stay with you here quietly? I don't think so," I countered, gritting my teeth and fisting my hands at my sides.

"When I said you'd be staying here with me indefinitely, I didn't mean to imply that it was optional, Maci," he said darkly, and his jawline tensed with enough anger to match my own.

"I don't want to be a part of your world. I just want to go back home," I replied hotly, and his expression hardened further.

"I didn't want you to be a part of my world *either*. I set you up so you would never be dragged into it. All you had to do was keep out of trouble and none of this would have ever happened," he snapped, his fury far more palpable now.

I took a step towards him, leveling him with a glare that was fit to kill. The room felt charged with tension, and I couldn't help but notice the way his eyes bored into mine, intense and unwavering. Despite the anger and frustration, there was something else in the air, something I willfully tried to ignore, but I knew what it was.

Desire.

My clit throbbed as Nikolaos cocked his head. His brow furrowed, but he remained silent.

"What do you mean this would have never happened?" I pressed.

"The only reason they found out about you was because I had to go bail you out of jail," he said, his frustration clear.

"You're serious right now?" I scoffed.

"As the grave, Maci-girl. All you had to do was not get busted and none of this would have ever happened."

"I can't believe you're mad at me about getting arrested when you're basically a fucking mob boss," I snapped, unable to hold back my anger.

The words hung in the air between us, and the room seemed to crackle with even more tension. I could feel the heat between us despite the rage and frustration still radiating off of each of us in spades. Our bodies were so close, our breaths mingling, and I couldn't deny the unfathomable desire that coursed through me.

I tried to suppress it. I failed.

His gaze darkened, and his fingers brushed against my cheek, a feather-light touch that sent shivers down my spine.

"Maci," he began, his voice low and husky, "I never wanted any of this for you. But now that you're in danger, I'll do whatever it takes to keep you safe, and if that means keeping you captive here in my home, then so be it."

"I can't fucking believe…" I began, but his hand jerked back to grab the hair at the base of my scalp. He fisted his fingers into my hair, and I cried out, a flash of pain radiating across my skull. With force, he pulled me in, and what came next was far more shameful than anything I could have ever imagined.

I *should* have resisted. I *should* have continued to argue, but in that moment, it was as if the world had melted away, leaving only the two of us.

Our lips met in a searing kiss, and all at once, it consumed me. Fiery passion ignited between the two of us, and I kissed him back, ignoring all the glaring red flags that should have stopped me.

He was my *godfather*.

And he was almost *twice* my age.

Not to mention he was also a fucking billionaire godfather mob boss or whatever the dangerous fuck he was.

And he kissed really, really fucking well. His lips pressed into mine as his fingers gripped the hair at the back of my head, not letting me go and forcing me to take every last second of that kiss, whether I liked it or not.

The problem was that I did like it.

I didn't *want* to like it.

But I *did*.

Our mouths moved with hunger, each of our tongues dueling for control. His fingers tangled in my hair, and his nails traced fiery paths of pain across my scalp. Then his teeth nipped my lower lip, biting me harshly enough to make me yelp out loud, and he swallowed the sound with another punishing kiss that left my jaw aching and my lips sore.

I didn't back down and just take it. I kissed him back, but as defiantly as I could. I bit down on his lip just as he had mine, and then he roughly pushed me down to my knees.

His hold on my hair tightened as he twisted my head to the side and pressed my cheek directly against his cock.

Oh my God.

He was hard. Like *really* fucking hard.

I swallowed with my own nervous arousal. A part of me liked that I'd made him that way, and another part of me was deeply ashamed, but also angry and defiant at the exact same time. I seethed down on the floor.

"I'm not going to fight with you, Maci. You're going to stay here with me, and that's just how it's going to be," he scolded huskily, his intentions dark from the tone of his voice.

I gazed up at him, meeting his eyes. His pupils were so blown out that his eyes were practically black, and I narrowed mine right back in his direction. In that moment, we teetered on the precipice of something perilous, where fury, desire, and an unsettlingly heated intent danced together, threatening to unravel the fragile boundaries that were keeping us apart.

Then I pushed it over the edge.

"Fuck you," I spat.

His cock throbbed against my cheek.

His stormy gray eyes darkened further, and his jawline tightened. His lips formed a thin determined line as his brow furrowed with anger, frustration, and something else that lit my own body on fire.

It doesn't make sense.

I shouldn't want this man, but I'd imagined a moment like this many times in the past, safe in the confines of my own bed late at night all alone.

But this is real...

I couldn't deny the heat simmering beneath my skin or the way my abs kept tensing with need, nor could I ignore the way his erection was pulsing with desire right against the side of my face.

My nipples pebbled inside my bra.

"Now, let me tell you how this is going to go," he growled, and I resisted just a little bit, but he pulled my hair more firmly, holding me in place despite my efforts as I cried out.

It hurt, but a part of me liked that it did.

"You can take my cock in your mouth, or you can take it down your throat. Make your choice," he continued, and I stiffened in his grasp immediately.

The absolute fucking nerve.

I'd never sucked a man's cock before. Sure, I'd seen one or two in a porn on occasion, so I at least knew the basics, but nothing in real life.

Fuck.

I opened my mouth to tell him off and cover up the fact that his threat was just a little bit intriguing, but he cut me off before I could say anything back.

"Think carefully before you answer, Maci-girl. I'm not going to give you a second chance," he declared firmly, and the heat in my body swirled inside of me like a bomb just moments away from exploding.

The use of my childhood nickname seemed even more shameful now that it was intertwined with whether or not I was about to take his cock in my mouth.

I shouldn't be aroused right now. I should be angry, furious even, that my godfather was pressing his hard cock against my cheek and threatening to fuck my mouth or my throat.

"But…"

"Choose," he demanded, leaving no room for negotiation in his tone.

I shifted from one knee to the other and licked my lips. His gaze followed the tip of my tongue, and a wicked smirk broke out at the corner of his lips, almost like he was imagining it running along the line of his cock.

Because *I* most certainly was…

"My mouth," I replied, my voice almost so soft that I could hardly hear it myself.

"Good choice, Maci-girl," he growled, and a surge of nervousness raced through me like a bolt of lightning as he reached down and unbuckled his belt. Gradually, he slid the tip through the buckle, and I watched as it drew apart. His fingers dropped to the button of his slacks, undoing it slowly before he moved on to the zipper. With a leisurely effort, he pushed his slacks down just enough to reveal a black pair of boxer briefs. Then, he freed his cock.

I couldn't tear my eyes away.

I'd imagined what it would feel like to see a man's cock, and specifically *his cock*, on several occasions, but I had never thought it would actually happen.

I couldn't deny it, especially right now when I was staring directly at it.

My clit zinged and I bit my lip, taking in the sheer size of his dick. It was far more intimidating up close like this than I thought it would be. A thick rim surrounded the head, and a bead of precum was already pebbling at the slit at the top. Veins throbbed to either side, and I swallowed hard, imagining it sinking in somewhere else that was definitely not my mouth.

It was the kind of big that made a girl nervous about taking it.

Down my throat.

Inside my pussy.

A strangled noise of disbelief escaped me, and I shifted on my knees, trying to reconcile with the way my own body was pulsating with a feverish heat.

I wanted this, but I *didn't*. I *shouldn't*. I didn't even really know.

"Open that pretty mouth," he demanded, and my abs tensed tight with desire. Every nerve in my body was simmering with it, and as much as I tried to push it all away, it sizzled right through anyway.

His fist tightened at the back of my scalp, and a delicious volley of pain blossomed across my skull as a shiver of decadent need raced down my spine.

I opened my mouth.

"That's a *good* fucking girl," he growled, and my body tensed with heated desire.

With a surprising amount of gentleness, he guided his cock in between my lips. My eyes flicked up to meet his, and the darkness within them took me aback.

No. It consumed me.

The taste of his arousal was instant. It was salty, yet somehow slightly sweet, and I swirled my tongue around his thick length, wanting more of it despite the fact that I knew this was wrong.

I *shouldn't* have his cock in my mouth.

Why did it feel so right then?

My movements were tentative at first, but I knew the gist of what to do, at least a little bit, so I bobbed my head back and forth and took him onto my tongue as far as I was able before I pulled my head away.

The expression of absolute bliss on his face was more than enough to spur me on, and I redoubled my efforts, sucking gently around the head of his cock until he gasped with pleasure. Then his hips surged forward, and he forced the length of his cock a bit further down my throat, making me choke a little before he jerked his hips back.

"That's right. Fucking take it," he growled, and my insides quivered with growing need.

His growl rolled down my spine like a warm summer rain, and I opened my mouth wider, tried to take him a bit deeper before his fist tensed and pain radiated down the base of my skull, shooting straight to my clit as I pitched forward just in time for him to thrust inside me. I gagged for a moment, and he pulled back out a little, giving me the briefest of seconds to collect myself before he pistoned back inside.

Every thrust into my mouth felt like he was possessing a part of my body that no one had dared touch before. Roughly, he enjoyed me, and I suckled around him, noting that my cheeks were beginning to get sore more quickly than I thought they would.

Fuck.

This was far more than I thought it would be. There was a part of me that kind of wanted it, that wanted more than just this, but I worried about how much it would hurt if he went further than this.

I knew the logistics of sex, but with a cock this big, there was no way that sex with him wasn't going to hurt.

Not to mention the fact that you're a virgin.

The more I thought about it, the more nervous I became, yet somehow, my body became even more alive.

Instinctively, I knew a fucking from a man like him wouldn't be gentle. He'd be rough and every single thrust would hurt just as much as the last, just like his punishing kiss.

I pressed my hands against his thighs, meaning to push back, and his grip pulled my head back far enough that his dick popped out of my mouth with an audible sound.

"I'm not through with you, Maci-girl. You're mine now, and I'm going to show you how I'll deal with you every time you fight me," he snarled, then forcibly lifted me up off the floor and tossed me over the back of the couch like it was the most normal thing in the world.

With my bottom high in the air, I tried to push up against the cushions, but his hand pressed down on my lower back, immediately holding me in place. I stiffened and swallowed hard.

"Deal with me… how?" I asked, my voice trembling with nervous energy. Maybe he knew that I'd touched myself while thinking about him. Maybe he even knew that I'd fantasied about him punishing me, but how? How could he know?

Maybe I was crazy. Maybe he wasn't about to spank me, and this was just preparation for the fucking I might have coming, but I didn't know. At least, I wasn't sure.

His other hand flipped up the back of my dress with ease.

"By introducing you to my belt," he said darkly, and I cried out, struggling with everything I had. My strength was no match for his, though, and he easily overpowered me and pushed me back into place. I kicked at his shins, but I missed, and he gripped the stretchy waistband of my leggings and yanked them down until they were around my knees, effectively binding my legs with my own clothing.

At least my panties were still up.

For now...

CHAPTER 10

M aci

"By introducing you to my belt."

His words echoed in my mind, over and over again, and I couldn't make them stop.

What panties was I even wearing? I knew they weren't mine. My clothing from the other day had seemingly disappeared, including my dirty underwear, leaving me with the pretty lacey numbers I'd found in the closet upstairs.

Pink lace, I remembered. Strappy and sexy enough to make me wonder who they'd belonged to before me. My heart squeezed painfully in my chest. Was I just another girl whose throat he'd shoved his cock down? Were there other women? Why did I care?

I closed my eyes and tried to quell the rising panic in me. Why wasn't I fighting harder? Why was my body at war with my mind over this? My pussy tensed, anticipating him inside me, and when his fingers traced down beneath the strings of my panties, every muscle in my body tightened along with it.

There was no stopping what came next.

With one firm yank, he tore through the strap at the side of my panties and then ripped through the other. He jerked the fabric away from my body, revealing my pussy to his view an instant later. I cried out and fought for everything that I was worth.

With embarrassing ease, he pinned my wrists behind my back. My leggings tangled around my knees, preventing me from kicking effectively. Bent over the couch like this, I was in no position to get back up, especially when he adjusted me forward just enough that my toes lifted right up off the floor.

I'd never felt so helpless and little in my life.

And now he can see your pussy.

I squeezed my eyes shut again as shame raced through me in spades. No man had ever laid eyes on my naked pussy before, and it felt even more embarrassing to realize that this wasn't even for sex, although maybe that would come, but for a spanking with my godfather's belt.

He was looking at my pussy because I'd pushed him, because I needed to be punished and we both knew it.

My pussy clenched hard, and a drop of arousal rolled down my thighs, making me exceedingly aware of something else for the first time.

I was *wet*.

Not just a little wet either, but soaking wet. The kind of wet that would make my pussy and my inner thighs glisten.

The kind of wet I can't even hope to hide...

"We could talk about this," I protested, pressing my inner thighs together as if it could help, even though I knew it was useless to even try.

My heart hammered in my chest, and my skin grew a bit clammy. It was almost as if I could feel the weight of his stare on my bare skin, that he was looking directly in between my legs at every one of my most private of places and there was nothing I could do to stop him.

"It's too late for that, little girl," he declared, and with a loud whoosh, he pulled his belt free from his slacks. I turned my head, watching him as he folded it in half and held the buckle in his hand.

This wasn't a fantasy anymore.

This was *real*.

As much as I could try to struggle and escape this, I knew it was futile. He was so much bigger and stronger than me, leaving me at a distinct disadvantage. Even if I did manage to escape him, where would I go? I didn't have a passport or money or any way to get back home to Pennsylvania. I was trapped here.

But if I didn't find a way to stop this, I was going to get a spanking with a belt for the very first time in my life. It didn't matter whether I wanted it or not. I was going to get it.

"Please, godfather. I'll do what you say," I protested, thinking that it was potentially possible to negotiate my way out of this. Maybe he would realize that he'd already pushed far enough, that maybe he shouldn't have fucked my mouth and maybe I shouldn't have wanted him to either.

Maybe he'd realize this was wickedly wrong and he'd put a stop to this whole thing.

Then again, maybe he wouldn't...

That's what you want, isn't it, you little slut?

"You will, and you'll do what I tell you with a bright red ass, Maci-girl," he declared, and my heart pounded that much faster. Even though he had a firm hold of my wrist, I tried to reach back and cover myself, but my hand barely moved an inch before he yanked it right back.

"I'll stay here with you," I continued, and he chuckled softly.

"You'll do that too. It doesn't matter if I need to belt this defiant little ass of yours every day, little girl. You're not in charge anymore. Now, you belong to me," he stated, his voice rumbling with heat.

"You don't need to use your belt," I whimpered.

"From now on, I'm going to be the one to decide what you need, Maci, and you've needed the belt for a long time, ever since that day I dropped you off at your house after bailing you out of fucking jail," he murmured, and my stomach dropped to the tips of my toes.

"Please," I tried one last time, but he didn't listen. Instead, he whipped the belt across my bare cheeks.

I wasn't prepared for that first strike. I wasn't even remotely ready for it.

A line of liquid fire arced across both cheeks and stole my breath away. Raw, stinging pain radiated from that first blow, intensifying with every passing second as I felt the resulting welt rise on my skin. A soft gasp escaped my lips, and I clamped them together, vowing to myself that I needed to stay quiet.

That I wasn't going to let him know how much the belt stung.

This was a spanking. Nothing more than that. A childish punishment, and I was a grown woman. I could take a belting, and I'd survive it. Hell, it might even make me stronger.

Mustering as much defiance as I could, I lifted my chin with a huff, only to be punished with another harsh crack of the belt. I swallowed back a cry as every muscle in my body tensed with pain before a third lash whipped across both cheeks.

I could take this.

The belt bit into my cheeks several more times before something unexpected started to brew deep in my belly. After every stinging lash, each wave of pain was inevitably followed by another much stronger one of pleasure.

I couldn't be enjoying this… *right?*

Even as I asked myself the question, my pussy spasmed as the belt cracked against my bare cheeks. Another drop of arousal rolled down my inner thighs. With another swing of the belt, the chilly air rushed over my wetness, making me keenly aware of every square inch of it.

My face heated with shame. I shouldn't like this. This was cruel, abusive even, but somehow still my body wanted it in some way.

Then my belting truly started.

I had thought he was using it harshly before. I thought each lash hurt. What came next made me realize how thoroughly gentle he'd been so far.

The next lash made me cry out.

The belt whipped across my bottom firmly and far more quickly than before. He lashed from the tops of my cheeks all the way down to the middles of my thighs, which I swiftly learned stung more than all the rest.

I tried to stay quiet.

I couldn't.

Honestly, I only managed to stay quiet for, at most, a few more lashes before my cries echoed off the walls. He didn't slow down once that began either.

In fact, the belt started falling that much faster.

It whipped the lower curve of my cheeks so thoroughly that I keened, the sting almost more than I could bear. The tip of the belt cut through the air again and again. I could feel the welts rising from every lash, burning hotter and hotter as my whipping went on and on for what felt like forever.

He thrashed me so thoroughly that my eyes started to water, and I started begging for mercy.

"Please," I pleaded, my voice breaking with emotion.

"I'm not through with you," he demanded, and another strike of the belt cracked against my bare cheeks.

I didn't care that he could see my pussy. I didn't care that I was probably wetter than before. I just wanted the belting to stop.

"Please, Nikolaos," I begged.

"Address me properly when I'm taking my belt to your bare ass," he growled.

"Please, sir," I whimpered, but my spanking didn't end there. Instead, he focused solely on my upper thighs, and the true gravity of how little control I had right now hit me.

This wasn't going to end when I wanted it to. It was already far past that. Now, it was only going to stop when he'd decided I'd had enough and not a moment before.

I was completely powerless.

A fresh wave of panic spiraled through me, and I struggled hard, but with the belt falling and his thorough hold on me, I couldn't escape even a single lash.

I couldn't make this stop.

He's in control, and that's what's making your little pussy so fucking wet right now.

I wailed as my pussy tightened, my abs clenching with desire. My eyes watered, and I tried to blink my tears away.

"You're going to let me take care of you, aren't you, Maci-girl?" he asked, his voice dangerously dark.

"Yes, *sir*," I wailed. I rocked my hips back and forth, and the belt bit down right on the fullest part, causing a surge of desire to race through my core.

"Good. Now I'm going to finish your belting and make sure you *never* forget that," he declared, and my stomach launched right up into my throat. Nervous anxiety roiled through me, but there was no time to think as that terrible leather strap truly began to punish me.

There was nothing other than my bare ass and his belt, nothing more in the world besides the two of us right now.

Every welt burned with fiery agony. My entire ass felt like it had been stung by a thousand needles or like I had sat straight down in a fire. I whimpered when one strike bit right underneath my right ass cheek and a matching one followed on the other side.

Pain twisted with pleasure, and I lost myself for a moment, freefalling in a place of helplessness with no end in sight.

With every lash, I cried out.

Soon my cries became sobs, and before I could do anything to stop them, tears were rolling down my cheeks. My body shook as I slumped over the couch, and my back arched, presenting myself for his punish-ment as much as I could in hopes he would grant me mercy.

He did *not*.

He whipped my bottom with the belt six more times, ensuring that every inch of my ass was thoroughly scalded before he was finally through with me.

When he was done, he tossed the belt beside me on the couch, and my tearful eyes stared right at it.

The black leather was well worn, and if I'd had the balls, I would have reached out and touched it. The scent of real leather wafted over to me, and for a moment, I could hardly believe that such an innocent thing could be so utterly painful.

His hand reached out, tracing along the lines of a single welt, closer and closer to the cleft of my ass and then down further still, all the way until he was mere inches away from my slit.

He didn't stop there.

His fingers journeyed further still until they brushed against the arousal between my thighs.

"You're soaking wet, Maci-girl. You enjoyed this, didn't you?" he observed, and I gasped, trying to get ahold of myself even through my tears.

"No," I breathed.

"Don't lie to me," he warned, and my pussy clenched so hard that my hips rocked. He dragged his touch back and forth as

I slowly tried to gain control of myself. I blinked quickly, my tears slowly drying on my cheeks.

"I wasn't…"

"Hush and take your fucking like a good girl," he growled.

My fucking…

Oh my god, this was really happening. This wasn't just happening in my head anymore. This was real.

"*Yes, sir,*" I whispered.

Drawing in several ragged breaths, I listened to the rustle of fabric behind me, and then his cock was pressed up against my virgin entrance. The heat of it felt like a fire brand against my naked flesh, and my hips bucked against him almost as if my body was seeking him out. I drew my lower lip in between my teeth and nibbled it.

I should have told him I was innocent, that no man had ever touched me, but I kept silent because a tiny piece of me wanted him to fuck me and thought that if I did tell him, he might decide not to.

I didn't want *that.*

I didn't say a word as his hands released my wrists and wrapped around my hips.

With his first thrust, I screamed.

The head of his cock pistoned right through my virgin barrier, and a flash of pain seared through me so intensely that my vision wavered and turned white. I keened and my entire body froze up, overwhelmed from the stinging agony burning through every inch of me.

Slowly, he pulled out and paused.

"You're a virgin," he murmured, his voice laced with shock.

"Yes," I whispered in return. There was no denying it now. Not when he'd taken it for himself. Hell, my virgin blood was probably slickening his cock right now.

He thrust into me again, and my pussy pinched tight, but his movements were slow, almost gentle even, gradually using my body as the pain from the taking of my virginity started to fade only to be replaced with something that much hotter.

My abs clenched and every nerve in my body began to tingle, demanding more, wanting more, needing more.

"We shouldn't…" I whispered.

"This sweet little pussy is so very tight," he murmured, and my cheeks flushed bright red just as my pussy clenched around his thick length. Every thrust was painful, stretching me painfully wide, and I gasped, my fingers digging into the couch cushions as I tried to hold on.

"Sir," I breathed, but with every inch of his cock, my protests grew weaker and weaker. In no more than a few moments, my words died on the tip of my tongue and pleasure steamrolled through me with a vicious force.

Fuck. He was so big that my pussy could hardly take it.

"Please," I begged, fully tipping over the edge into the world of desire. My hips arched back, and I took him a bit deeper now.

His slow, leisurely thrusts began to gradually pick up speed, possessing more and more of my body with every stroke.

I began to enjoy it.

Far more than I thought I should…

Each inch of his cock sunk into me, grinding against a place deep inside me that drove me crazy with need, and I pulled in a shaky breath. His hands gripped my hips tighter, and I whimpered, feeling my core squeeze hard. My inner walls gripped at him, trying to pull him in at the same time that they tried to push him out.

This felt far better than it should.

Everything in my head was fighting against it, but my body was already on the precipice of something truly great. My fingers and my toes curled. My back arched, and his cock sunk inside me that much deeper until my world felt like it was practically vibrating.

I shouldn't like this. I shouldn't want to come with my godfather's cock deep inside my pussy.

But even I knew that I was fighting against the inevitable.

He slapped my right ass cheek, and my clit pulsed hard. My thighs began to tremble, and I keened, trying to fight the rising wave of pleasure, but it was useless.

I felt like a freight train about to barrel off its tracks, like I was going to lose control at any given moment and there was nothing I could do about it.

Desire simmered through me, ready to boil over, and I finally gave in completely.

My orgasm crashed into me like a tidal wave. Pleasure wove its way through the strands of my every nerve, fraying me at the seams and tearing me apart from the inside out. With a keening cry, I arched back as he thrust into me. With every savage stroke of his cock, he possessed my body more completely than I could have ever known.

I writhed beneath him, rocking my hips back and forth as he fucked me. With my head in the clouds, there wasn't much I could do other than take every last ounce of pleasure he forced upon me, and then some. Passionate need surged within me, an intoxicating current that seemed to consume every fiber of my being. It was an electric rush, igniting my senses and leaving me breathless, my heart racing in tandem with the fiery intensity of my desires.

I surrendered to the sweet torment of passion that enveloped every inch of me from my head all the way to my toes. Swept away by the current, I soared as exquisite bliss burned through me in one wave after another. My pussy spasmed around his cock, and he groaned, letting me know without a doubt that he could feel it.

My cheeks burned, but I was too caught up in ecstasy to give it any thought.

"Did you come good and hard for me, Maci-girl?"

"Yes," I breathed, my face blazing with shame. I stared down into the couch cushions as he pushed in and out of my body, taking me as he saw fit. My heart hammered in my chest and my blood rushed through my ears. A sheen of sweat glistened on my skin as I drew in one ragged breath after another, and I closed my eyes, just trying to gather myself as the seconds ticked by.

"Good, but you should know I'm far from through with you. You're mine now, and I'll fuck you as hard as you need to be fucked, needy girl," he threatened, and my body came alive at the same time that my nerves clenched up tight. I opened my mouth to protest, but he thrust into me so hard that my body jerked forward from the force of it.

Oh fuck.

"I've been gentle with you so far," he purred, and the sound of his voice rolled down my spine like a cool drink of water.

"Please," I pleaded, feeling the need to beg for mercy from whatever came next without even knowing what it was.

"I've been waiting a long time for this. I'm through with being gentle," he rasped, and he slammed into me with vicious force. My pussy still burned from his massive size, but it hurt more now that he was fucking me this hard.

Wait. He's been wanting me this whole time, too?

The cadence of his thrusts quickly spiraled into something brutally vicious. He fucked me so hard that he threw me into another mercilessly hard orgasm in moments rather than minutes.

I screamed through it, but I also came harder than I'd ever come in my life. I came undone, the threads of my soul unraveling one by one.

In that moment, time itself seemed to stand still as I lost myself in the whirlwind of sensations. His touch was both a torment and a lifeline, each caress setting my skin ablaze and sending shivers of pleasure cascading down my spine.

My breaths came in ragged gasps, and I clung onto the couch as if it was my anchor in a stormy sea. My heart pounded, the rhythm matching the tempo of his thrusts. Before I knew what was happening, my eyes were rolling back in my head and my legs were quivering with white hot euphoria.

Holy shit.

I'd never come more than once before, and now I was coming for a third time, and there seemed to be no end in sight.

A lightning bolt of pleasure cracked through me as every muscle in my body froze up with heated bliss.

My head soared up into the clouds, lost in a veritable web of sensation that struck down deep into the pit of my soul. By the time I came down, every inch of me was shaking and I couldn't make it stop.

He didn't slow down either.

My fucking continued with ruthless vigor, and I realized with a panicked gasp that he hadn't come yet. In fact, he didn't even seem close.

"Sir, please," I begged.

"I'm enjoying myself, Maci-girl."

His cock dove in and out of my pussy, slamming deep inside me. The initial burn from his taking had faded, leaving nothing more than mind-numbing pleasure and the residual burning stretch of his thick girth inside of me. My nipples pebbled, still safely encased in my bra, and then he slammed into me one last time viciously hard before he pulled out.

"You're not on birth control, are you?" he asked, his tone a bit annoyed.

"No…" I wailed.

His hands left my hips and one of them closed over the back of my neck. I cried out as he lifted me off the sofa. Before I knew what was happening, he'd placed me back on my knees.

"Open your mouth. You're going to suck my cock and swallow everything I give you," he demanded.

My eyes glanced down at the swollen red beast right in front of me. It seemed even larger than before, and I pulled away before I realized what I was doing. Using his body, he pinned me against the couch. With the back of my head flush against it, his cock seemed even more imposing up close, and I shook my head.

"Be a good girl. And. *Open. Your. Mouth,*" he growled, and I shivered with nervous arousal. I tried to sit back, but there was nowhere for me to go. I was trapped by his cock, and it jumped right in front of my face as I glared up at him.

"You're an asshole," I snarled.

"You can either open your mouth, or I can whip that freshly fucked pussy with my belt. Your choice, Maci-girl," he barked.

I gritted my teeth before doing as he bade me, but I scowled back at him with as much spite as I could muster.

My clit throbbed like it had its very own heartbeat the whole fucking time.

The tip of his cock slid into my mouth, dragged against my tongue, and pressed against the back of my throat.

I gagged, but he didn't pull back this time. He just let me suffer as he fucked my mouth much more savagely than he had the first time.

I tried to push back against his thighs, but with my body up against the couch, there was nowhere for me to go, and he knew it. Eventually, he pulled back a bit and let me gather myself, but that period of time was unmercifully short. Then he thrust back inside of me and pushed the tip of his cock past the barrier of my throat, and I gagged again.

He didn't care.

He just *fucked* my face.

Every thrust was rough. He gave me no time to gather myself, simply stroking his cock in and out of my mouth like I was just some fuck toy, and my pussy burned with need because of it.

The taste of myself was rife along his thick length. Sweet and tangy and slightly metallic from my virgin blood. I blushed hard, thoroughly ashamed at such a wicked thing.

He fucked my throat hard enough to leave it sore in mere minutes, then he fucked it some more. His hand wound down to grasp the back of my throat as he took what he wanted and then some, possessing me so completely that I knew I would never be the same after this.

Soon, my panic started to well up inside of me. I pushed a bit harder against his thighs, but it accomplished nothing.

He still fucked my face anyway.

My eyes watered and spittle dripped down my chin.

"Play with your clit while I fuck your face. I'm not going to come until you do," he said darkly, and in that moment, there was no room for hesitation or doubt. I just gave into the intoxicating blend of passion and surrender that enveloped me.

If he wanted a wild filly, I'd give him one.

I reached down between my legs and started at what I found. The wetness there was seeping down my inner thighs. My fingers glided along my arousal, and I sucked in a breath, trying to swirl my tongue around his dick at the same time. I choked, and he thrust into me a bit more viciously, but then my fingertips danced across my clit, and a magical sheen of pleasure pierced straight through me.

My sensitive little bundle of nerves was really hard beneath my fingers. Using the flats of two fingers, I circled over my clit as he fucked my face, moving faster and faster until I was on the edge of climax once more. Gagging, I tried to open my throat as he pushed past the back of it again and again, but it was difficult to concentrate on his cock when my fingers were between my own thighs.

I knew how to touch myself. My fingers worked faster and faster as he pistoned into my mouth, taking me like I was his with a vicious fervor. I choked and gagged, but he didn't slow down, and I eventually figured out a rhythm for breathing that timed with the rough cadence of his thrusts.

The room was filled with the heady scent of our passion, a blend of sweat and desire that hung thick in the air.

My thighs pressed together, my fingers moved faster, and all of a sudden, the tidal wave of pleasure was almost more than I could bear. It slammed down over me and swept me away in an instant.

As I surrendered to the overwhelming pleasure, my heart raced in concert with the rhythm of our bodies. I clung to him, lost in the tempest of our passion, unable to find solid ground. I drowned in the depths of sensation, my body writhing as he fucked my mouth and groaned.

That guttural, masculine noise was like a siren's call, drawing me deeper into the whirlpool of pleasure. It was the sound of his own desire, his hunger, and his devotion, all rolled into one intoxicating melody that echoed through the depths of my soul, leaving me utterly captivated and consumed by him.

His cock jerked faster into my mouth, owning my throat, once and for all. His grip on the back of my throat tightened as he fucked me, surging deep inside with one final thrust.

His cock throbbed on my tongue.

Oh fuck. He was about to come in my mouth.

I wasn't ready for it, but he wasn't waiting for me. Instead, his seed spurted into the back of my throat, filling it up and choking me. Left with no choice, I swallowed everything that I could, even as his come was still surging against my tongue.

My own orgasm burned on, taking me by storm and refusing to let me go. As I submitted to the overwhelming waves of passion, I felt a fiery intensity coursing through my veins, igniting every nerve ending in my body. The sensation was all-consuming, a relentless blaze that left me breathless and trembling. My heart raced in time with the electrifying rhythm of our bodies, each beat urging me further into the abyss of ecstasy.

His hands on the back of my neck, his cock pressed deep into my throat, it was as if we had become one, our souls entwined in a passionate dance. I clung to him desperately, breathing through my nose as my nails dug into his thighs and I arched into his touch, craving more of the intense pleasure that he effortlessly delivered.

The world around us faded into obscurity, and there was only the two of us, lost in a realm of sensation and desire.

By the time my orgasm ended, a burning tingly numbness reigned over my body.

Slowly, he pulled his cock free from my mouth and pulled me up by the back of my neck to my feet. My dress fell back into place, covering me at least for the moment.

I wavered back and forth, dizzy with pleasure, and he held me steady for a moment as he stared into my eyes. His other hand reached around to cup my cheek.

His thumb gently brushed against my lips, wiping my mouth in a loving and tender gesture that spoke volumes about his intentions.

His gentleness took me by surprise.

I watched as a storm of emotions played out on his face. In his eyes, I saw a fierce battle between tenderness and something darker, something he was desperately trying to suppress.

It was as if he wanted to hold me and push me away at the same time.

I leaned in closer towards him, wanting his arms around me more than anything.

Finally, he sighed, and I watched as he shook his head. His fist tightened around the back of my neck as he spun me around, lifted my dress, and slapped my bare welted ass hard enough to sting. The pain took me by surprise, and I cried out, reaching back with my hands to quickly cover my bare cheeks.

"Go take a shower and get ready for dinner."

Asshole.

I dipped down and grasped my leggings, pulling them up with a huff, and then I stormed off with the taste of his come still fresh on my tongue.

CHAPTER 11

ikolaos

I lost myself in the blue green lagoons of her eyes, the soft, gentle, caring soul within them screaming up at me to take care of her in the way a gentleman would.

I wanted to be gentle with her. I wanted to take her in my lap and comfort her, but I didn't because I'm a fucking asshole that takes what he wants whenever he wants despite the consequences.

Just like you did with her.

I wanted to hold her. The desire to protect her, the need to take her in my arms and shelter her from the dangerous world I inhabited, warred with the stark reality that this was her life now.

There was no fairy tale ending for us, no marriage, no happily ever after. This was not a Disney movie, and I couldn't even remotely pretend that it was.

I couldn't make her my wife. That would put an even bigger target on her back.

She was in my world, and there was no way out. If I made a wrong move, if I let my guard down, it could cost us both our lives. The stakes were high, and I couldn't afford to indulge in fantasies of a simpler life. I had to be the strong one, had to make hard decisions to ensure her safety and mine to make sure we both stayed alive.

As I looked at her, a complex mix of emotions swirled within me. I wanted to be the protector she needed, the one who would keep her safe no matter what. But I also knew that this world demanded a different kind of strength. It was Game of Thrones now, and I had to play it smart.

With a heavy heart, I resisted the urge to pull her into my arms and instead took a step back.

This *was* her life now, and she had to get used to it. There was no room for sentimentality in our world, only the cold, hard truth of survival.

So, I grabbed her, turned her around, and stared down at her bright red ass before I slapped it hard enough to make her cry out.

I played the part of an asshole because that's exactly what I was.

"Go take a shower and get ready for dinner," I barked, and she jumped. She looked over her shoulder with the same pouty, defiant look that had just gotten her fucked, and I narrowed my eyes in her direction. With a huff, she pulled up her leggings over her swollen pussy and flounced off to her room, and I gritted my teeth—annoyed, aroused, and feeling like the biggest dick in the world.

I shouldn't have fucked her. I should have had more self-control than that. Hell, I hadn't even known she was a virgin, but by the way she'd looked at my cock for the first time, I should have known. And then the feeling of being the first man inside of her had taken over my every waking thought.

I lost control and it's all her fault.

Maybe a part of me had known, and I'd just willfully ignored it, wanting to be the first and last man she ever had inside her. That's what had caused me to lose control. It had to be.

I should have stopped, but I was only a man, and she was a woman that needed a good fucking more than she needed anything else.

Her sweet little cunt had hugged my cock like it had been made for it, and I hated and adored that at the same time.

She shouldn't have felt that good.

But she did, and now I wanted more.

I wanted her full of me at every hour of every day and every night because she was mine now, and I couldn't ever let her go.

My world. *My* woman.

I couldn't afford the luxury of marrying her, at least not now. I needed to become more established, more secure in this world where danger lurked around every corner. The thought of making her mine in every sense of the word was tantalizing, but it was a risk I couldn't take at this moment.

For now, she couldn't be anything more than my little secret fuck toy until my name struck fear in all those that dared to rise up against me.

I closed my eyes, envisioning the image of her welted red ass bent over that couch, right before that perfect pink pussy swallowed up my cock like the perfect fucking little vice. The more I thought about that delectable red bottom, the more I felt like an absolute dick. It was petty of me to get angry at her for my mistake. I should have been more careful with my movements around her so that she wouldn't have been discovered in the first place, but it was well past time for regrets.

That still didn't change the fact that I wanted to take her into my arms and comfort her like a daddy would comfort his little girl after a scary dream, but that wouldn't help matters either.

With a ragged sigh, I tucked my cock back into place, then buttoned and zipped up my slacks.

There was a knock on the door and Andreas walked in, took one look at me, and said, "Oh you fucked her, didn't you?"

"That obvious?" I asked, a bit bashfully. He knew me well.

"It's practically written all over your face," he chided, cocking his head with a bit of a judgmental glare, which faded almost immediately.

"I shouldn't have fucked her, should I?" I asked with a sigh. My regret felt thick enough to cloud up the room.

"No, but it's too late for that now, isn't it?" he sighed, shaking his head with a playful grin.

"You're just jealous that I have a way with the ladies," I jabbed back.

"If that's what you want to call it, boss," he smirked. "Did you at least use a condom? The last thing we need is Niko-laos Kaligaris Junior running around the house, you know."

"No, but I came in her mouth," I scoffed, feeling slightly chastised.

"Of course you did," he replied with a heavy sigh, "So, what now?"

"Besides fucking her again?"

"Yes, besides that, boss," he said, his tone a bit exasperated.

"We take care of her. She's mine now and she will accept that. If she doesn't, she will, in time."

"Of course, boss," Andreas nodded, and he left the room, leaving me with my thoughts as I sat down on the same couch that I'd just fucked Maci over and groaned.

It felt wrong not to have her in my arms right now.

I longed to take care of her, to protect her from the dangers of my world, but I knew that I couldn't. It was a life-or-death situation now, and I had to ensure her safety, regardless of her feelings for me.

Or mine for her...

As much as I desired to be close to her, to feel her in my arms, I had to be strong and make the difficult decisions that would keep her alive.

One thing was certain though.

Maci Williams belonged to me now.

She was mine.

Forever.

CHAPTER 12

 *aci*

That asshole.

That goddamn *dick*.

That absolute fucking jackass of a man that just fucked my mouth and my pussy and made me come harder than I'd ever come in my life.

Fuck him.

Fuck him right in the nuts with a fucking rusty screwdriver.

I sat down on my bed with the most glorious pout I could have ever imagined and crossed my arms over my chest with a snarl. I stared out the window and shrieked with frustration as I watched the sea crashing against the coast down below.

Nikolaos Kaligaris was the villain, Lex Luther in a fucking toga practically, and he had the audacity to get angry at me and whip my ass with his belt for getting into trouble with the law. Sure, maybe the Pappas family would have never found out about me if I hadn't gotten in trouble, but how could I have known?

I couldn't believe he fucking had the balls to get mad at me for that when he was who he was—*and* when it was his own fucking people that had messed up and hadn't hid me well enough.

I glared around my room, or better, my luxurious jail cell, each fine detail of the room all cruelly mocking me. The plush bed, the elegant furnishings, and the stunning view of the sea felt like a slap in the face. It was all a facade, an illusion of freedom that hid the truth—I was trapped in a gilded cage and there was no key in sight.

I couldn't accept a life where I had no say, no control. I'd be damned if I allowed myself to become a pawn in his dangerous game.

But *fuck*, did the man know how to use his cock.

I pressed my fingers to my lips, remembering the touch of his thumb as if it had just been there seconds ago.

Despite my anger, there was no denying the intensity of our connection, the way our bodies had responded to each other. I couldn't help but wonder what was going on inside his head, what conflicted emotions were churning beneath his stoic facade.

What was I to him? Just some quick fuck when his cock got hard? Was there anyone else?

A sharp pang spiraled in my chest, and I shook my head. Was this jealousy? No. It couldn't be.

As I paced the room, I couldn't help but think about the undercurrents of tension that had been building between us. He was infuriatingly stubborn and overprotective, and it grated on my nerves.

Yet, there had been a vulnerability in his gaze, a longing that mirrored my own desires, and I hadn't missed that when his thumb had grazed across my lip, like he'd wanted to take me into his arms, hold me, and kiss me sweetly like I deserved to be kissed.

I reached up and traced the path of his thumb, his touch still tingling along my lip, and sighed.

But I refused to give in to him completely.

I couldn't.

I had to stand my ground. I couldn't give in to him, not when I was in the midst of a world that I never wanted to be a part of. My resolve was my shield, my determination my armor, and I couldn't let him breach those defenses, no matter how much I craved being around him.

Or how much you crave his cock...

I paced over to the window, annoyed at myself, and him, and at the entire world for putting me in this situation. I shouldn't have to worry about when and where someone might kill me. This shouldn't even be fucking real, but as much as I wanted to fight it, the evidence of this world was damning.

Fuck me, I still had very pale marks on my wrists from the handcuffs.

Plus, the welts on my ass…

I reached back, the warmth of my punished cheeks searing through the thin fabric of my leggings, and I drew in a shaky breath.

But a part of me liked those…

And the fact that *he* had been the one to give me each one of them.

CHAPTER 13

 *ikolaos*

I paced back and forth in my study, replaying the events of the last twenty-four hours in my mind over and over on repeat. I couldn't shake myself of my rage.

The more I thought about what they had done to her, the more disturbed I became. They had dared to touch her, and they deserved to pay for that. Not only that, but they'd made a move against me, one that demanded that I retaliate in kind.

I started seeing red.

As I paced, a dangerous sizzling fire burned in my chest. I had been patient, playing the waiting game and slowly building my reputation as patriarch to the Kaligaris family, but now it felt like the Pappas family was mocking me. They had underestimated me, thinking they could get away with this without consequences, but I wasn't going to let that stand.

I needed to do something. I couldn't just sit back and let them insult me like that.

My jaw clenched, and I knew that simply keeping Maci safe with me wasn't enough for me anymore. I needed to do more. They needed to pay for what they had done. I couldn't let them think they could mess with my family and get away with it. It was time to take deliberate action. They had awakened a beast, and now they would face the consequences.

The more I thought about it, the more I realized that there was only one course of action.

War.

War would be dangerous, but I had no choice. This demanded a strategic response, and I needed to step up and take it. If I didn't, my reputation would take a hit, and I couldn't stand for that.

I sat down at my desk, my mind a whirlwind of angry thoughts. I needed a plan, and I needed it fast. I reached for the phone and dialed Andreas's number, asking him to come to my study right away.

I waited, my anger seething that much hotter. The more time that passed, the more my rage intensified, until I couldn't stand it anymore.

When the door finally opened a few minutes later, Andreas walked in, his usual composed demeanor in place. His grey tweed suit gave him a confident edge, and I immediately felt better as soon as he stepped into the room. We would decide on a course of action together.

"You wanted to see me, boss?" he asked.

I nodded, gesturing for him to take a seat. "We need to discuss our options regarding the Pappas family. It would be lax of me to let this slide."

He nodded, his expression serious. "I've been giving it some thought as well."

I leaned back in my chair, frustration, rage, and determination burning in my eyes.

"They've crossed a line, Andreas. They've touched what's mine, and I won't stand for it. I can't afford to," I growled.

Andreas looked at me closely for a moment before he nodded in agreement. "I understand, boss. We can't let them think they can get away with this."

I leaned forward, my voice heavy with steadfast resolve. "We're going to war. We have to."

Andreas, always the voice of reason, studied me carefully. "I understand your anger, boss. But we need to consider the risks and consequences of a full-blown war."

I clenched my fists, my jaw set in resolve. "I don't care about easy, Andreas. I care about vengeance. They've crossed a line that can't be uncrossed, and I'm going to make them pay for it."

Andreas sighed, knowing that he couldn't dissuade me. "Very well, boss. We'll prepare for war. But remember, it won't be easy. We need a strategic plan to ensure our victory."

I leaned forward, my voice low and unwavering. "I want you to gather all the information we have on the Pappas family—everything, every connection, every vulnerability. We need to be one step ahead of them so we can make our move."

Andreas nodded again, jotting down some notes. "Consider it done. I'll also reach out to our contacts and see if we can gather any more information on their recent activities."

I nodded, feeling a surge of energy as I began to form a plan. "Good. We'll hit them where it hurts, Andreas. I'm going to make them regret ever crossing me."

Andreas met my gaze with a determined nod. "We'll show them, boss. They won't know what hit them."

* * *

Several hours later, Andreas knocked on my office door, and I called out for him to enter. When he walked into my office, his expression was grim. Immediately, I didn't like it.

Hastily, I gestured for him to take a seat, my heart already heavy with anticipation. "What is it, Andreas?"

"I've come across some information that you should know," he began. His expression was cautious, a little bit shocked even, and he cleared his throat.

"Well, spit it out then," I replied, my own impatience building.

He cleared his throat before speaking, his voice measured. "It's not just the Pappas family that took Maci. They were acting on behalf of the Stefanidis family, under their orders."

My brows furrowed in surprise and anger. "Stefanidis? As in, Antonios Stefanidis?"

What the actual fuck? I had just secured an alliance with the man, and he'd been actively moving against me the whole time? Was he playing me for a fool?

Fuck that.

Andreas nodded solemnly. "Yes, boss. It seems he hired the Pappas family to target Maci to get to you."

I leaned back in my chair, seething as I tried to process this new information. I clenched my fists, before pressing them against the surface of my desk, trying to keep calm, but it was futile.

"How did you find out?" I questioned.

"One of the mobsters involved in Maci's kidnapping was captured and adequately *convinced* to give up the information," Andreas explained, his calm demeanor making the whole thing seem less barbaric. "Amongst every detail we could squeeze from him about the men he worked for, he revealed the connection to the Stefanidis family. Antonios Stefanidis paid a lot of money to Alexander Pappas for the successful delivery of your goddaughter as collateral to hold against you throughout the terms of your negotiation."

"You're sure of this?" I pressed, not wanting to believe it, but knowing that it was likely the truth. Treachery amongst the reigning Greek families was not uncommon, which was exactly why I had been trying to secure myself against it in the first place.

The truth was, I should have seen this coming.

"We captured one other mobster that was involved in the kidnapping, and he confirmed the information before we disposed of him too," Andreas answered.

My fists clenched involuntarily at the thought of what they had done to Maci and the web of deceit that extended even further. I remembered the look of terror on her face when she'd first laid eyes on me in that shipping crate and my vision turned red.

Antonios Stefanidis was going to rue the day he moved against me.

"We can't let them get away with this, Andreas. They both will pay for what they've done."

Andreas nodded, his eyes determined. "We'll need a comprehensive strategy, boss, one that takes into account both families and their connections. We can't take any rash actions, not without fully understanding the consequences."

"Prepare our forces, Andreas. We're going to war, and this time, it's not just the Pappas family. We're going after the Stefanidis family as well," I agreed, crossing my arms over my chest.

Andreas glanced at his watch, the silver gleam catching the soft lighting in the room. It was almost as if he was waiting for something, but I didn't know what.

"What is it?" I pressed, furrowing my brow with curiosity.

"I've brought someone in that you should meet," he answered, and he walked to the door and swung it open.

As the patriarch of the Kaligaris shipping family, I'd faced many formidable figures in my time, but few commanded the room quite like Dimitris Kostas, kingpin to the Kostas mafia family.

Even though I'd never met him in person, I'd heard of his dangerous reputation. He was known as a ruthless mafia boss, a man who wielded power with an iron fist cloaked in a velvet glove. Few dared to stand against him; those who did rarely lived to tell the tale. His name alone evoked a mix of respect and fear in the underworld.

He was a figure who embodied an aura of controlled power and understated menace. In his early forties, he possessed a rugged handsomeness that was both striking and intimidating. His hair, dark as midnight, was always impeccably styled, giving him a look of polished sophistication. His face was marked by sharp, angular features. His icy blue eyes seemed to measure the room with disconcerting precision. Dressed in a black tailored suit, he was the spitting image of ruthless professionalism.

I understood why Andreas had brought him in. With him at my side, we actually stood a chance against the Stefanidis and Pappas families.

Andreas stood to greet him. "Dimitris," he said with measured respect. He knew, as did I, the gravity of this meeting.

"It's been a while, Andreas," Dimitris responded, his voice a blend of silk and steel. His eyes, sharp as a hawk's, briefly met Andreas' before settling on mine. "It's nice to finally meet you, Nikolaos. It's an honor."

Dimitris took a seat, and I remained silent, a spectator in my own domain.

"I've heard you've got yourself a problem," Dimitris began.

"The Stefanidis family have overstepped, and they need to be dealt with," I answered, my voice firm and clipped.

Andreas glanced at me before speaking. "Antonios Stefanidis hired the Pappas family to take Nikolaos' goddaughter. A young woman, just out of high school. They kidnapped her with the intent to use her as a bargaining chip. We intercepted before it was too late, but they need to answer for it. Involving a woman is a new low for them."

A scowl crossed Dimitris' face. "Bringing a woman into our world... it's positively shameful. The Stefanidis and the Pappas seem to have forgotten their honor."

I nodded in agreement, feeling a surge of anger when I thought of the red marks on her wrists and the ones on her ankles. Immediately, I wanted to go upstairs and tend to them, make sure that she wasn't hurting. The idea of going upstairs sparked something else though, and I shook my head, not trusting myself to be gentle with her right now.

If I went upstairs to her, she was going to get fucked again.

"She's an innocent. This act is beyond the bounds of our world's unspoken rules. It's not just an attack on my family, but a grave insult to our code of conduct."

Dimitris slammed his fist on the table, his disgust evident. "They have no respect for tradition. They play a dangerous game, breaking the rules that have kept a balance in our world for years."

I gazed intently at Dimitris, sensing the pivotal moment unfolding between us. "With the combined strength of our families, we are not only formidable; we become an indomitable force against the Stefanidis and the Pappas."

Dimitris extended his hand, a gesture signifying the solidity of our alliance.

"To a new era then, Nikolaos. The Kaligaris and Kostas, standing shoulder to shoulder. Let those who oppose us do so at their peril," he grinned, a hint of mercilessness glinting in his eyes.

I interjected, my voice firm, "We must respond, but with strategic precision. Our move must remind them of the lines that shouldn't be crossed, especially involving those who are not part of this life."

Dimitris nodded, his expression turning calculating. "We need to send a clear message and take them down a peg. One that speaks of our values and our strength. The Stefanidis must realize the cost of their dishonor."

"Agreed," I said.

"Perhaps we should consider targeting Marco Stefanidis, their chief enforcer," Dimitris suggested, his voice tinged with strategy. "He's been a thorn in my side for far too long."

Andreas chimed in, "Or Alexi Vardalos, their top money launderer. His loss would disrupt their financial operations significantly."

I listened to their suggestions, weighing each name for their value within the Stefanidis family, but none of them felt right.

Dimitris pondered for a moment, then added, "While we're at it, we should also consider key players in the Pappas family. Men like Yiannis Petridis, their main arms dealer. He's been supplying them with more than just conventional weaponry for ages."

Andreas quickly followed up, "And let's not forget about Nikos Argyris, their chief strategist. He's the brains behind many of their recent territorial expansions. Taking him out could cripple their strategic capabilities."

I listened intently, each name resonating with the power and influence they held within their respective families. "These are significant names, no doubt, but our response needs to be more than just eliminating key players. We need a show of force that speaks louder than any assassination."

Dimitris nodded in understanding. "So, we're looking at a strategy that not only cripples their operations but also sends a clear warning to anyone who might think of crossing us."

"Exactly," I affirmed.

"This is about sending a message that resonates within our world. We need to do something that has never been done before," I replied, my voice contemplative. My mind started to whirl with ideas, and soon, one took the forefront well over anything else.

Dimitris leaned back, his icy blue eyes narrowing in thought. "Nikolaos, while I agree we need a strong response, we must also consider the repercussions. Going too far could ignite the kind of war we're not prepared for."

Andreas nodded in agreement. "We must tread carefully. The balance is delicate. We risk everything if we overstep in our response."

I stood up, feeling the weight of my position. "I understand your concerns, but our hand has already been forced. We will respond in a way that upholds our honor and terrifies our enemies. I will lead this personally. It's time they remembered why the Kaligaris family name commands respect."

Dimitris and Andreas exchanged a look, a mix of respect and worry in their eyes. They knew I was set in my decision. I was about to make a move that would redefine the rules of our world, and I was going to ensure it was done *my way*.

I stood up and paced the room, an idea forming in my head.

"Dimitris, I want you to pay off some dock workers to look the other way. Then, we'll have a team of scuba divers plant explosives on the hulls of a number of Stefanidis' ships in port. We take down several at once, so it's unmistakably a hit. A precise, calculated strike," I instructed.

Dimitris raised his eyebrows, a hint of admiration flickering in his icy blue eyes. "That's a *bold* move, Nikolaos. Are you sure you want to take it to this level?"

I met his gaze squarely. "I am. We hit them where it hurts, Dimitris—their fleet, their lifeline, right in their deep pockets."

Dimitris leaned back, the corners of his mouth twitching into a wry smile. "I have to admit, that's pretty badass, Nikolaos. Blowing up their ships will cause a stir they can't ignore. It'll be a message loud and clear."

I allowed myself a small smirk. "It's just a trifle few million dollars in damage. A small price for them to pay for maintaining our honor and sending a clear message. They need to learn that actions against the Kaligaris family come with a price."

Dimitris nodded, his expression now one of resolved determination. "Consider it done, Nikolaos."

"I want this done tonight," I demanded, my voice resonating with an urgency that left no room for doubt.

Dimitris nodded, a look of grim determination settling over his features.

"Tonight, it is then. I'll get my best men on it. The dock workers will be paid off, and our divers are already the best in the business. They'll make sure the job is clean and untraceable," he said thoughtfully.

Andreas, who had been quietly taking notes, looked up. "I'll coordinate with our contacts in law enforcement to ensure they're looking the other way. We can't afford any slip-ups on this."

I leaned forward, locking eyes with both of them. "Remember, this isn't just about revenge; it's about sending a message. We're not just another family to be trifled with. I am Nikolaos Kaligaris, and my reach and influence go far beyond what they've seen so far."

Dimitris's expression hardened. "They'll realize they've awoken a sleeping giant. The Stefanidis and the Pappas families will rue the day they decided to take a shit on the rules of our world."

I stood up, signaling the end of the meeting. "Good. Keep me updated on every detail. Remember, precision and stealth are key here. We strike hard and fast, and then we vanish into the night."

Dimitris cleared his throat, and I turned back to him.

"What is it?" I asked.

"What about the Pappas family?"

"They'll get what's coming to them. Don't worry," I replied, and he nodded once before getting up out of his seat.

As they left to set the plan in motion, I sat back in my chair, contemplating the imminent shockwave this would send through our underworld.

Taking out their ships was a bold move, but necessary. In our world, respect was currency, and I intended to show that the Kaligaris family's wealth was immeasurable.

It was time to make my move.

And everyone was going to see it.

 ikolaos

The first light of dawn was creeping through the curtains when I woke up. Immediately, I sat up as thoughts of last night's decisions raced through my head. My mind should have been preoccupied with the Stefanidis family, but thoughts of the young girl sleeping in the other room popped into my head instead.

My Maci...

All of a sudden, my phone rang, shattering the morning quiet. There was only one person who would call me at this hour, and I answered it immediately.

"Andreas," I greeted, my voice steady and calm, my eagerness for news only just held at bay. I needed this plan to go off without a hitch. It had to be done perfectly the first and only time.

"Good morning, Nikolaos," Andreas replied, a subtle tone of victory in his voice, and I sighed with relief. "The operation was a success. The Stefanidis ships have been hit. All three targeted vessels are at the bottom of the harbor. Our divers executed the plan flawlessly, and there were no casualties on our side. It's already causing ripples through their ranks."

A momentary sense of relief washed over me, followed quickly by a reassertion of my usual mask of composure. "And the repercussions?"

"As expected, there's chaos in the Stefanidis camp. They're scrambling to find out who's responsible. Our involvement is still hidden for the moment, but I suspect it won't be long until they figure out it was us. Law enforcement is treating it as an unfortunate accident, thanks to our initial ground-work. It couldn't have gone off better, boss."

"Excellent work, Andreas. Keep a close eye on the develop-ments. I want hourly updates. You and I both know that this is just the beginning. The Stefanidis family will be planning their next move, and we'll need to be ready for whatever they throw at us."

"Understood. The team is on high alert. I'll keep you informed of every single detail."

"Good. I don't care how small. I want to know."

As I ended the call, I stood by the window and looked out at the rolling ocean, the early morning light glinting off the water's surface like a handful of glittering diamonds. My heart was pounding in my chest, and I slowly turned my head, gazing in the direction of Maci's room.

I wanted to go to her, but I held back for a long moment.

I *shouldn't*, right?

For a moment, regret seeped into my head. Maybe I should have been gentle with her, taken her virginity sweetly instead of hard and fast like a savage beast, or maybe I shouldn't have touched her at all. I should have been a gentleman and held her close, comforted her after I had taken her so roughly. Something, *anything* really…

None of that mattered now.

I closed my eyes, imagining the scintillating scent of her lavender shampoo and the way it had driven me wild, and I drew a breath in through my teeth.

She was young, innocent in many ways to the world I commanded, and I was a man who bore the weight of a legacy written in power and sometimes in blood.

She was mine now. That much was certain.

She had become a part of my life, a beacon of something pure and untainted shining amongst the shadows of my existence, and a part of me wanted to keep it that way. Her innocence was like a breath of fresh air, and I never wanted it to go away.

I wanted to keep her. A man like me shouldn't be allowed to keep an innocent like her, but I didn't play by the rules.

I made my own.

I would do anything to keep her safe, to shield her from the harsh realities that lay outside the walls of my home. In a life where trust was a rare commodity, and weakness and vulnerability could be fatal flaws, my desire to protect Maci would be forever unwavering.

I knew that the path ahead would be fraught with challenges. But one thing was clear—I would protect what was mine.

And Maci was *mine*.

Knowing it was still quite early, I quietly made my way towards her room. The house was silent, the only sounds the distant murmurs of the ocean and my own measured footsteps against the hardwood floors. As I gently pushed open her door, I soundlessly held my breath.

The soft morning light filtered through the curtains, bathing her face in a soft light. In sleep, Maci seemed to be in a world far away from the dangers and complexities of our reality. Her features were relaxed, a stark contrast to the deliciously defiant intensity that often marked her gaze when she was awake.

She looked like a perfect angel.

In this moment, she was just my Maci, my sweet, innocent goddaughter that was untouched by the shadows of my world.

Untouched by me.

I approached her bed, my gaze lingering on her every curve. Her chest rose and fell in a steady rhythm, the very picture of serenity.

Noticing that the covers had slipped slightly, I reached out to take them between my fingers as gently as I could. Carefully, I pulled the blankets up, ensuring she was snug and warm. As I tucked the blanket around her, a warm, foreign feeling surged within me.

Standing there, watching her sleep, I felt a rare moment of peace amidst the constant storm of my life. In her presence, I found a semblance of solace, a glimpse of what life could be beyond power struggles and looming threats.

A happily ever after...

No.

That wasn't in the cards for me. I had to be realistic. I shook my head, shaking off the idealistic pipedream of happiness and put my mind back where it was supposed to be.

In the game. *Forever* in the game.

I lingered for a moment more, committing the sight of her to memory—the way her eyelashes fluttered and caressed her cheeks in her sleep, the soft, rosy blush that crept over her face, the gentle curve of her chest as it rose and fell. Then, silently, I retreated from the room, closing the door gently behind me.

I stood there with my back to the door for a long moment, just wanting to be near her for a moment longer.

Returning to my room, I let the remnants of that quiet moment with her remain in my mind before I finally made myself push it aside.

It was time to prepare for the day ahead. I had just entered into a war with two prominent families, and I needed to be prepared for their inevitable strike back.

I stepped into the shower, letting the hot water wash over me, cleansing not just the persistent remnants of sleep but also allowing me a moment of solitude to gather my thoughts and steel myself for whatever challenges the day might bring.

After the shower, I dressed meticulously in a fine black tailored suit. Then I made my way downstairs to the kitchen. The house was just waking up, the early morning light radiating its golden hue through the windows. I decided to prepare breakfast—thinking that Maci might appreciate the kind gesture especially with how rough I was with her yesterday.

Even though I'm certain she enjoyed it. I made sure of it.

Over... and over again...

My thoughts drifted back to yesterday afternoon, and my cock jumped, remembering how her snug, virgin pussy had spasmed around my cock with every orgasm, the tiny little gasps she'd made right before she came and the sound of her screams as she shattered and bucked beneath me.

Every bit of it was fucking delicious.

Fuck. I shouldn't let her get to me. I was a strong man before she came into my life, and I would remain that even with her in it.

I vowed that to myself.

As I cracked eggs into a pan and started whisking them into a scramble, the aroma of coffee and cooking slowly filled the kitchen. I was just adding a handful of herbs to the scrambled eggs when I heard the gentle pitter-patter of tiny feet. Turning around, I saw Maci entering the kitchen, her expression a tad hesitant, which was understandable.

She was dressed in a simple green wrap dress that complemented the blue-green hue of her eyes. The color accentuated her natural beauty, giving her an ethereal quality that was both striking and endearing, and for a moment, she took my breath away. The morning light seemed to catch and dance in her eyes, making them sparkle with a life and vibrancy that utterly captivated me, and I found that I couldn't look away.

I swallowed hard, eventually making myself turn back to the eggs.

"Good morning," I greeted her, trying to hide my inherent interest in every inch of her body.

"Morning," she replied, her voice soft, a small smile gracing her lips. She moved closer, her presence filling the kitchen with a lightness that contrasted starkly with the usual hard intensity of my life.

Seeing her there dressed so simply yet looking so beautiful, I was reminded once again of the stark dichotomy of our lives—the danger and power of my world, and the simplicity and purity of these moments with her. In her I'd found an unexpected sanctuary, a reminder of a life that could be, of a peace that was so rare in my world.

In truth, a part of me adored that about her.

As I continued with the breakfast preparations, Maci moved towards the small television set perched on the kitchen counter and flicked it on. The room was suddenly filled with the crisp, professional tone of a news anchor. Her voice rang clear, narrating the morning headlines and I tuned it out, at least until she started talking about the port.

"In breaking news, a series of mysterious ship sinkings has occurred at the local harbor. Three vessels, all belonging to the Stefanidis shipping line, were found sunk early this morning. Authorities report that the sinkings appear to be targeted, though no group has yet claimed responsibility. Investigators are currently exploring all possibilities, including foul play. This incident has sent shockwaves through the maritime community, raising concerns about security and the potential for a deliberate attack..."

As the news story unfolded, I felt Maci's gaze on me. Turning to face her, I saw the knowing look in her eyes. I didn't say anything, wanting her to bridge that gap first.

"*You* did that, didn't you?" she asked, her voice steady, her gaze unwavering.

For a moment, I contemplated denying it, but looking into her eyes, seeing the understanding that lay there, I decided against it. And honestly, I was impressed that she'd figured it all out on her own.

Her ability to connect the dots, to discern my involvement in such a covert operation, was remarkable. It wasn't just her intuition that struck me, but her courage to confront the truth head-on with me that really sunk down deep into my heart. In that moment, I saw not just the little girl

I had protected all her life, but a sharp, perceptive woman that could potentially navigate the complex layers of my world.

Maybe...

I wasn't yet convinced though.

I turned off the stove and moved to sit at the kitchen table, motioning for her to join me. I slid a plate of food in front of her, and she dove right in. Enraptured, I watched her eat for a moment with a sense of appreciation.

Honestly, it was refreshing. Most women I interacted with were too worried about their figures to do anything but pick at a salad in front of me, but not Maci. She wasn't afraid to eat her fill, and I found that I really liked that about her.

I had to be careful.

I couldn't get attached. I needed to protect her, but I couldn't be anything more to her than that. Not when it put her at risk.

"Yes, I did," I finally admitted, meeting her gaze directly. "It was necessary. A message had to be sent. They made a move against me. They dared to touch you, and they needed to answer for it."

Maci listened intently, her expression contemplative. I could see the wheels turning in her mind, trying to reconcile the man she knew with the actions I had just confessed to right to her face. It was a delight to watch.

"You're quite the little detective, aren't you?" I said, my tone lightly teasing yet edged with a hint of concern. "It's impressive, really, how quickly you've pieced that together."

Her eyes narrowed slightly, a spark of defiance lighting them up. "I'm not a child, Nikolaos. I understand more than you give me credit for," she replied, her voice steady yet charged with an undercurrent of challenge.

My cock grew rigid in my slacks.

Why was I so enamored with her?

"Oh, I don't doubt your intelligence," I responded, maintaining a casual demeanor while observing her reactions closely. "But this world, our world now, it's complex. Every step we take needs to be careful, calculated. There are dangers you can't even imagine."

"And you'll shield me from them forever?" she asked, her tone laced with a mix of sarcasm and genuine curiosity.

I couldn't help but chuckle softly. "Forever is a long time, Maci. But I will protect you, yes."

Her gaze didn't waver, and the air between us grew thick with an unspoken tension. The challenge in her eyes made my cock rock hard, and I didn't even try to hide it. Instead, I sat back and unabashedly allowed my gaze to peruse the length of her body.

"And what if I don't want to be protected? What if I want to understand, to really be a part of your world?" she pressed.

I couldn't allow that. It was too dangerous. Just yesterday, she'd wanted to go home and now she wanted to stay, and not only that, but she also wanted to be a part of everything?

The conversation had taken a turn, and I could feel the atmosphere shifting between us, charged with a blend of frustration, curiosity, and an undeniable undercurrent of desire. It was a dangerous cocktail, and I wanted to take another sip.

Fuck. I wanted to down the *whole* damn drink.

She glared back at me like she wanted the same, and I shifted in my seat, my dick aching to empty inside of her, to feel her tight sheath clenching around my cock as she broke apart.

"Maci," I began, my voice lowering, "You don't know what you're asking. It's far too dangerous for a girl like you."

"A *girl* like me? I'm not afraid. I can handle whatever you throw at me. I got fucking kidnapped and I kept a level head," she countered, her voice firm, her eyes locked onto mine.

"The answer is no. Not yet, Maci-girl," I replied, and her eyes sparked with challenge.

Her response was quick, tinged with a healthy dose of frustration. "And when will I be 'ready'? When you decide? Don't I have any say in my own life? My own future? You already took my home away from me. My damned virginity too. What more do you want from me?"

I couldn't help but admire her spirit and her unwillingness to back down. "It's not that simple. You're not just anyone, Maci. You're important to me, more than you realize. My world… it can be cruel. I can't let it harm you. You're just going to have to accept that."

Her expression softened slightly, but the defiant challenge in her eyes remained. "I can handle more than you think, Nikolaos."

The air between us was thick with a charged energy that seemed to snap and crackle with every word we exchanged. Her fire stoked my arousal far more than I'd expected. My cock was hard as a rock, and I wanted nothing more than to sink back into her, again and again until she screamed my name as she writhed beneath me.

And she kept looking at me like she *wanted* it too.

It took everything in me to remain in my seat and not yank her up out of her chair, bend her over the table, and fuck her absolutely senseless.

"Strength isn't the only thing required to survive in my world, Maci. It's about knowing when to strike and when to hold back, when to reveal and when to conceal. It's a chess match, and the stakes are extremely high, more than you can possibly imagine."

She moved closer, her determination more than a little evident. "Then teach me. I want to learn, to be a part of it."

Her proximity was intoxicating and utterly addictive. I could see the passion in her eyes, mirroring my own, and I wanted to snatch the hair at the back of her head and kiss that beautiful mouth. I wanted to steal away her every waking breath, taste every bit of that fire and take it for myself.

"Maci," I said, my voice low and steady, "this isn't a game. The decisions I make, the actions I take... they have consequences, sometimes grave ones."

"Listen, I'm already stuck here. I'm ready to face whatever comes our way, *with* you, whether you let me or not," she pressed, her frustration building, and I shook my head, standing my ground.

The more defiant she was, the more I wanted to fuck it right out of her.

"The answer is no, Maci-girl. You don't need to be involved in my world," I answered decisively.

She wasn't ready, but the truth was, I wasn't ready either.

She growled in frustration, and I stared at her, my blood boiling with desire. Within her anger and annoyance though, I saw something else.

Her arousal. It was painted all over every inch of her.

Her pretty cheeks were flushed a bright rosy pink, and the pupils of her eyes were fully dilated. Despite her frustration, she was leaning in towards me, like a moth drawn to a flame.

If she wasn't careful though, she was going to get burned.

Her bra was thin, and her nipples were so hard that they pebbled right through it. The flush that graced her cheeks descended down the length of her neck, and I suddenly got the urge to rip her dress down the front just to see how far down that rosy pink went. I licked my lips.

Fuck it.

If she wanted it, who was I to deny her?

"No. That's not what you need, is it?" I murmured.

I let my gaze slink up and down her body again, and she shifted nervously in her seat. I wondered, was her ass still sore from my belt? Would I find little pink welts left behind from yesterday?

"What do I need then?" she answered, her voice clipped and her brow furrowing in heated suspicion. Her lips opened just a little bit, almost like she was waiting with bated breath to see what I said next.

I stood up with a subtle smirk, shifting towards her, but she didn't pull away. Instead, she leaned in towards me like she was seeking me out, and I knew I made the right decision.

"Let me tell you, princess."

CHAPTER 15

M aci

I was right.

He was a dick, and an asshole, and a fucking powerful bastard, so why did I want him so much? Why did I want him to reach out, tear my clothes off, and fuck me just as hard as he had yesterday? Why was I itching for his touch, on my skin, between my legs, over every inch of me as I fell apart with the type of orgasm that only he was capable of giving me?

I'd tried last night. My orgasm hadn't even come close.

I hated him. I didn't understand why I wanted him, why my body was calling out for him to take me and ravage me senseless.

I glared at him, trying to hide how much I needed him. I focused on my anger, on my hate, and lifted my chin with as much defiance as I was humanly capable of.

On the one hand, he was praising me for figuring out that it was him that had blown up the ships, but on the other, he'd been kind of talking down to me while he did it, which I didn't like at all. I understood it was coming from a place of concern, but fuck that.

I could hold my own. I could handle a lot. He just needed to give me a chance.

"It's impressive, really, how quickly you've pieced that together."

My pussy could only focus on his praise. It was like it had a one-track mind of its own, and the only thing that it wanted was the man's big cock inside of it, making me come just as hard as he had yesterday.

My lip tingled where he'd touched it yesterday, and I almost reached up and touched it just to feel that same fire again, like I'd done a million times last night.

With our every interaction, my body reacted this way, and that was annoying in and of itself. With his every word, my pussy flooded with heat, whether I wanted it to or not, and there wasn't anything I could do to stop it.

As I stared up at him, I couldn't help but focus on that infuriating smirk playing on his lips, and despite my irritation, my body responded, coming alive in a way that was both exhilarating and maddening.

I wanted him to reach out, grip my hair, and punish my lips with his until I moaned his name. I wanted him to bend me over, tear my panties off, and take what was his whether I liked it or not.

I was caught in a whirlwind of emotions and desires, a tumultuous sea that I was thoroughly unprepared to navigate, and I didn't know what to do. The more I thought about it, the more I realized that there was a depth to my feelings that was quickly becoming deeply unsettling. He wasn't just my godfather anymore; he was becoming someone who meant much more to me than ever before.

Shit. I couldn't allow that.

This was nothing.

This was just meaningless sex, right?

A man like him didn't have feelings for a woman. I was nothing more to him that a pretty little fuck toy, and right now, my body didn't care about anything more than that.

My heart raced, and I could feel the heat in my cheeks. It was as if every nerve ending had awakened, attuned solely to him.

I was angry at myself for this undeniable attraction that defied all logic and reason. He was a dangerous man, a man whose life was a labyrinth of power plays and dark dealings. And yet, here I was, drawn to him like a bee to honey, unable to resist our every interaction. I shouldn't want him. Wanting him was shameful. He was my fucking godfather, for Christ's sake. Nothing was ever supposed to have happened between us, but here I was, wanting him to sink that massive cock right in between my legs just like he had done yesterday.

It was maddening. It was wickedly taboo and so terribly wrong. What would my parents think? What would my grandmother say?

He's your fucking godfather.

His turbulent grey eyes locked onto mine, and in them I saw a reflection of my own turmoil. It was a look that spoke of a deep, primal connection, a mutual understanding that whatever was happening between us was inevitable, that it was a force of nature that neither of us could control.

And sooner or later, the two of us were going to clash. It was simply a matter of time now.

I swallowed hard and lifted my chin, making a decision in the blink of an eye. I was going to stand my ground whether he liked it or not. Because I needed to. Because I wanted to.

If he wanted me, I was going to make him take me.

As I grappled with the tumultuous mix of my own shame and my simmering arousal, Nikolaos began to stride towards me. Each step he took seemed to echo in the charged silence of the room. His commanding presence was overwhelming. The closer he got, the more I could feel a tangible energy emanating from him, enveloping me in a way that was both intimidating and intoxicating all at once, and I couldn't get enough.

I wanted so much more.

I tried to steady my breathing, to maintain some semblance of control in the face of this onslaught of emotions, but it was futile. The shame that I felt for wanting a man like him—so powerful, so enigmatic, and so out of reach—clashed violently with the raw arousal that surged through me.

I wavered on my feet.

His eyes never left mine as he approached, and in them I saw the same intense desire that was coursing through me. There was something undeniably captivating about him, and I found that I couldn't look away no matter how hard I tried.

As he stood before me, his towering figure seemed to over-shadow my own, yet it was not just his physical presence that overwhelmed me. It was the aura of authority he exuded, the unspoken power he wielded. It made him both dangerous and alluring, a combination that was utterly irre-sistible. My heart raced, and a part of me wanted to retreat, to protect myself from the inevitable.

I could feel my resolve weakening. His proximity to me made me feel like a flame to dry tinder, igniting a fire within me that I was powerless to extinguish.

And I just let it happen.

I swallowed hard, lifting my chin and standing toe-to-toe with him. I wasn't going to go down without a fight this time.

This time, I'm going to get what I want too.

His hand wrapped around my upper arm, and he spun me around, effortlessly pinning both arms behind my back with only one of his own. My shoulders arched back, and I strug-gled, but there was no breaking his hold. He was that much stronger than me, and I didn't make any headway. He just waited, letting me fight and truly letting it sink in how powerless I was against a man like him.

He was a monster.

"I hate you," I whispered.

"No, you don't, princess. Don't lie to me," he chided.

"I'm not lying," I snarled.

"You are. If I ripped your panties down right now, your pussy would tell me different, wouldn't it?"

I didn't dare say a word for fear that it would confirm that he was right. Even now, I could feel how soaked through my panties were already, that my arousal was practically leaking from my pussy, and I gritted my teeth, trying to stay strong even in the face of a powerhouse like him.

"Are you ready to hear what you need, Maci-girl?" he asked, and a shiver raced down my spine at the heated intent in his voice. His body pressed against my back, and I realized that the way my arms were angled meant that my hands were pressed right over his very, *very* hard cock.

"What do I need?" I growled, not doing anything to hide the anger in my tone. I hoped it was enough to cover up the rampant desire pulsing through my veins.

"You need another *hard* fucking," he said blatantly. It wasn't a question, but a statement, and I gritted my teeth, wanting to tell him exactly where to shove it while also wanting to tell him I wanted it, but I kept my mouth shut.

I wanted to say yes. I should have told him no, yet I said nothing at all.

His cock throbbed underneath my hand, and it took everything in my power not to cup it, to really feel how hard he was for me, how much he wanted me, and everything that he was offering. I closed my eyes, and my fingers twitched. His sharp intake of breath was the only thing that alerted me to my accidental movement, and I felt a blush creep up onto my cheeks.

What was I doing? Why did I want this?

His free hand roamed up and down my body, slowly exploring every inch of the front of me and then finally settled over my right breast. Roughly, he cupped it, squeezing it just hard enough to take my breath away, and I bit my lip, trying to keep quiet.

I didn't want him to know how much of an effect he was having on me. That would be too much, too embarrassing, too shameful, too wicked. My chest rose and fell with the difficulty of staying still, and his fingers cinched tighter and possessively around my breast as a breathy little cry finally escaped me and my body practically hummed with desire.

"Do you need a fucking, *my pretty little slut?*"

Oh, my fuck.

His words shouldn't have this much power over me. My lips parted and a soft moan escaped me before I could stop it. Almost immediately, I bit the inside of my cheek as his hand roamed over me again, this time just sliding over my mound and then traveling back up to cup my other breast.

He wanted me to answer.

I wasn't going to.

With a quiet intake of breath, I wavered back and forth, brushing my hand against his cock, and my eyes practically rolled back in my head. I felt almost like I was floating up in the clouds, like my body had taken over and my mind was just coming along for the ride. It was utterly intoxicating, and I couldn't get enough.

With deliberate intent, he released my breast and reached down to my waist, slowly taking the tie to my wrap dress within his fingers and pulling it loose. Inch by inch, it came undone until he let it go, completely untied. The fabric of my dress parted slightly, and he reached up to bare my chest, revealing the matching lacey bra I had chosen this morning.

The lace cups lifted my breasts seductively, or so I had thought, but he didn't turn me around to appreciate them. Instead, he just scooped his hand into my bra and lifted my left breast clean out of the cup. He did the same with the other side.

I felt like my breasts were obscenely displayed, and it did nothing but turn my body even more molten.

His fingers closed around my left nipple, and he pinched lightly enough to cause a slight glimmer of pain to race through me. I trembled a bit in his arms, and I could have sworn that his cock felt even harder than it had before.

Fuck me... I urged him in my head, not daring to say the words out loud. I wasn't going to give in that easily. I was strong and I could stand toe-to-toe with him. I would show him that I was just as powerful as he was.

"Answer me, *my* little slut."

My legs almost buckled underneath me at his possessiveness. I didn't want to answer him. I just wanted him to take me, to overpower me and fuck me just like he had yesterday. I wanted the pain. I wanted the pleasure.

I was *almost* desperate enough for another round of his belt.

My clit throbbed at the thought. I drew my lower lip in between my teeth, trying to maintain some semblance of control over myself, but nothing seemed to work.

My body felt like a volcano, moments awake from erupting. My fingers tingled and my toes curled. Every nerve in my body seemed like it was ready to fire all at once, and my legs trembled, giving me away whether I liked it or not.

Still, I defied him.

I refused to answer. I lifted my chin higher, pulled my shoulders back a bit further, and struggled in his hold. I knew I wasn't going to escape him, but that didn't really matter.

I just wanted to show him that I wasn't the compliant, perfect little submissive that he wanted, that I was a force to be reckoned with all on my own.

His fingers tightened, pinching my nipple that much harder, and I gritted my teeth, pain radiating across my breast and striking right down into my core like a bolt of lightning. My back arched, inadvertently pressing my hands and my ass against his cock, and he growled.

His growl was a low, rumbling sound, primal and deeply resonant, so much so that it caught me by surprise. It started like distant thunder, a sound that seemed to originate from the very depths of his being. It was as if the sound carried with it an electric charge, igniting every nerve ending it touched, and I couldn't get enough of it.

"Nikolaos," I breathed.

His hand moved to my other nipple, and I sucked in a breath, trying to calm myself for what I knew was coming, but I couldn't prepare for it. He took my nipple between his fingers and clamped down on it so hard that I saw stars, the delicious agony reigning through my body like a sudden storm, and I cried out.

Why was I fighting this again?

He pulled his hand back, releasing my nipple, and I breathed a sigh of relief. The pain escalated for a second, but eventually it started to fade, and I slumped forward, but then the flats of his fingers slapped my tit, right on top of the tip of my nipple, and I yelped out loud.

Then he spanked the other side just as firmly, making my breasts jiggle, but my mind was reeling from the stinging agony more than the shame of what my tits looked like as they bounced.

He spanked them hard several more times. My head went blank, solely focused on the terrible sting the flats of his fingers wrought on my naked breasts. I glanced down, seeing the pink flush his hand left behind, and I gasped, only just holding back one yelp after the next. Then he paused, the scalding hot burn radiating across my breasts, and my chest heaved up and down as I tried to catch my breath.

Fuck. That hurt almost as much as his belt. Maybe even more so.

"Tell me. You need a fucking, don't you, my little slut?"

In the heated moment, a part of me wanted to fight him, to push against the overwhelming tide of authority and dominance he represented. My mind screamed for a semblance of control, to assert my independence against the pull of his commanding presence, but as the waves of desire crashed over me, they eroded the very foundations of my resistance.

Each thought of defiance became hazier, more distant, as the all-consuming flame of desire grew within me. It was a battle between my will and the sheer force of the attraction I felt towards him, which was rapidly overpowering every rational argument I had. His nearness, the intensity of his body around me, the deep timbre of his voice—all of it was dismantling my resolve, piece by piece.

I was losing myself in the tidal wave of desire.

He was offering exactly what I wanted. Why was I fighting him in the first place?

Fuck it.

I would get what I wanted either way.

"*Oh my God*, yes," I finally breathed.

His dark chuckle chilled me to the bone, and my legs quivered with need. As I stood there, caught in the gravity of his presence, a part of me was relentlessly trying to gauge how far he would go. His every move was like a carefully played chess piece—deliberate and calculated. Would he push the boundaries even further? My mind raced, analyzing each subtle shift in his movements, every nuanced tone in his voice saying something more.

There was an unspoken question hanging in the air that neither of us dared to voice. Would he be more savage than he was yesterday? Harsher? More brutal?

Would he hold me after it was all over?

His grip on my arms loosened and my mind raced. What was going to happen next? Would he take me up to the bedroom? Would he fuck me right here?

With a quick turn, he spun me around to face him, and I got my first good look into those wild grey eyes of his.

They were like turbulent seas, deep and fathomless, and I lost myself in them. His gaze locked onto mine, intense and unyielding, and in that instant, the world around us seemed to fall away.

Then, without warning, he closed the distance between us. His lips found mine in a punishing kiss that stole my breath away. His kiss was a whirlwind that engulfed me, leaving no room for thought or resistance. His breath became mine. It was as if he was imprinting himself onto my very soul, marking me as his in a way that words could never achieve.

The intensity of the kiss drowned out everything else. His hands were firm on my back, pulling me closer, leaving no space, no air between us. I was lost in the taste of him, in the urgent press of his lips against mine. The world spun, and I spun with it, caught in the orbit of his overwhelming presence. It was a clash of souls, a battle and a surrender all at once, and I both loved and loathed it in the same breath.

Then he grabbed my dress and yanked it open, revealing the rest of me in a matter of seconds. I tried to knock his hands away, suddenly overwhelmed by anxiety and arousal, but it was like I was trying to bat away a fly. His grip was too strong, and in less than a blink of an eye, he'd stripped my dress off of my shoulders and tossed it to the floor. His arm wound around my waist, holding me in place as he unclasped my bra and tossed that aside too, leaving me in nothing more than a pair of ballet flats and my panties.

Somehow a part of me knew I wouldn't be wearing those much longer either.

As his hands moved over me, there was a surprising roughness in his touch. His grip was firmer, more insistent than I had anticipated, betraying a raw, unbridled intensity that lay beneath his composed exterior. It was an intensity that spoke of deep passion and unrestrained desire, a side of him that was both startling and exhilarating at the same time.

"You make me crazy, Maci-girl," he growled.

At first, the fervor of his handling took me aback, sending a jolt of surprise through my senses. But as the initial shock subsided, I found myself being drawn into the fire of his embrace. A part of me, a part I hadn't fully acknowledged until now, reveled in this newfound intensity.

There was something undeniably thrilling about being wanted with such force, such ardor. It ignited a fire within me, a wild and untamed response that matched his own.

I embraced it.

He gripped my panties and yanked them so hard that the lace parted as though it was made of paper. I yelped as the fabric pinched at my swollen folds, and I pitched forward, but he was there to catch me. In a flash, he spun me back around and roughly bent me over the table. I tried to push up against the wooden surface, but his hand pressed down in the middle of my back, holding me firmly in place.

Fuck.

He was being way rougher than I thought he'd be. He was treating me like his little fuck doll, and there was something about that that made my insides burn with overwhelming desire.

His hand was like fire on the small of my back. I stole a heated breath, pushing against the table and trying to fight with everything I had left, which wasn't a lot. Bent over the table like this, I was at a distinct disadvantage, and no matter how much strength I put into the fight, he easily held me in place. I snarled in response, and he pressed down a bit harder, like he was silently reminding me that he was in charge, and I was not.

It was maddening.

It was arousing.

It was *fucking perfect.*

CHAPTER 16

$\mathcal{M}$aci

I shouldn't want this. I shouldn't want more of what he was giving me. I felt like a slut, more specifically, his slut, and my body came alive.

Every bit of me was vibrating with energy, and when I heard the sound of him unbuckling his belt behind me, it nearly undid me. The metallic click of the buckle being released was like a key turning in a lock, unleashing a flood of emotions and desires that I had tried so hard to keep at bay. It stripped away the last vestiges of my restraint, leaving me exposed, vulnerable, and achingly wanting.

Each second stretched into eternity as I waited, breathless and on the edge.

The fabric of his slacks rustled behind me, and the sound of his zipper going down made my heart pound frantically in my chest.

I could feel my wetness seeping down my thighs, practically dripping down my heated flesh. The cool air from the overhead fan brushed against my soaked pussy, making my face burn with a shameful heat. Why was I so aroused? Why did I want him to fuck me? Did I really want that?

Then all of a sudden, the heat of his cock brushed against my pussy and an involuntary moan broke free from my lips. My hips jerked, not away from him, but towards him, and I hated my body for giving away how much I wanted him.

The head of his cock pressed against my entrance. If I expected him to tease me or draw this out, I received none of that. Instead, he thrust into me hard and fast and took me far more brutally than I could have ever expected. With a shriek, I tried to crawl away, but my hips butted up against the table, and he plunged into me even deeper.

My pussy burned from his massive girth, stretched open wide without preparation, but my shame was a thousand-fold as my own wetness eased his journey inside of me. The wet squelch made my face burn hotter, and I hated that every inch of him felt just as good as I knew it would.

He fucked me hard though, far harder than I thought he would.

He pounded into me, sinking his full length inside me so firmly and so fast that his balls slapped against my wet folds, punishing my pussy with every inch of him. I thought he had fucked me senseless yesterday.

That *paled* in comparison to this.

His hands wound around my hips, protecting me from the corner of the table as he plunged into me. He drove into me ruthlessly hard, the tip of his cock bouncing off my cervix and reminding me that he was the one *doing* the fucking and I was the one *taking* it.

Over and over, he plowed into me, taking everything that he wanted and more. His fingers dug into my hips, and I knew without a doubt that they were going to leave marks, but a part of me liked that. A low moan escaped me as my body very slowly accommodated to his size, but the more he impaled me on his cock, the more I slowly realized something else.

I wanted to come.

Badly.

With every brutal thrust, I moaned, and soon my moans became screams. Every nerve in my body quivered with unreleased tension, and no matter how much I tried to hold it back, I barreled closer and closer to orgasm.

"Please," I begged.

"You're going to take my cock like a good little girl," he growled.

"It hurts," I pleaded.

"Then don't be coy with me again, naughty girl, and I won't have to punish you with my cock," he said darkly, and I felt my pussy nearly spasm around his thick, punishing length.

I hadn't meant to be coy. I'd just wanted to stand up and fight against him for a moment, to stand toe-to-toe with him, but it was hard when his cock kept impaling me again and again, driving me mad with desire. My back arched, taking him deeper and deeper as his cock possessed me, and I dug my fingers into the table, trying to claw at the wood but finding nothing to hold onto as I quickly spiraled out of control.

In that singular moment, my desire soared, unbridled and unrestrained, propelling me into a realm where only raw, untamed passion existed. It was as if a dormant volcano within me had erupted, sending a cascade of fiery need coursing through every vein.

The intensity of my arousal was like a rocket, shooting straight into the stratosphere, leaving the mundane world far below. Every nerve ending was alight, every sense heightened to an almost unbearable degree. The air around me seemed charged with electricity, each breath I took saturated with an aching hunger for him.

My heart pounded like a frenzied drum in my chest, its rhythm echoing the tumultuous whirlwind of emotions that swept me along in its vortex. The world around me became a blur, leaving me breathless, exhilarated, and soaring into a realm where only pure, unadulterated desire reigned supreme.

"Nikolaos," I breathed.

"You'll call me sir when my cock is ravaging this sweet little pussy," he snarled, and my inner walls clutched at his thick length like it was made for it.

"Yes *sir*," I wailed.

I kept trying to figure out how far he would go, how brutally hard he would fuck me, and then it would keep getting more ruthless, harsher than I could ever have imagined. My pussy burned from each punishing stroke, and when it got harder than I could have ever thought possible, I started to beg.

"You're going to be a good girl the next time you want a fucking, won't you?" he asked.

"Yes, sir," I whimpered.

He pulled my hips back, pounding into me so firmly that the table scraped against the tile floor beneath me. He yanked my hips back a bit further and slid one hand underneath me, capturing my clit between his fingers in an instant.

"That's my good girl," he purred, and my heart skipped a beat. His praise did something to me that I didn't want to admit, and I wanted so much more of it.

"I'll be your good girl, sir," I breathed.

My tits still burned from his punishing slaps, and my nipples pebbled against the table, terribly tender and needy, and I reached for them and took one in between my fingers as he fondled my clit. He circled over my needy little bundle of nerves and my body nearly quaked against the table.

"You're going to take my cock no matter how hard I give it to you, my little slut," he growled, the timbre of his voice rolling down my spine like a sip of fine wine.

"Yes. Yes, sir!!!"

"Then be a good girl and come for me," he demanded.

I shattered.

My eyes rolled back in my head, and I pinched my nipple firmly, pain and pleasure spiraling through me in spades. I writhed beneath him, seeing stars and losing my head so far up in the clouds that I wondered if I would ever come back down again. My body broke and everything inside me burned with pleasure.

Every nerve ignited in the same moment, blaring red hot and blinding me with white hot euphoria until I thought I was losing my mind with pleasure. Sheer ecstasy ricocheted through my body, making my fingers tingle and my toes curl and everything I held dear unravel.

When my climax finally began to fade, I caught my breath, but his fucking didn't stop.

It didn't even slow down.

He plunged into me with even more vigor than before, and I found myself on the precipice of yet another release. There was no fighting it this time. There was simply taking it.

When I came again, I came hard.

As the waves of desire crashed against me, I felt myself being swept up in a current of relentless passion. It was as if a wildfire had ignited within the core of my being, its flames licking every corner of my soul, setting me ablaze with a fervor that knew no bounds.

With each heartbeat, the endless bliss intensified, ascending swiftly, like a falcon taking flight into the sky. My senses were overwhelmed, each touch, each breath, amplifying the burning need that consumed me from within.

I was adrift in a sea of pleasure, riding the crests of waves that brought ecstasy beyond imagination. Every sensation was magnified a thousandfold.

His cock sunk into me so hard and so fast, and when he finally pulled free of me, I felt empty. Lonely. I wanted him back inside of me.

I heard the ripping of a wrapper and the sound of a condom snapping into place around his cock and when he pressed himself at my entrance once again, I froze.

"Wait."

"What is it, my needy little slut?"

Slowly, I pushed myself up off the table and turned around, my sore pussy throbbing and somehow still wanting more. Hesitantly, I took his cock into my hand, and I glanced up at him, locking my eyes with his stormy grey depths.

"Can I ride your cock instead?"

I didn't know what had come over me. Maybe I was feeling bold after taking such a hard fucking and surviving it, but he cocked his head and glanced down at me with a wry grin that told me he didn't hate the idea, that maybe a tiny part of him liked it.

He gently cupped my face, his fingers tracing the contours of my skin with a touch that was both delicate and deliberate. Then his hand shifted, finding its way to the back of my head, where his fingers entwined themselves in my hair.

His grip was firm, commanding, a stark contrast to the softness of his initial touch. It was a possessive gesture, one that spoke a thousand words without a single one being uttered.

In that charged moment, he leaned in, and his lips met mine in a kiss that was anything but gentle. It was a punishing kiss, a clash of wills and desires, fierce and unyielding. His lips moved against mine with an intensity that was overpowering, yet I found myself melting into it, surrendering to the overwhelming sensation.

It was as if with that kiss, he was staking a claim, marking me as his in a primal, unspoken agreement. Every ounce of restraint I had tried to maintain crumbled under the assault of his kiss.

I loved it.

When the kiss finally broke, my lips ached, and the rest of my body was pulsing with the blood rushing through my veins. He reached to the side and pulled out a chair, sitting down. His fingers found mine and pulled me towards him.

"Climb on top of my cock, Maci-girl," he demanded.

"Yes, sir," I blushed.

My gaze dropped down to his cock. Though covered with a condom, it was rock hard and throbbing just for me. The latex was clear enough so that I could see the deep purple head and the slit at the top. Veins were pulsing on either side of his cock, and I started.

My pussy clenched nervously.

A droplet of wetness rolled down my inner thigh as I crawled on top of him. Slowly, I pressed my hand beneath me and guided the tip of his cock to my entrance. Gradually, I sunk down and took his cock inside me, his gaze mesmerized by me the entire time.

He felt so much bigger this way.

As he watched my face, his gaze intense and unwavering, I felt a warmth flood through me. In his eyes, I could see his utter captivation that made my heart flutter. It was in the way his eyes traced the contours of my features, the softness in his expression, and the slight parting of his lips as if he was drinking in my presence, like he couldn't get enough of me either and wanted more.

For the first time in what felt like an eternity, I felt like the most beautiful woman in the world.

Maybe, just maybe, there was something more here, something beyond the fiery passion and unspoken tensions. Could there be a possibility for something deeper, something lasting after all this was over?

His eyes held a promise, a hint of something more, igniting a flicker of hope in the depths of my heart. Maybe there could be something beautiful between us, maybe not.

I didn't know.

I sunk down a bit deeper, taking more and more of him until I was completely full. I bit my lip, my pussy aching as his cock stretched me wide open, yet I wanted so much more.

His cock was a monster, and I just sat there with him inside me for a moment, too anxious to move for fear it would hurt. My pussy burned with fire, stretched wide open by his monster of a dick, and I mewled nervously.

I couldn't believe I was doing this.

With unending dominance, his fingers wrapped around my waist, and he slowly guided me forward, teaching me how to roll my hips as the head of his cock brushed against a place deep inside me that nearly made me come apart right then and there.

Slowly building my confidence, I fell into a rhythm, grinding my hips back and forth as he slipped his thumb in between us and caressed my clit.

I lost all sense of reason.

In an instant, my orgasm came crashing down, painting my vision a vivid white, blinding me and tossing me into the white-water rapids of my own desire. His other hand swept behind my hair, pulling it taught and making me cry out as a fissure of pain splintered through my desire.

It was fucking delicious.

I rode him hard and fast, gradually increasing the pace until my body took control. His thumb worried my clit, forcing my pleasure to the surface again and again until my body was slick with sweat and my breathing turned ragged.

"Fuck, princess. Ride me harder. Take my cock like the needy little slut you are," he purred, and I couldn't help but give him my every surrender.

Pain and pleasure warred within me, an endless battlefield of sensation that tore through me like lightning. His grip on my hair tightened, and he wrenched my head back, thrusting up and filling me more completely than I thought possible.

The battle within me was intense, each side vying for dominance, each sensation as potent and strong as the other. The pain spiked through me again and again, while the desire edged onward, a siren song promising ecstasy intertwined between the two.

I fell.

Agony and ecstasy became one and the same. My mind went blank as I writhed on top of him, taking my pleasure for myself as he thrust up into me.

I ground up and down on his cock like a piston, up and down, over and over again.

Then, all at once, one last final orgasm tore through me, my inner walls clutching around him and milking him for everything he was worth. He roared and the hot feeling of his seed spurted up into the thin condom, filling me up even more completely than I thought possible.

I unraveled and his arms wrapped around me, clutching me tight in direct opposition to the way he had left me yesterday. His arms tightened as I came down from my orgasm, and he didn't let go.

His cologne, rich and intoxicating, wrapped around me like a luxurious cloak. It was a complex scent, deep and masculine, with notes of smoky cedarwood, a hint of spicy black pepper, and the subtle undertone of cinnamon and nutmeg.

As I nestled closer, I could smell the faint traces of his sweat. Every breath I took was filled with him. And then, he leaned in and sweetly kissed my forehead.

My heart practically stopped beating in my chest.

I don't know how long he held me, but it was a long time. It was like he didn't want to let go and nothing in his power would take me away from him.

I *liked* that.

After a long while, he finally lifted me off his cock and settled me back down on my feet.

"I would stay with you for the rest of the day, but I have several meetings that I can't move this afternoon, Maci-girl," he explained, the tender look in his eyes a bit sad.

Did he mean that? Did he really want to stay with me?

"I'll go back to my room," I whispered.

His hand found the back of my head, his fingers weaving through my hair with a possessive roughness that sent shivers down my spine. He held me firmly, a silent command that was both thrilling and startling at the same time.

"That's not your bedroom anymore," he said, his voice low and resolute, echoing with a dominance that resonated deep within me. "My staff will have your things transferred to our room right away," he continued.

The words, simple as they were, struck a chord within me. There was something profoundly arousing about his assertiveness, the way he claimed me. It was as if he was marking his territory, staking his claim in a manner that was both primal and deeply romantic.

I was left standing there, momentarily dazed, my heart racing with a mixture of surprise and anticipation. In that simple declaration, he had opened a new chapter for us, one where the lines of passion and romance intertwined.

Maybe there could be something between us after all.

I allowed myself to hope.

"Yes sir," I whispered.

 ikolaos

I shouldn't have come to any of these meetings.

The only thing I could think about was the tight grip of Maci's pussy as I took her hard over that table, of the sweet look in her eyes as she rode me to orgasm again and again, and the tender hope painted all over her face when I'd announced that my room was now our room.

As I sat in the midst of yet another crucial business meeting, my mind should have been focused on the intricate web of decisions and strategies being discussed. I was a man known for his steadfast attention to detail and my formidable presence in the boardroom. But today, my usual ironclad concentration was besieged by a relentless distraction—*her*.

The image of her, the memory of her touch, the scent of her that still lingered on my skin—it was as if she had cast a spell over me and I couldn't break free of it.

It was unsettling. I wasn't a man accustomed to being swayed by emotion, to allowing personal matters to intrude upon business *ever*, and here I was, letting her cloud my mind like a vision.

I was caught in a vortex of thoughts and feelings that I couldn't seem to escape. Her smile, the sound of her laughter, the way she looked up at me with those captivating eyes.

She was perfect.

I found myself analyzing every moment we shared, every exchange, every touch. There was an intensity between us that I couldn't shake off, a connection that seemed to be growing stronger with every passing moment.

Honestly, it was dangerous. It was making me rash.

Maybe blowing up those ships took it a step too far...

I tried to refocus, to bring myself back to the present, but it was futile. She had infiltrated my thoughts, a sweet and potent distraction that made the numbers and reports in front of me seem entirely inconsequential.

I couldn't wait to be free so that I could return home to her.

Finally, when the endless meetings and discussions drew to a close, I was left with a profound sense of relief.

I couldn't wait to hold her again.

Upon arriving home, I found that the house was quiet, a stark contrast to the hustle of the day. It was late as I made my way to the bedroom, where I found her already asleep, her form a peaceful silhouette in the soft glow of the moonlight filtering through the curtains.

She was so beautiful.

Gently, I climbed into bed beside her, careful not to wake her. As I drew her into my arms, her warmth and softness were a welcome comfort. Her hair, spread across the pillow, released a delicate scent of lavender from her shampoo. It mingled perfectly with her own unique scent, a fragrance that was inherently Maci—subtle yet utterly enticing.

Her skin was soft under my touch, smooth and inviting. I ran my fingers through her silky hair, marveling at its softness, each strand slipping through my fingers like fine threads of the most expensive silk.

As I lay there with her in my arms, the trials of the day melted away. The simple act of holding her, of feeling her nestled against me, made the end of my day absolutely perfect.

I didn't know why I allowed myself this small comfort. I didn't know what it was about her that made me feel this way.

But I did.

I allowed myself, *for tonight.*

* * *

The next morning, I woke up with Maci still nestled in my arms. I took a moment to simply watch her, to appreciate the quiet beauty of her presence. Her breath was a soft, rhythmic whisper against my chest.

The warmth of her body against mine was heavenly. The scent of lavender still lingered in her hair, now mixed with the faint traces of our shared pillow, creating a scent that was uniquely ours.

As I lay there holding her, I was struck by a sense of awe at how naturally she fit in my arms. It was as if she was always meant to be there.

I shook my head. I shouldn't be letting myself feel these things, but with her in my arms, I felt a contentment that I'd never known before.

I swallowed hard.

She stirred awake and turned to face me, her eyes fluttering open to reveal those captivating depths that had ensnared me from the start. In those first moments of wakefulness, her gaze held a mix of vulnerability and inquiry, searching mine as if unsure of what the new day held for us, almost as if she didn't know what to expect from me after the intensity of the previous few days.

The truth was, I didn't either.

I didn't say anything.

Leaning in, I just gave in and kissed her.

Her response was immediate, a soft yielding that melted into the tenderness of the moment, and I kissed her a bit harder and more possessively, and she molded to me like a vine wound around a tree.

"Good morning," she breathed.

"Good morning, Maci-girl," I answered. I moved to climb out of bed, but she nestled closer to me, and I couldn't bring myself to pull away from her, at least not yet. She shifted against me, her expression one of curiosity as she leaned away from me just far enough to see my face.

"What are you going to do today? Plot your next bombing? Take over the world? Negotiate an unbreakable alliance with another shipping family?" she asked, a certain playfulness twinkling in her eyes.

The little minx was testing me, and it made my dick really fucking hard. I didn't care if she could feel it either.

In fact, I liked that she probably could.

"Just because you figured that out yesterday, it doesn't mean that anything will change, Maci-girl. You're safe outside my world and that's where you're going to stay," I chided, but I was still pretty fascinated over her figuring that out, even though it was the day after. She was smarter than I gave her credit for.

I wouldn't make that mistake again.

"I know that they're going to hit back after you sank their ships. What are they going to do in return? Have you started a war? How will it end?" she asked, lifting her chin and searching my gaze, and I was once again hit with pride about how intelligent she was.

Maybe she could be an asset in my world after all.

"How it ends all depends on how hard they hit me back," I answered carefully. I was giving her just enough, but not too much. I wanted to watch as she figured it all out on her own once again.

"What are they going to do?" she pressed.

Her curiosity was endearing, and I found myself enjoying every second of it. In fact, I wanted to play into it a bit more, so I decided to test her.

I was going to enjoy this.

"Well how do you think they'll hit back?" I asked, raising my eyebrow.

Her face scrunched up in thought, and it was the cutest thing I had ever seen. Her eyebrows drew together, and she glanced down, thinking, before her gaze popped back up to mine.

"Wouldn't they just not hit back at all? I mean, you sent a clear enough message, I would think..." she tried, and I shook my head. Her brow furrowed once again.

"No, they have to do something in retaliation. It would destroy their reputation if they did nothing at all," I answered patiently.

"Yeah. I guess you're right... Well, I guess they wouldn't want to hit back as hard as they could because that would escalate the war, but then they could try to hit back hard enough to save face."

My pride in her reached a new level, and I decided to keep pushing her. How far could this go?

"What do you think they would do to achieve that?" I questioned, reaching for her and casually brushing a lock of hair out of her face and tucking it behind her ear.

"Maybe they'll just kill a few of your guys but no one really important," she guessed.

I smiled, unable to hide how stunned I was with how quickly she was learning. "Little miss crime lord, I'm not just going to let them kill my men. What kind of patriarch would that make me?"

"Well, what then?" she pressed, her eyes lighting up adorably bright.

She was enjoying this too.

"We blew up three of their very expensive ships. If I were them and I wanted to hit back, not too hard, but just right, I would blow up some of our trucks, maybe expose one of our safe houses. That way, they still hit just hard enough not to puss out and destroy their reputation, but not hard enough to start a full-blown war."

"I understand. And what would happen after that? Would you hit them back again?"

"No. Then I'd let things lie. I've already proven I can hit them hard, and then the war between us will settle," I explained.

"Next time you plan with Andreas, can I come along?" she tried.

"No, I don't think the time is right for that," I said as I gently shook my head. She pouted a little, and I cupped her chin pulling her into another sweet kiss. By the time I pulled away, her eyes were dazed, and all thoughts of crime had seemingly melted away from her face.

I wanted to stay in bed with her all day, but I needed to talk to Andreas. My phone beeped on the nightstand, and I knew it was him without even looking.

"Sleep in, princess. I'll have breakfast sent up to you shortly."

"Don't mind if I do," she quipped, her smile lighting up her face, and I spent a moment admiring her beauty before I pulled away from her and climbed out of bed.

I hated leaving her, but I had an empire to run. Now was not the time to show weakness.

I needed to be strong.

I couldn't let anyone know how weak she made me because then everything might crumble.

 aci

As he climbed out of bed, I couldn't help but let my gaze linger on his perfectly carved body. The broad expanse of his shoulders spoke of power, tapering down to a waist that hinted at his physical prowess and discipline. The way his muscles moved under his skin, flexing and relaxing with each movement, was almost hypnotic. There was an elegance in his movements, a poise that belied the raw power he possessed, and I couldn't get enough of it.

I let my eyes drop to the round bubble of his ass. I licked my lips, allowing myself to simply appreciate his masculine body. A part of me wondered if he knew I was looking, but that didn't really matter to me.

He probably knew.

It was obvious that he was the kind of guy that took care of his body, that spent hours in the gym each week lifting and toning those strong muscles, and I sincerely appreciated it.

A part of me wanted to sink my teeth into his shoulders as I rode his cock or scratch my nails down his back and leave my mark on his own skin just like he'd left his on mine.

I grinned and he chose that exact moment to look back over his shoulder at me, catching me looking, and my cheeks heated immediately. He smirked and disappeared into his closet, his rock-hard cock bouncing with every step.

Even though my pussy was still sore, I wanted more of him, but I would never admit it. At least not out loud…

When he came out, he was dressed in a tailored suit.

His suit was clearly the work of a master artist. It hugged his frame perfectly, showing the attention to detail that only the finest tailors could provide.

It was a deep, rich black that seemed to absorb and reflect light in a way that gave it an almost velvety sheen. The jacket was structured yet not stiff, with sharp, clean lines that accentuated his broad shoulders and tapered waist. The lapels were just the right width, not too wide nor too narrow, lending an air of modern elegance.

His shirt was a crisp, pristine white. The collar was sharp, framing his jawline in a way that was both commanding and stylish. He paired it with a richly colored grey tie, its fabric a beautifully fine silk. As he adjusted his cufflinks—understated yet undoubtedly expensive—the entire outfit came together in a display of effortless elegance.

Honestly, he looked sexy as fuck.

"Keep looking at me like that, and you're going to get fucked," he warned, and I giggled, because a part of me desperately wanted that.

"My pussy is too sore," I whined, already knowing him well enough that he probably would still fuck me anyway, and that made my pussy clench hard.

He breathed in through his teeth, took one last look at me and growled under his breath. With what seemed like extreme reluctance, he peeled his eyes away from me and picked up his phone from the nightstand.

"That won't save you from getting fucked later, Maci-girl," he purred, and I squealed in delight. "Now be a good girl and go back to sleep. I'll be back in a bit to take care of that needy little pussy."

I dove under the covers for a split second, but then peeked over them as I watched him walk out of the room.

"See you later, sir," I whispered, unable to keep myself from smiling so wide it hurt my cheeks.

* * *

Nikolaos didn't return until a few hours later. By that time, I'd drifted back into a light sleep, woken up, eaten breakfast in bed, enjoyed a nice hot shower, and watched a movie on the massive television mounted on the wall across from the bed. Honestly, it felt like having my very own private movie theatre in the middle of a high-end hotel room.

His room was even more ostentatious than my previous one.

"That's not your bedroom anymore."

His words echoed in my mind, and I couldn't help but smile as I looked around the room.

The centerpiece of the room was undoubtedly the massive king-sized bed. Its dark blue quilted headboard added a touch of elegance to the space. The bed was dressed in the finest linens, crisp and white. The duvet was fluffy and lightweight, yet incredibly warm, enveloping me in a cocoon of comfort. Scattered across the bed were plush pillows, each encased in silky, high-thread-count pillowcases that felt luxurious against my skin.

Beside the bed stood sleek, contemporary nightstands, each holding minimalist lamps that illuminated the room with a warm, ambient light. Across from the bed, the large windows were dressed in heavy, dark blue drapes that could be drawn to block out the morning light or opened to reveal a breathtaking view of the ocean.

The room also featured a seating area with a comfortable, modern sofa and a coffee table, both in tones of dark blue and grey, creating a perfect spot for reading or enjoying a morning coffee.

Adjacent to the bedroom was the en-suite bathroom, a spa-like space that wouldn't be out of place in a high-end hotel. It featured a large, walk-in shower with a rain shower head, a deep soaking tub, and his-and-hers sinks set in a sleek, marble countertop. The towels and bathrobes were fluffy and white, adding to the spa-like experience.

I wore nothing other than one of those robes until he returned. Honestly, it kind of felt really good to be that free.

Much of my time alone, I thought about how much I wanted to stand by his side and be a part of his life.

I wanted power. *With him.*

I could handle his world. I wanted him to see me not just as a little girl to be protected, but as a partner, an equal who could stand tall amidst the complexities and challenges of his life.

In my mind, I rehearsed conversations where I would express this to him, showcasing my understanding of the delicate intricacies of his world. I was aware of the dangers and the power plays, the delicate balance of strength and diplomacy required.

I wanted to show him the strength I possessed. There was a part of me that knew I could be powerful at his side, an ally who could navigate the treacherous waters of his world with a grace he might not yet be accustomed to. I had so much to offer him, and he'd be foolish to let that be swept under the rug.

I believed in my ability to adapt, to learn, and to contribute. All I needed was a chance, an opening for me to show him how we could be stronger together.

In the time he was gone, I decided that they wouldn't expose one of his safehouses. They'd hit his fleet of trucks.

When he finally came back, I looked up from where I was lounging and said with as much confidence as I could muster, "They hit a fair number of your trucks after all, didn't they? More than you thought they would?"

The moment the words left my mouth, I saw a flicker of surprise cross his face, quickly replaced by an unmistakable look of admiration, and my heart leapt up into my throat.

Maybe he would let me into his world after all. I knew I could handle it. I just needed to convince him.

He paused for a moment, studying me with a gaze that seemed to delve into the very core of who I was. I could almost see the wheels turning in his mind, reassessing me, perhaps acknowledging that I was more than just a little girl who needed protecting.

His expression softened.

"You're right," he finally said, his voice tinged with a mix of resignation and quiet admiration. "I am impressed, Maci-girl, and you know what, that makes my cock rock fucking hard."

He stood up and prowled towards me. As he approached, I could feel the atmosphere between us shift, a heated sense of anticipation building in the air, and I held my breath, my heart skipping a beat with anxious arousal.

Methodically, Nikolaos reached up and began to loosen his tie, his fingers deftly untying the knot with ease. He then proceeded to remove the jacket of his suit, revealing the white shirt underneath that hugged his frame. Then he unbuttoned his cuffs, rolling them up one by one as I fidgeted and waited for him to approach.

Then he climbed onto the bed, his movements fluid and assured. He positioned himself over me, his eyes locking onto mine with an intensity that made my heart race. The air between us crackled with an electric tension, and I finally let out the breath I was holding all at once.

In that moment, I was acutely aware of every line and curve of his body, especially his rock-hard cock that was pressing right against my center.

"You were my very good girl today, weren't you?" he purred, and my breath hitched in the back of my throat.

"Yes, sir," I whispered. Drawing my lower lip in between my teeth, I couldn't tear my eyes away as he slowly untied the waistband of my robe and drew each side of it open, baring my body slowly.

Reverently.

"I think I should reward you for being such a good girl," he added next, and my thighs trembled a bit with exhilaration.

"I think I'd like that," I answered, my voice trembling just a bit with nervous energy.

His eyes held mine as he crawled backwards and lowered himself between my legs, his eyes locked with my own the entire time.

Then he looked down, and in an instant, my shameful arousal slapped me right in the face. He was looking at my pussy.

Like really looking.

He'd be able to see every inch of what was between my legs, from my wetness leaking from my pussy, to my swollen clit, to my entrance.

Everything.

I tried to close my legs and he swiftly used his arms to wrench them apart.

"Never try to hide this beautiful body from me, princess. If I want to look, you'll show me, unless you want to end up over my knee instead," he warned, and my pussy practically spasmed with heat.

"Yes, sir," I blushed, and just to show him that I could handle it, I opened my legs a bit wider, and his resulting grin was more than worth my own personal embarrassment over him seeing something he'd already fucked twice.

Like he wanted to push me, he took his thumbs and spread my lips open to reveal my swollen bundle of nerves, and I quivered, my shame escalating immediately. My cheeks burned with heat, and I turned away, unable to meet his eyes, but when the wet warmth of his mouth settled over my clit, my eyes jerked right back.

I gasped.

I'd never felt anything like it.

He pulled away for just a second and locked his gaze with mine.

"You're going to come for me. You won't get to decide how many times or how hard. I will just make you come as hard and as long as I want," he growled, and my breath stuttered in the back of my throat.

Before I could say a word, his mouth returned to my pussy, and in an instant, my eyes rolled back in my head.

His tongue was absolute magic.

The tip of it circled my clit. The wet heat was mesmerizing, and my thighs clenched, trying to stay open even as fissures of pleasure spiked through me with wild abandon. With every lash of his tongue, my pleasure escalated higher and higher, until my head was high up in the stratosphere amongst the clouds and I knew I wasn't going to come down any time soon.

My world was completely rocked by an all-consuming desire. It was as if a dormant volcano deep within me had erupted, sending waves of fiery need coursing through every fiber of my being.

The air around us seemed to thicken with this raw, palpable hunger, a magnetic pull that drew me irresistibly to him. Every nerve ending felt supercharged, alive with electricity that only his presence could generate.

My heart raced, pounding against my ribcage like a wild drum. The room, the world outside, everything else faded into a distant blur, leaving only the overwhelming sensation of wanting him, needing him in a way that was primal and urgent.

He ate my pussy like it was his last meal and before I knew what was happening, my world flashed vivid white and wave after wave of pleasure rocked my senses from the inside out.

That first orgasm was magical. My body writhed beneath him as his hands wound around my hips, his body settling between my legs so I couldn't close them even as every muscle within me tensed with mind-bending pleasure.

His tongue flicked and teased my clit, and before I knew what was happening, I was coming again.

And again.

And *again.*

At first, each orgasm was pleasurable, but soon, each one spiked with pain. My clit was oversensitive and my body along with it, every nerve firing over and over until I thought that they couldn't anymore and then they would again.

Pain and pleasure battled one another, and the more I came, the more the latter started to win out.

I loved it.

With every touch, every movement, Nikolaos guided me through a dance of sensations that left me breathless. The pain, when it came, was like a sharp, electrifying jolt, and then the waves of pleasure inevitably followed.

It was a strange, intoxicating mix that heightened every moment of heated bliss, making each moment more vivid, more intense. And the pleasure that came after was like a soothing balm, a wave of joy that washed over me, erasing everything else. I found myself craving the contrast, wanting more, needing more.

I loved every second of it, every pulse of pain, every surge of pleasure, until I thought I couldn't take anymore.

He didn't stop.

I writhed. I screamed. I shattered beneath him into a million different pieces.

When he finally came up for air, my entire body was covered with a sheen of sweat and my heart was nearly pounding out of my chest, my breathing ragged.

"That's my good girl. You came good and hard for me, didn't you?" he asked.

"Yes, sir," I blushed, my voice a breathy whisper.

He climbed back over me and captured my lips with his, the taste of my arousal still sharp on his tongue. It was sweet, slightly musky, and extremely taboo, but I didn't care.

I kissed him back just as hard. When he finally pulled away, I looked up into his eyes and took a deep breath. It was time to stand my ground.

"So, next time I can come to your meetings?"

I caught a fleeting glimpse of shock crossing Nikolaos' face, his usually composed features momentarily giving way to surprise. But almost as quickly as it appeared, the shock was replaced by amusement.

His lips curled into a knowing smirk, and a twinkle of mischief lit up his eyes. He shook his head slightly, a silent chuckle escaping him before he grabbed my legs and lifted them straight up, exposing my ass without even a second's delay. His hand smacked my left cheek and then my right, stingingly hard, and I cried out, the pain catching my over-sensitized body by surprise.

"You're a feisty little crime lord, aren't you?" he growled, and I cried out as several more stinging slaps struck my cheeks.

Almost as quickly as the spanking had started, he stopped and gently put my legs back down. I fidgeted against the bed, my bottom scalded just enough to make me whimper.

Leaning down, Nikolaos brought his face close to mine, his breath warm against my skin. With a playful yet seductive movement, he gently bit my ear, sending a thrilling shiver down my spine. Following the playful nip, he brushed his lips softly against my cheek, a kiss so feather-light yet so charged with emotion that it made my heart flutter.

Then, in a voice low and resonant with promise, he whispered, "Next time, princess. I promise. Right now, though, you're about to get fucked."

CHAPTER 19

 *hree weeks later*
       Nikolaos

She was positively exquisite. I couldn't take my eyes off her.

Watching Maci diligently pore over the acquisition files, I found myself increasingly impressed by her innate ability to navigate the complexities of my world. True to my promise, I had involved her in several meetings with Andreas, and in each one, she had excelled.

Initially, I'd harbored hesitations about introducing her to the intricate details of my operations. However, her adaptability and keen intellect swiftly alleviated my concerns.

Whenever I directed a question towards her, subtly steering her towards a specific conclusion, she consistently reached it on her own. More than that, she often enriched the discussion with her unique perspective, adding things I hadn't anticipated and sometimes even beating me to the punchline.

It was impressive.

Observing her in these meetings, seeing her analyze, question, and understand the nuances of each deal, was not just reassuring—it was an absolute joy.

And it made my cock rock fucking hard.

Even now as she poured over an extensive file of recent local acquisitions, she was the picture of elegance.

Her focus was absolute, her eyes scanning the pages with a deep intensity. The way she occasionally chewed the end of her pen, lost in thought, only made my cock that much harder.

Her hair fell in soft waves around her face, occasionally obscuring her view as she leaned closer to examine a particular detail. Each small gesture, whether it was the furrowing of her brow in concentration or the slight smile that played on her lips when she came across something interesting, made me want to take her right then and there.

I cocked my head, imagining her screams as she came for me, over and over until she collapsed on my desk.

I cleared my throat, keeping my thoughts to myself. She wanted to be included in my business, and I needed to let her.

There would be time for fucking later.

"So, Maci," I began, my tone casual yet probing, "looking at these property acquisitions over the past few months, what pattern do you notice?"

She leaned over the table, her eyes scanning the documents thoughtfully. "There's a concentration of purchases around the downtown area," she observed, pointing to the marked locations on the map. "And they all seem to encircle these three key ventures we've been interested in."

"Exactly," I nodded, encouraging her to delve deeper. "Now, considering the buyers, what strikes you as unusual?"

Maci furrowed her brows, her gaze moving back and forth between the documents. "The buyers are varied, but the transactions are brokered by the same set of lawyers and agents. It's almost as if they're coordinated."

Andreas chimed in, "Coordinated by whom, do you think?"

She paused, connecting the dots in her head. "It's the Stefanidis family, isn't it?" she finally said, her voice laced with confidence. "They're the common link. They're buying up these properties to block us from these ventures."

I couldn't help but smile at her accurate conclusion. "Precisely, Maci. The Stefanidis family has been trying to corner the market ever since I blew up their ships, subtly boxing us out."

Her eyes lit up with realization and understanding. "So, they're not just expanding their portfolio; they're strategically undercutting us. This is more than just business expansion, isn't it? It's a power play."

Andreas raised his eyebrows and looked at her. I knew him well enough to see that he was visibly impressed. "Exactly. They're trying to weaken our position," he confirmed.

"If the Stefanidis family is boxing us out of these ventures, why don't we turn the tables on them?" she suggested, her eyes alight with strategic thinking.

I furrowed my brow and narrowed my eyes, suddenly more than a little intrigued. "Go on," I prompted.

"Well," she started, her fingers tracing potential moves on the map, "instead of directly competing for these properties, what if we start acquiring businesses that are peripheral yet essential to the ventures Stefanidis is interested in? We could control resources or services that their new properties would depend on."

Andreas and I exchanged a look, both impressed by her line of thinking. "You mean, take over supply chains or smaller businesses that are crucial to operating those properties effectively?" Andreas asked, leaning in. He was just as mesmerized by her as I was.

"Exactly," Maci replied, her confidence growing. "By doing this, we not only create leverage over the Stefanidis family, but potentially open up new revenue streams for us. We might even force them into a position where they have to negotiate with us on our terms."

I nodded, considering her strategy. "That's a sharp move. It turns their aggression into an opportunity for us. Not only do we protect our interests, but we also expand them, making a much bigger profit in the long run."

"And it's subtle," added Andreas. "It doesn't directly confront the Stefanidis family, which minimizes the risk of escalating tensions even further, but it's enough to send a message if they're smart enough to figure it out."

"I'm proud of you, Maci," I purred, and she beamed in my direction, a sense of accomplishment written all over her face. Her radiant smile lit up her features, and her eyes twinkled with glee. With a confident shake of her head, she pulled her shoulders back and smirked in my direction.

"I told you I was ready," she replied, and I couldn't help but chuckle at her forwardness.

"That you are, princess," I said darkly, and her cheeks reddened.

It was clear that she was beginning to grasp the intricacies of my world. Her insight was not only spot on but showed a depth of understanding that went well beyond surface-level analysis.

Maybe, *just maybe*, I'd found my queen.

She had the potential to hold her own at my side, and that aroused me more than I cared to admit.

"Andreas?"

"Yes, boss?"

"Leave us. There's some urgent business that I need to discuss with Maci," I said darkly, and her cheeks flushed a deeper rose red.

"Of course," he replied. With a sense of urgency, he stood up and took his leave, leaving the two of us alone together. Once the door shut, I cleared my throat.

"Bend over the desk, princess. You've got a hard fucking coming," I began, and her sharp intake of breath told me everything I needed to know.

Without a word of defiance, she stood up, holding her head high as she gracefully bent over my desk. I moved behind her and slowly lifted her skirt, already knowing that her pussy was bare underneath because I hadn't allowed her to wear panties this morning.

When I ran my fingers between her thighs, I found her already soaking wet for me.

Fuck. She was perfect.

Mine.

Forever mine.

"Do you know how proud of you I am, my little queen?"

"Yes, sir," she murmured, and I slapped her ass, hard. Instead of pulling away, she gasped and arched her back like a cat. The sight of it made my balls ache, and I wanted nothing more than to sink inside of her this instant, but she deserved so much more than that.

She deserved to come hard, and I was going to make certain that she did.

"Spread your legs," I demanded, and she obeyed, visibly trembling before me. She wasn't afraid. She was already shaking with need.

"Look at this soaking wet pussy, so wet for me, and I've hardly even touched you," I murmured, and she mewled with something that sounded a lot like shame.

"Sir," she breathed, her voice quivering a little.

"Were you thinking about my cock sinking into this tight little cunt?"

"Yes," she moaned, and I lightly slapped her beautiful pussy, eliciting the most delicious yelp of pain from her that shot straight up the length of my dick.

"Naughty girl. You were supposed to be concentrating on the acquisitions file, weren't you?"

"Yes, sir," she whined.

"I should spank this needy little pussy bright pink, but today I want to spoil you, so I'm just going to make you come hard for me, over and over again until you beg me to fuck you," I growled, sliding my fingers in between her folds until I found the hard little nub of her clit.

She shuddered against the desk, and I slapped her cunt once more, just hard enough to sting a tiny bit. Her back arched and her legs spread wider as she offered her body to me, and I spanked her pretty little pussy once more before I found her clit.

Using only my fingers, I forced her to the edge of orgasm, enjoying the way her body bowed as if she was seeking me out, and the way her breathy little gasps quickened right before she lost control, and the quivering of her legs as she closed in on her climax.

I didn't let her come yet.

Instead, I teased her, taunting her with pleasure but not letting her reach climax. I wanted that first orgasm to break her.

I must have brought her right to the edge no less than half a dozen times before she began to beg.

"Please, sir. Please let me come," she pleaded, her voice shaking with her need.

It was the sexiest thing I'd ever fucking heard.

"How badly do you want to come, my little queen?"

"Please, I need to come," she whispered, her voice hoarse. Her hips bucked a little against the edge of my desk, and I yanked them back just far enough that she wouldn't hurt herself.

"You deserve to come hard for me, don't you?"

"Yes, sir," she wailed, her body trembling harder than ever.

"Then come for me," I demanded.

Immediately, I pressed a bit harder on her clit, forcing her orgasm to a head, and she threw her head back, grinding against my fingers as she found her pleasure.

I'd never tire of the sight.

She started to scream, her body writhing against the desk. Her toes curled and slid along the floor, and I quickly wound my arm around her waist, supporting her through her climax. I didn't stop rubbing that needy little clit.

Instead, I made her come hard.

Again.

And again.

My cock was like iron in my slacks, and I wanted nothing more than to sink into her wet heat.

"Please fuck me," she whispered as though it was hard to speak, and I smiled, knowing I had her exactly where I wanted her.

"Be more specific, my little queen. What do you need?"

"I need… your… your… *cock*," she finally managed.

"You deserve my cock, don't you?" I pressed.

"Yes, sir," she murmured, moaning as I teased that delicious little cunt. She was dripping for me at this point. Her arousal was all over my fingers. When I finally pulled them away, I wiped them off on her gorgeous little bottom, and she hummed with her shameful need.

Quickly, I unbuckled my belt and freed my cock. I didn't waste any time. With a need of my own, I lined up the head of my cock with her cunt and plunged in deep.

"Then you're going to get it," I vowed, and she cried out, my dick stretching her vicelike pussy wide open.

I thrust in all the way to the hilt before I pulled out. There was no mercy for her as I took her over that desk, pounding her delicious little pussy so hard that I knew she'd be sore the rest of the day.

As she should be.

By the time I was through with her, she was not only going to be sore, but she'd be dripping with my come.

CHAPTER 20

 *week later*

Maci

As I stood in front of the mirror, adjusting the delicate fabric of the gown I'd chosen for the charity ball, a wave of excitement coursed through me.

Tonight was going to be something special, like really fucking special, and I was feeling so giddy with excitement that I nearly skipped around our bedroom like a child at recess.

With a hard shiver, I tried to calm myself, but it only did so much.

Tonight, I would stand by Nikolaos for the first time as his date.

It was going to be our first public outing together, a step that felt significant given the recent strife between him and the Stefanidis family, and it felt particularly special because I hadn't gotten the chance to leave the house since I arrived.

Truthfully, there hadn't really been a need for me to go anywhere, especially since Nikolaos saw to my every need, not only in the bedroom but outside of it. Plus, there was the matter of my safety to consider too. It had been too dangerous for me to venture around the city, and I understood that.

Thankfully, tensions had calmed down, and the situation had seemingly stabilized enough for Nikolaos to feel it was safe to take me out.

He was finally going to show me off, at his side for all to see, and maybe—just a little bit—to announce to the world that I belonged to him.

My breath caught in the back of my throat whenever I thought about it.

I was his and he was mine.

I thought about all the sweet moments between us—how he had made me breakfast on several occasions, how there were fresh sunflowers on the table every day because he knew I loved them, how his face lit up with a smile that reached his dark stormy grey eyes as he handed me a plate of perfectly cooked eggs and a cup of coffee just the way I liked it, or the way he held me after a particularly hard fucking, not to mention the handwritten notes he left me. I thought about the last one he'd given me. It was a simple 'thinking of you' but it had brightened my day even though he was away at meetings for much of it.

I took a deep breath and tried to calm myself by studying my reflection and trying to figure out how everything in my life had led to this moment.

I swallowed hard, fingering my dress.

What if this was all it would be? What if this was the happiest moment of my life and nothing else that came after this came close?

A flicker of uncertainty crept into my mind. I couldn't help but wonder about what Nikolaos and I were to each other. Was I something more than just his goddaughter? Could I be more to him than that, or was I just a fleeting presence, a fuck toy he'd soon tire of, and then where would I be?

Just as my doubt started to really take hold of me, the door swung open, and Nikolaos strode into the room.

I sucked in a breath, hoping he would like what he saw. The gown I'd chosen was a deep, enchanting blue, its fabric flowing like a gentle wave around my body. It was both elegant and bold and the color of the dress accentuated the blue in my eyes, making them stand out with a vivid intensity, and I hoped he would notice.

At the sight of me, he stopped in his tracks. For a moment, he just stood there, his gaze taking me in. I could feel my heart pounding, waiting for what he would say.

"Maci…" he began, his voice trailing off as if words had momentarily escaped him. He took a step closer, his eyes never leaving mine. "You look… you are the most beautiful thing I've ever seen."

I felt a blush rise to my cheeks at his words. "Do you really think so?" I asked, a mix of happiness and disbelief coloring my tone.

"Absolutely," he replied, his voice firm and sincere. "Your eyes… they're like jewels tonight. Fuck. You're absolutely stunning, my sweet girl. In fact, you're lucky the limo is already waiting outside or else I'd rip this dress right off of you and fuck you just like you need to be fucked."

I shivered, a fissure of desire racing straight down my spine. Feeling a bit bold, I leaned in towards him and cleared my throat. "Later then?"

"If you're a very good girl, I just might let you ride my cock," he growled, and I trembled with delight.

"I'm not wearing any panties," I sassed, and his growl deepened in timbre, igniting the heat coiling within my core and setting it ablaze.

"Very naughty, little girl. It sounds like you're going to need a spanking before your fucking tonight then, doesn't it?"

"Maybe, sir," I breathed, and his hand slinked around my neck as he pulled me in for a sweet, but ravenous kiss. Our breaths became one and my head danced with pleasure. His tongue sought out mine, claiming my mouth as his once and for all, and I loved every second of it. When he finally pulled away, his expression was one of raw desire and reluctance, and I imagined mine was much the same.

"Then you're going to need to decide whether you want just my hand or my belt before I fuck you to sleep tonight, my naughty girl."

"Promise?" I grinned and he turned his gaze on me.

"Sassy girl, I think I'm going to need to take you in hand before we even walk through those doors. Perhaps, I'll even take you over my knee in the limo," he murmured, and I bit my lip.

"You wouldn't dare," I replied, my voice husky with my own arousal. I knew he would before the words even fell off my lips, but I didn't want to wait until after the ball.

I was needy now.

His dark answering chuckle told me he was definitely going to, and I couldn't hide my anticipation. His touch lingered on my hip, drawing back and forth just above the place where I should have had a panty line and deceptively close to the juncture of my thighs.

My body tingled with arousal.

He took my hand and led me out of our room, through the house and to the waiting limo just outside the front door. Like the perfect gentleman, he opened the door for me so I could climb inside before he slid in next to me. As soon as he shut the door, he turned his gaze on me. Without a word, he grabbed my upper arm and tossed me over his knee. I didn't really put up that much of a fight as he pressed his hand down on my lower back, while the other cupped my ass.

My pussy clenched hard.

"It's awfully naughty of you not to wear anything underneath your dress, my little slut," he scolded lightly, his tone serious but somehow still playful, and I shivered with delight.

"I know," I hummed nervously as he reached down and lifted the long skirt. Slowly, he raised the fabric up the backs of my calves all the way to my knees. He gradually bared me, exposing me inch by inch and making my anticipation soar that much higher.

"I didn't think you'd need your bottom reddened this quickly, princess," he chided, lightly slapping my left cheek and then my right.

I struggled a little bit, and he held me tighter. My thighs slipped against one another, already slick with my own arousal. My shame spiraled through me, but my desire pulsed even hotter.

"I'm not sorry," I breathed, egging him on.

"Then we'll need to correct that, won't we?" he purred, and then he started spanking me. His palm bit into my bare cheeks as the limo pulled down the driveway, and I squeezed my eyes shut, fully aware that someone might hear it as we drove by, which only seemed to heighten my need. The windows were tinted pitch black, so I hoped they couldn't see through.

Nikolaos spanked me hard, but I found myself lifting my ass with every strike, seeking him out and wanting more. His palm peppered every inch of my naked bottom, making sure it was thoroughly red before his fingers dove in between my thighs.

"You're soaking wet, my naughty girl," he growled, his possessiveness making my nipples stiffen against the leather seat. I wiggled a little bit, and his fingertips just grazed my clit. A lightning bolt of desire swept through me, and my breath caught in the back of my throat.

"Sir..." I whispered, my voice hoarse, but then his rough fingertips teased me again. Soon, he was lightly circling my clit, not hard enough to make me come right away, but just enough to taunt me.

Every inch of my body sizzled with heat. The more he teased me, the more intensely my entire being blazed with heat. Feeling the hard length of his cock beneath me only added to my building passionate need, and I didn't know how much longer I could stand it.

"Please," I began, my yearning quickly spiraling out of control. My legs quivered and I bit my lip, trying to keep still even though it was useless. Before I knew it, my hips were shamefully rocking back and forth, seeking out his touch with every movement, and I whined with embarrassment.

"Are you going to be a good girl at the ball?"

"Yes, sir," I breathed. "I promise!"

"A very good girl?" he pressed, and I gasped, a piercing cut of denial flashing through me as his fingers drew away from my clit.

"I'll be your very good girl," I vowed, breathing a sigh of relief as soon as his fingertips returned to their rightful place.

"If you're naughty, Maci-girl, my cock isn't going to fuck this needy little pussy," he said darkly, and I tensed over his knee, edging dangerously close to orgasm, but not quite.

"Sir?"

"Where is my cock going to fuck if you're naughty?" he pressed.

I opened my mouth, confused for the briefest of moments before it finally hit me.

"You can't mean to…" I began and he cleared his throat, effectively cutting me off, and my heart pounded in my chest. Reflexively, my muscles tightened, and I closed my eyes, too ashamed to keep them open for fear that what he was saying might be real.

"Say it, naughty girl. Tell me where I'm going to fuck you," he pushed, his fingers worrying my clit a bit more roughly, and I teetered on the precipice of what promised to be a powerful climax.

I needed just a little bit more, and he knew it.

"But…"

"If you want to come, you're going to tell me," he threatened and I knew I couldn't delay the inevitable any longer, no matter how wicked and salaciously enticing it sounded, no matter how much I kind of wanted to know what it was like.

"My ass," I whispered, my voice hardly audible, and he growled with approval just as his fingers pressed a little harder, just enough to send me sailing right over the edge.

"That's right, my needy little slut. Now come for me," he demanded, and my body had no problem being obedient.

My orgasm hit me like a freight train as the image of his big cock sinking into my tight virgin asshole took over my every waking thought. My inner walls clenched as I rode out the white waves of bliss rolling through me, writhing over his lap like a cat in heat. I moaned low, the sound of my pleasure vibrating between us, and his fingers pressed a bit more firmly, forcing my climax that much higher.

Exquisite euphoria pumped through my every nerve, my blood surging with heat. Sizzling sensation burned through me, and when I finally stilled, my breathing was ragged.

"Such a good girl, coming so hard for me," he murmured, and his praise caused another lightning bolt of pleasure to pierce right to my clit.

Then he grasped my bottom cheeks and spread them open, exposing my dark hole to his gaze.

Heat rushed to my face, and I tried to reach back and block his view, but he easily grabbed my wrist and pinned it behind my back.

"I want you to remember my warning, Maci-girl. When I fuck your bottom, I won't be gentle," he said softly, and I could feel the limo slowing down, which only made my panicked shame that much hotter. My chest squeezed tight as I whined and struggled against his grip, but he held my bottom open with ease.

With his fingers still slickened by my arousal and without any warning at all, he forced a single finger into my asshole.

In an instant, my body fought back, trying to force him out as I keened, the foreign burning stretch overwhelming for several long seconds. The pain was fierce at first, deeper than the spanking, and far more mortifying. My legs trembled with it, the feeling almost more than I could bear.

Worst of all, my pussy had clenched hard at the same time, and when he slowly started pumping that single finger in and out of my bottom, I loathed that a part of me started to enjoy it.

I detested that my body kind of wanted more.

When he pulled his finger free, I felt empty in a way I hated and loved, and as if my body was mocking me, a droplet of arousal slid down my inner thigh.

"Remember that, naughty girl," he chided, and I gulped so hard he could probably hear it.

"Yes, sir," I whimpered.

Carefully, he pulled my dress back into place. Then, he lifted me up off his lap and arranged me so that I was sitting next to him. It stung just a little to sit, but I managed, although I squirmed a bit. What was worse was my sore bottom hole though, and no matter what I tried to think about, thoughts of him fucking my ass raced through me like crazy.

My clit throbbed and I knew that if he took me home and fucked my ass right now, I would come while he did it.

Nikolaos smirked knowingly, and I dropped my gaze, unable to look out the window as the limo pulled up in front of the red carpet. When we eventually came to a complete stop, I finally lifted my eyes and looked out the window.

My excitement returned in a rush.

This was our night.

He climbed out first and rounded the car to open my door for me, offering me a hand as I blushed and felt my arousal dripping down my thighs as I took my first step out of the limo.

"Remember, be my good girl," he purred in my ear as he pulled me close, weaving his arm around my waist. His fingers dug into my side a bit possessively, and I curled against him, hiding my face in the crook of his shoulder simply because it felt right.

"Yes, sir," I breathed, my face burning that much hotter. A camera flash shuttered somewhere to the right, forever capturing the moment of my surrender for all to see.

Being forced to submit to him in such a public place made my body burn with fire.

He grinned like he knew exactly what I was thinking.

I broke eye contact with him and tried to shake it off, stealing a moment to take in my surroundings since I'd been so caught up in everything that was him.

The red carpet beneath our feet stretched out like a luxu-rious scarlet ribbon, leading to the extravagant carved wooden doors of the grand hall at the end of it. Flashes from photographers' cameras twinkled like vivid stars, capturing the glamour and elegance of the night as each couple made their way down the red carpet.

I would have felt out of place if I wasn't on his arm.

Everything seemed magnified, the air charged with a mix of excitement and sophistication. The red carpet was lined with onlookers, paparazzi, and reporters, their eyes eagerly taking in the parade of guests arriving in their finery. Even the venue itself was a sight to behold, with towering pillars and grand windows that gleamed under the soft glow of the evening lights, and I pulled in an unsteady breath.

I told myself that I belonged here too, that out of all the women in the world, Nikolaos Kaligaris had chosen me as his.

I was the one on his arm.

As we walked, I couldn't help but notice the wide array of beautiful women and men all around me dressed to the nines. One woman glided past in a deep emerald silk gown that shimmered like the sea under moonlight, its skirt flowing in smooth, liquid-like waves. Another twirled in a gown of delicate lace, its ivory hue glowing softly in the bright lights.

The men were equally impressive in their tailored tuxedos and sharp suits, the epitome of classic style and poise. One gentleman wore a midnight blue tuxedo, the jacket perfectly tailored to his frame, with a subtle satin sheen that caught the light with each movement. I watched another move through the crowd in a charcoal grey suit, his slender silver tie adding just the right touch of modern flair.

Being amongst it all was the most incredible feeling in the world.

Everywhere I looked, there were jewels glittering against skin, hairstyles that were both artistic and flawless, and makeup that accentuated the natural beauty of all the perfectly beautiful faces it adorned. The air was filled with a subtle blend of exquisite perfumes and colognes, creating an almost intoxicating ambiance.

I loved it.

Nikolaos guided me through the crowd. His hand on my back was incredibly reassuring. I could feel all eyes drawn to us, almost as if there was a sense of intrigue and admiration directed our way. He drew me closer, as if he could sense their gazes too, and I enjoyed the possessiveness in his touch.

It made me feel like I belonged to him too.

"Are you ready?" he asked, a boyish grin lighting up his features.

"I'm ready," I grinned.

Then, without any warning at all, he stopped right in the middle of the red carpet and pulled me in close. His lips sought out mine, and he kissed me like he wanted to fuck me, right there in front of the cameras for everyone to see.

"Nikolaos Kaligaris! Who's the woman on your arm?" a reporter called out and Nikolaos grinned.

"This is Maci Williams and she's mine," he growled, and I couldn't help but lock eyes with him, my adoration for him written all over my face.

"Nikolaos," I breathed, and he pulled me in close.

"I love you," he said softly enough so that only I could hear, and in an instant, a warm feeling ricocheted through me at his pronouncement.

This night couldn't be any more perfect.

"I love you too," I whispered, and his grin nearly split his face in two.

"Come now. It's time for me to show you off," he declared, and he took my arm and led me forward.

I was giddy with happiness as he guided me inside.

My mind reeled from his profession. Could he really feel that way? Instinctively, I knew that it was true. Nikolaos had never lied to me, and that was one of the things that I liked most about him.

Pulling my shoulders back, I took a deep breath. It was time to dive into his world with him at my side.

And I couldn't wait.

 ikolaos

The sight of her took my breath away.

She was more than just beautiful; she was a vision, radiant and captivating, absolutely the most stunning thing I'd ever laid my eyes on. The deep blue of her gown highlighted the unique color of her eyes, making them sparkle with the same intensity that had drawn me to her in the first place. She carried herself with grace, and she was the most gorgeous thing on the red carpet.

There was no question about it.

As we walked into the charity ball, I couldn't ignore the eyes of other men on her. Their gazes were lingering a tad too long for my liking and I couldn't shake it off.

How dare they lay eyes on what's mine?

I felt an unfamiliar twinge in my chest, a tightening that I didn't recognize, at least not at first. As we moved through the crowd and my gaze caught other men leering at my Maci, a primal urge to tear them apart simmered just underneath the surface, and the sudden need to claim her more thoroughly thundered through me.

Acting on impulse, I slid my hand from her back to her waist, pulling her subtly yet firmly closer to my side. The message was clear: she was mine, and I was not willing to share even a glance.

When I reached a more visible spot, where the lights from the cameras and chandeliers shone brighter, I stopped and turned to face her. Without a word, I leaned in and kissed her. My lips moved against hers with a certainty and ownership that left no room for doubt who she belonged to. She kissed me back just as fervently, almost like she was laying claim to me too, and I couldn't help but lightly nip her lower lip to remind her who was in charge.

Her quiet whimper immediately made my cock rock hard, and suddenly the image of her writhing over my lap with my fingers between her thighs flashed before my eyes, and I growled, the sound low and steady in the back of my throat.

As our lips parted, I could feel the weight of the crowd's eyes on us, but none of that mattered. All that mattered was the woman in my arms.

That she belonged to me.

That no one else would ever touch her again.

And that I was the only one that would *ever* see what was underneath her beautiful dress.

Right now, I'd much prefer to have her back in my bed, writhing underneath me as she took my cock in that sweet little pussy like a good little girl, but I wanted her to be more than just my little fuck toy. I wanted her on my arm.

Permanently.

I hadn't meant to tell her I loved her. It had just come out, and now I wouldn't take it back for the world.

Her response to those words, the emotion in her eyes, only cemented my resolve. She was meant to be with me, and I was ready for everyone to see and respect the powerful bond we shared.

I guided Maci through the crowd, my hand at the small of her back. My fingers glanced against her bare skin, and a powerful shiver raced down her spine. I loved that I had that effect on her. When I glanced down, her arms were covered with gooseflesh, and I smiled with delight, leaning in close to her as I pulled her to the dance floor.

"Dance with me, Maci-girl," I dictated, and she smiled.

"I'm not sure how," she admitted, her brow furrowing rather adorably with her concern.

"You don't have to know how. All you have to do is let me lead, but you already do that quite well, don't you?" I replied, and her cheeks blushed a bright rosy pink, the same pink I'd spanked her perfect little ass on the ride here.

My cock hardened like a spike.

She was going to get fucked so hard tonight.

"Sir," she whispered, her voice hardly audible, and I grinned widely, spinning her around and pulling her in towards me so that my chest collided with her bare back.

"I wonder if anyone else needed to be put over their man's knee before they came here," I said quietly, just low enough so that she was the only one who would be able to pick up on the sound of my voice.

"Nikolaos," she blushed, her cheeks red as a cherry tomato now, and my balls ached.

If we were at home, I'd have put her down on her knees and fucked that pretty face until she swallowed every drop.

Then my focus suddenly shifted to those around us as I began to catch fragments of hushed conversations that were most certainly not meant for our ears.

"...did you see them? He's old enough to be her father," one voice murmured, barely audible over the hum of the gathering. I could tell Maci had heard too because I saw her stiffen for the briefest of seconds before she moved in a bit closer to me. I gripped her waist harder, trying to comfort her in silence, but then I heard another shrill voice begin to speak.

"She must be his escort for the night. Have you seen how she looks at him? It's probably all about the money."

The words were like a slow poison, each syllable laced with bitter judgment and raw speculation. My chest tightened as a flare of irritation ignited within me. I wanted to confront them, to shatter their narrow-minded assumptions with the truth of what Maci meant to me, but I restrained myself, knowing that any outburst would only fuel their gossip further.

I slowly moved us off the dance floor and ushered Maci towards the bar, wanting to get her as far away from them as possible. She needed a glass of champagne, and I wanted a bourbon.

As we moved through the crowd, the insulting whispers seemed to follow us, like a persistent buzz that was increasingly grating on my nerves. I found myself growing progressively more annoyed, but I tried to ignore it. I was successful for at least a little while, but then I heard another group talking among themselves.

We'd only just reached the bar when another woman leaned in towards her friend and cleared her throat.

"He's always had a taste for younger women, but this… this is a bit much, don't you think?" another voice suggested, thinly veiled disdain coloring the words.

My grip on Maci's back tightened involuntarily. It was one thing to endure scrutiny about myself, but to hear Maci being spoken about in such a demeaning way, and to know that she could hear it too, was unbearable.

She was more than they could ever comprehend—a woman of intelligence, depth, and significance in my life, not some shallow arm candy.

She was so much more than my fuck toy.

She was *mine*.

As I scanned the crowd, I could barely contain my rage, and another voice cut through the murmur, cruder and more insulting than the rest.

It came from a young man lounging against a pillar, a glass of bubbling champagne in his hand. He was a known figure in our circles—Alexios Demetriou, a Greek trust fund baby notorious for his silver spoon upbringing and the entitled attitude that came with it.

"Look at that," he said loudly, a smirk on his face, his eyes fixated on Maci and me. "Kaligaris has really outdone himself this time. Picked up a slutty little whore from the nearest street corner, has he?

That comment was the final straw. I stopped, turning slightly to confront him, my eyes cold and hard.

My vision went red with rage.

Without a word, I strode towards him, my steps measured but filled with a barely contained fury. The room seemed to hold its breath as I approached him, but I ignored them. His words played over and over in my mind, and I couldn't make them stop.

I didn't say anything at all. I let my fist do the talking.

I landed a punch squarely on his smug face, the impact echoing through the hall. I moved so quickly that he didn't have time to lift his arms to block the blow, and the unexpected look of surprise on his face was well worth whatever consequences came with it.

Alexios staggered backwards, his hand flying to his nose. It felt extremely satisfying to see a stream of blood flowing from between his fingers. My breathing was heavy, each inhale and exhale echoing throughout the silence of the hall.

It was as if everything had come to a complete stop. No one else said a word, their breaths and the soft sound of violins playing in the distance the only sounds audible in the entire place.

"How dare you?" Alexios snarled.

"Next time you open your mouth and speak disrespectfully about my woman, I'll kill you," I growled, and I reached for Maci's hand, leading her away from the scene. As we walked away, I could feel the weight of every gaze upon the two of us, but none of it mattered.

Only she did.

* * *

A week later

Adjusting the cuffs of my suit, I took a moment to compose myself. With a deep calming breath, I lifted my chin and shook off my nerves.

You're Nikolaos Kaligaris, patriarch of a massive, powerful ship-ping empire. This is nothing.

Yesterday, the Secretary-General of the Ministry of Justice, Christos Georgiou, had called me to request a face-to-face. It had been less of a request and more of a demand.

I'd agreed to the meeting, nonetheless. I had to maintain some semblance of power.

I knew I looked good. Appearance mattered in meetings like this; it was part of the language of power and respect.

My suit was impeccably tailored, a deep navy blue that contrasted with the crisp white of my button-up shirt. I straightened my tie, a subtle but richly colored beige piece that complemented the suit perfectly. Every inch of my appearance spoke to my power, and I liked it that way.

I need it today.

As I walked through the halls of the Ministry of Justice, my steps were measured, my expression neutral yet confident. I was no stranger to high-stakes meetings, but the context of this one, following so closely after the charity ball as well as the tensions between myself and the Stefanidis family, added an extra layer of complexity.

I was keenly aware that the outcome of this meeting could make my life very difficult, but I held the kind of power men only dreamed of.

Upon entering the meeting room, my eyes immediately settled on the Secretary-General of the Ministry of Justice. He was a man around my age, possessing an air of authority and gravitas that was befitting of his position. His appearance was striking—he had a handsome, well-defined face, characterized by sharp, angular features that suggested both intellect, determination and a shrewd business acumen that could prove dangerous to the unsuspecting.

His hair, neatly combed back, was peppered with hints of grey at the temples, lending him a distinguished look that spoke of experience and wisdom gained over the years. His eyes were sharp and observant, a deep blue that seemed to miss nothing, surveying the room and its occupants with a practiced ease.

He strode over to me and offered me his hand. His hand-shake was firm, an equal match to mine, and his voice, when he greeted me, was calm and collected, at least on the surface.

"Nikolaos Kaligaris, thank you for coming," he said.

"Secretary-General Christos Georgiou, it's my pleasure," I replied, maintaining a polite facade.

"Bourbon?" he asked.

"Certainly," I grinned, and he moved over to a cart of glass-ware and several very expensive decanters of liquor. He picked up one with a beautiful dark amber color and poured two generous glasses before handing one to me.

He raised his glass slightly. "To good taste, and to straight talk," he proposed.

"To both," I agreed, and we each took a sip. The bourbon was exceptional, its complex layers of flavor unfolding with each passing second. Notes of vanilla and caramel emerged, mingling with hints of oak and a subtle smokiness that spoke of its aged refinement. The smoothness of the bourbon was complemented by a warm, spicy undertone, providing a depth that was both rich and satisfying. The ensuing burn was positively delightful as we both took our seats, the leather armchairs both creaking softly as we settled.

"I must say, Nikolaos, your recent escapade at the charity ball was quite the talk. You're lucky young Alexios Demetriou didn't press charges. It could have gotten quite messy for you."

I nodded, acknowledging the incident without betraying any emotion. What he said was true, but I wasn't going to give him the satisfaction of being right, not this early in our meeting.

"Alexios and I had a difference of opinion, but we handled it as men should."

Georgiou raised an eyebrow. "Indeed, but it's important to keep one's composure, especially for someone in your position. Isn't it?"

His words were a clear warning, and in that moment, I recognized the need for diplomacy. I cleared my throat and dipped my head a bit apologetically.

"I see your point, Secretary-General. It was an unusual situation. I'm sure it won't happen again," I replied.

He leaned back, eyeing me carefully. He was sizing me up, and I did the same to him, sitting back in my chair. I took another sip of bourbon, knowing what he was going to say next. I wasn't an idiot.

He hadn't called me here to admonish me for punching Alexios. If anything, he probably supported it. I knew the trust fund baby had been a thorn in his side on more than one occasion.

No. This was about the Stefanidis ships.

An incident like that would have created a mountain of work for him. After some reflection, I had admitted to myself that it might have been a bit of an overly rash decision, and that I'd let my feelings for Maci cloud my judgement in handling the situation.

A smaller hit would have certainly sent the message I wanted, but I would stand by my decision regardless, especially in the face of the Secretary-General.

"Speaking of unusual situations, there's been quite a stir about the Stefanidis shipping incident. Three ships, wasn't it? Quite an expensive loss. Some are even calling it an act of terrorism. There's been a lot of speculation about who might be responsible from Al Qaeda to pirates. There's even been a few hints that link it to organized crime."

"Yes, I heard about that. A tragedy, indeed. But I fail to see what that has to do with me," I said boldly, keeping my expression neutral. I wouldn't admit to anything. There was nothing that could tie the explosions to me. I'd made certain of it.

Georgiou's gaze was unwavering. "Oh, nothing directly, of course. But in our circles, rumors can be telling. And the rumor mill suggests your involvement. You understand how such speculation would be... well... *problematic* for me as well as for you."

I met his gaze squarely. "Rumors are just that, Secretary-General. You know as well as I do that speculation without evidence is a dangerous game, especially for men like us to play."

He nodded slowly. "True, but sometimes speculation is grounded in reality. And reality can sometimes be... incredibly inconvenient for people like you and me."

"Speculation is not proof, Secretary-General. I trust the Ministry is more interested in facts than rumors, or at least, I hope it would be."

There was a pause as we reassessed each other. I was exceedingly aware that the balance of power in this conversation was delicate, and by the look on his face, I knew he did too.

"Of course," Georgiou finally said. "Facts are what's important, but let's be pragmatic. Sometimes, ensuring that certain... rumors remain just rumors... can be beneficial. For all parties involved."

"I deal in reality, not in idle gossip," I answered, setting down my glass and cocking my head. Was he seeking out a bribe? If so, maybe the two of us could come to some sort of arrangement after all.

The tension between us was thick, and with every passing second, it was growing thicker.

He studied me for a moment, then nodded. "Fair enough. But remember, realities can always change. And when they do, it's often wise to have friends in the right places."

"Truer words have never been said," I replied, purposefully keeping my answer vague.

I couldn't help but consider the types of problems we could cause for each other if things turned sour during the course of this meeting. In my world of business, both legitimate and otherwise, I had the power to mobilize a network of resources and information that could make life very difficult for a man in his position.

My connections ran deep, and my knowledge of the darker corners of our society gave me an edge that could unearth secrets and disrupt political careers, especially if he aspired to seek out a promotion and become the next Minister of Justice.

On the flip side, Christos, with his powerful role in the Ministry of Justice, held a different kind of influence. He wielded the machinery of law and government, capable of initiating legal nightmares and bureaucratic entanglements that could entrap someone like me for years to come. His access to confidential information and legal tools, not to mention his ability to sway judicial proceedings, posed a significant threat to me. His power lay in the system, in the labyrinth of legal processes and political maneuvers that could easily ensnare a businessman like me, no matter how savvy.

"And then there's one more thing, the matter of your new companion, Maci," Christos began, a sly edge to his voice. "A young girl like that, in your company... it does lead one to wonder. People talk, Nikolaos. They see a man of your stature with someone so... inexperienced. They might get the wrong idea. Some might even say she's nothing more than a whore."

The implication hit me like a physical blow. My grip on my glass tightened, and a surge of protectiveness mixed with anger coursed through me.

"Fuck you, Christos," I spat out, the veneer of civility cracking under my rising rage. "You can sit there and insinuate whatever you like about me, but I will not tolerate such disrespect towards her. Keep her fucking name out of your mouth."

Christos leaned back, a smirk playing on his lips, clearly pleased at having struck a nerve. "Nikolaos, calm down. I'm only speaking of perceptions. But you know as well as I do that perceptions in our circles can be as damning as reality."

"You're treading on dangerous ground," I warned him, my voice low and menacing. "If you or anyone else dares to slander her name, you'll find that I'm not someone who takes such things lightly. This is your only warning."

Christos raised an eyebrow, unphased. "Threats are a dangerous game, Nikolaos. Remember, I have resources at my disposal that could make things very difficult for you. It would be wise to consider how you speak to me."

I stood up, my anger barely contained. "I don't need to hear this bullshit."

Fuck it.

With that, I turned and walked out, leaving Christos Georgiou behind.

CHAPTER 22

 *ikolaos*

I sat back at my desk and sighed.

I probably shouldn't have told the Secretary-General off like that. It hadn't been one of my finest moments.

As a direct result of that meeting, there had been sudden, unexplained delays in getting approvals for new projects, a large amount of highly unusual scrutiny of our financial transactions, and a marked increase in regulatory audits—all of which could be traced back to the influence of the Ministry.

I felt a twinge of regret for how the meeting had unfolded. My reaction, though justified in defense of Maci, was impulsive—a deviation from the calculated and disciplined approach that had always guided my actions. This wasn't the first time either. Blowing up the Stefanidis' ships, though a strategic move, was a bold play that invited scrutiny and risk at a much higher level than I allowed typically, and then there was the incident with Alexios Demetriou at the charity ball...

I'd paid off his father, and with his agreement, we'd pushed it under the rug.

I had always prided myself on being a disciplined man, one who weighed every decision with precision and foresight. But ever since Maci came into my life, I found this discipline slipping. It was as if her presence had awakened a different side of me, one that acted on emotion rather than cold logic.

I didn't like it.

"What's happened to you, Nikolaos?" I muttered to myself, feeling the weight of my own question. Maci had become my weakness, a chink in my armor that others could exploit. I had let my guard down, allowing personal feelings to influence my decisions in a realm where such emotions could be costly.

There was a knock on the door.

"Come in," I called out.

Andreas walked in and took a seat opposite me as I let out a heavy breath. I had already told him about the outcome of the meeting days ago and he hadn't been happy about it either, which honestly was a fair reaction when I considered it.

"We need to talk about a few things, boss," he began.

"Go ahead," I sighed. I knew that it probably wasn't good news, especially by the look on his face.

"We've hit a few snags in getting the new shipping licenses," he explained, his frustration evident. "The process, which used to be straightforward, has become unnecessarily complicated. The paperwork has doubled, and there are constant requests for additional documentation, some of which seems irrelevant to the actual licensing requirements. It's as if every step forward is met with a new hurdle."

"Is that all?" I pressed, my heavy sigh echoing throughout the room.

"There's also the issue of our regular tax audits, which used to be routine and predictable. Now, they've turned into something much more invasive. It's like they are digging for something, scrutinizing every transaction, every record, far beyond the usual scope. It's become an inquisition rather than an audit. This level of scrutiny is unprecedented," he continued.

With a heavy sigh, I pressed my hand to my forehead in frustration.

"It's retaliation, Niko. You already know why." Andreas offered, lifting his eyebrows in a bit of chiding way. He was the only person in the world that could get away with that, especially when he was right. Even so, a sliver of annoyance raced through me, and I swallowed it down. He was simply the messenger, and this was one hundred fucking percent my fault.

"We need to strategize. Push back against these bureaucratic games without escalating things further," I replied with a curt nod, my hands clasped together on the desk.

"Listen Niko... We need to talk about Maci," he replied quietly.

"What about her?" I said quickly, immediately feeling myself go on the defensive.

"If she's the reason you're this fired up, why not just go all in? Marry her. Flip everybody the bird and show them she's more than what they paint her to be. Who cares what they think? You're Nikolaos Kaligaris. Put your fucking dick on the table and show them who you are. Make her your fucking wife."

His suggestion caught me off guard.

Why couldn't I marry her?

The more I considered it, the more it made sense. Marrying her wouldn't just be about protecting her or making a statement. It would be about accepting that she was as much a part of my world as I was, and that together, we were stronger.

It didn't just make sense, it felt right.

Like everything had suddenly just fallen into place and I knew why.

Because not only did I love her, but she also deserved it.

"You know, Andreas, you might be onto something," I said, a new sense of clarity emerging.

Andreas grinned. "Sometimes the best defense is a bold move nobody expects."

"Get me a meeting with the best jeweler in the country," I demanded.

"I already set it up for you," he smirked.

CHAPTER 23

ne week later

Maci

I sat by our bedroom window, a small note from Nikolaos folded between my fingers. I glanced down at it, unfolding it and reading it for what felt like the thousandth time.

"I love you, my sweet girl—N."

It was thoughtful, a small gesture that showed he cared, but as much as these little things—the notes, the way he said he loved me, the way he held me close after fucking me senseless, his kisses—meant to me, I couldn't shake off a growing sense of discontent.

Over the past few months, I had been feeling like an accessory in Nikolaos' life. Yes, he involved me in some aspects of his business, but it didn't feel like enough. He took me to meetings, and showed me a part of his world, but it always felt controlled, measured.

I needed more.

When he held me, there was a tenderness in his touch and a genuine affection that I couldn't even begin to doubt. His kisses were filled with passion, and when he looked into my eyes, I felt like the only person in the world. I knew he cared about me.

I adored him, truly, and perhaps that was why this situation was so frustrating. I wanted more from him, more from us. I wanted to be involved in the real, gritty parts of his life, to stand beside him not just as a woman to be protected but as his equal.

I shifted in my seat, my bottom still sore from this morning. My cheeks flushed as I thought about how he'd made me breakfast. For whatever reason, I had been feeling particularly feisty this morning and I had sassed him right into a spanking with a wooden spoon as a result.

I grinned, pressing my thighs together, the image of him fucking me over the same table we'd just eaten at still fresh in my mind. My clit throbbed knowingly.

Shaking my head, I tried to push thoughts of this morning out of my mind and focus on the plan for the day. I needed to talk to Andreas about the escalating situation between the Secretary-General and Nikolaos. Since Nikolaos had first brought me into his meetings with him, I had been building my relationship with Andreas too. In some ways, he felt like a proud father figure, and I really liked that about him. I'd never really had a presence like him in my life, and it was more fulfilling than I could have ever expected.

Most importantly, though, I'd been making allies in all the right places, from high social society all the way to the wait-staff that cleaned the mansion on a weekly basis.

With a determined stride, I tucked the note into my pocket and left our bedroom, my mind a whirlwind of thoughts.

As I walked through the corridors of Nikolaos' expansive home, I paused when I overheard two members of the cleaning staffs speaking among themselves. They were talking in hushed, excited tones, and my ears instinctively tuned in.

"Did you see the size of that diamond? It's massive!" one of them whispered.

"And so beautiful," the other replied. "Do you think it's for her? For Maci?"

My heart skipped a beat. A ring? For me? The thought sent a flurry of emotions through me—surprise, excitement, and a touch of disbelief. Could Nikolaos really be planning to propose?

"Who else would it be for? He's been head over heels for her ever since she arrived," the first one replied.

I blushed. Were they right? Could everyone tell but me?

I'd heard enough. I'd get answers soon, but they were going to be directly from him.

With a soft smile, I slipped down the hall without them noticing my presence, heading straight to Andreas' office on the first floor. Without hesitation, I knocked and then confidently strode in, taking a seat across from him like I owned the place, which I knew Andreas would appreciate.

"Andreas, I need an update," I said directly. "What's the latest on the escalating situation with the Secretary-General? Nikolaos mentioned some difficulties he was facing this morning at breakfast, but I want specifics."

Andreas looked up, a hint of surprise in his eyes, quickly replaced by respect. "Maci, I'm glad you're taking an interest. The situation is more strained than we'd like. Just yesterday, the Secretary-General's office sent back our shipping license application. Again. Third time this month."

I nodded, absorbing the information. "This is more than just bureaucratic red tape, then. It's a deliberate move to hinder our operations."

"Exactly," Andreas agreed. "Nikolaos is doing his best to handle it, but it's a delicate situation. We're walking a tightrope."

I leaned forward, my mind working through the problem and coming up with a solution all on my own. "This situation might need a different approach. Something unexpected…"

Andreas raised an eyebrow. "What do you have in mind?"

"A woman's touch," I said with a slight smile. "I might not have Nikolaos' experience in these matters, but I bring a different perspective. Sometimes, a fresh take can make all the difference."

Andreas looked thoughtful, his gaze narrowing in on mine. "How do you plan to convince Nikolaos? He can be... rather... set in his ways."

I returned his gaze with confidence. "Don't worry about that. I have my ways too," I said, the corners of my mouth turning up in a sly smile.

I already had a plan in mind.

* * *

Later that night, I was just getting out of the shower when I heard the sound of footsteps climbing the stairs. I paused, listening closely and recognizing the cadence of Nikolaos' steps. With a deep breath, I lifted my chin and pulled my shoulders back. This time, I was going to take control and show him that not only was I a woman that was worthy of being his wife, but his equal in more ways than one.

Even in the bedroom.

Maybe especially in the bedroom.

I knew he could fuck me into submission. He'd done it time and time again, and I'd loved every second of it, but this time was different. Tonight, I wanted to see if he was the kind of man with the strength to put his trust in me so that we could both come out on top.

I had a plan, and I was going to see it through.

As I wound a towel around my chest, I positioned myself in the doorway between the bathroom and the bedroom. My stance was casual yet calculated, designed to catch his gaze the moment he walked in. I leaned against the frame, a playful yet defiant expression on my face.

The door opened, and Nikolaos stepped into the room. For a moment, he said nothing, his eyes quickly finding mine. There was a pause as he took in the sight of me standing there, draped in nothing but a towel. His gaze turned seductive and predatory, like a lion that had just spotted its next meal, and I pulled in a deep, steadying breath. His eyes said everything that words couldn't.

I smiled coyly, holding his gaze. The air between us was charged with an electric tension.

I couldn't get enough of it.

I remained in the doorway, the smile still playing on my lips as I basked in the intensity of his gaze.

"I missed you," I began.

"I missed you too, princess," he murmured, watching me intently.

He took a step closer, closing the distance between us. The space of the room seemed to shrink, focusing entirely on us. His proximity was captivating, his presence commanding yet utterly intoxicating.

His gaze roved up and down my body, but there was an air of hesitation written in the movements of his body.

"Is something the matter?" I asked, cocking my head to the side and taking a step towards him.

"Are you happy, Maci-girl?" he finally murmured, his voice soft and a bit tentative.

"I could be happier," I answered coyly, taking another seductive step in his direction. I could tell something was off about him, that he had something on his mind other than simply fucking me senseless.

Maybe it was the ring. Maybe it was the Secretary-General, or maybe it was something else.

"What do you want?" he asked quietly, his predatory gaze assessing me.

"I want more," I whispered, striding up close to him and dragging my finger down the length of his collar, only just brushing against the hair on his chest. His eyes darkened, and a subtle smirk graced his mouth at my touch.

"More, you say. I can certainly give you more…"

He reached out to me and clasped his hand around my wrist, pulling me in so that my body was flush against his. The scent of his cologne surrounded me, smokey cedar and bergamot, and all things that were him. It was a heady sensation, and I found myself leaning into it as his arms wrapped around me.

"Yes," I breathed.

"How much more, my sweet girl?" he asked. His hand wound around the back of my neck and gripped tight, holding me in place, and I lifted my chin to look up into his eyes.

I didn't let him take control. At least not this time.

I wrapped my fingers around the lapels of his suit jacket and pulled him flush against me. His cock was already rock hard, and I grinned to myself, fully enjoying the fact that I had that much of an effect on him.

I felt powerful.

I didn't wait for him to kiss me. I kissed him first, pressing my lips against his with a confidence that surprised even me. His initial reaction was one of astonishment, but he quickly responded, his own assertiveness matching mine.

Nikolaos tried to take the lead, his hands moving to my waist to pull me closer. But I was not ready to relinquish control just yet. I deepened the kiss, my hands moving up to his face, guiding the tempo and intensity. It was exhilarating to feel him respond to my assertiveness, to sense his usual dominance give way to my initiative.

As we continued to kiss, it was clear that I was the one setting the pace. He finally yielded to my lead, his body responding to my every move. In that moment, I was not just his equal; I was the one in control.

I pressed my hands against his chest, slowly leading him backwards toward the bed. He let himself be led, which made my heart twitch with emotion.

There was nothing stopping him from picking me up and throwing me on the bed, so he could fuck me as hard as he wanted. He could rip my clothes off, bend me over the mattress, and plunge his cock into me, but right now, he was letting me take control and that made my body burn with heat.

One step backwards. Then another and another until the backs of his legs collided with the bed, and then I used all my strength to push him back. With a dark, knowing grin, he allowed it and sat down on the bed. He pressed his palms to the bed and cocked his head, watching me intently as I approached him.

Boldly, I reached for his tie. My fingers delicately grasped it, pulling it loose with a gentle yet firm tug. The silky fabric slid easily, and the tie came undone, falling away from his neck. Next I moved to his suit jacket, sliding it off his shoulders with careful precision.

Finally, my hands moved to the buttons of his shirt, undoing each one slowly.

Deliberately.

As the fabric parted, I was rewarded with the sight of his bare chest, his muscles flexing with anticipation.

He smirked wider, his gaze contemplative as he tried to guess what I was playing at. Not wasting any time, I dropped my hands to his belt and unbuckled it, gradually sliding the leather through the clasp and pulling it taught before the metal tab released.

"What do you need, my pretty little slut?"

I didn't say a word as I knelt down and untied his black leather shoes. I pulled them off, removing his black knit socks next.

He leaned back far enough so that I could unbutton his pants, not moving as I slid the zipper down and tugged them down his waist. It seemed like both of us held our breaths as I gradually freed his cock. My breath hitched in the back of my throat at the sight of it.

I would never get used to seeing the monstrosity of his cock.

With my heart pounding in my chest, I yanked his slacks and his boxer briefs down his legs and tossed them aside with the rest of his clothes. I didn't bother to fold them.

With grace, I pulled the corner of the towel free and dropped it to the ground, baring myself in one smooth motion. His gaze feasted on my bare flesh. Every bit of his restraint was written all over his face, and I reveled in the feeling of that.

I was the kind of woman that was going to bring him to his knees.

With the grace of a panther, I approached him, each step slinking towards him slowly and surely. My hips swayed, but his eyes remained locked on mine, almost like he was trying to figure out exactly what I was thinking, like he was trying to discern exactly what had gotten into me, but he didn't have a clue.

Without a word, I climbed on top of him. His hands settled on my waist as I positioned myself just above his cock. In that moment, it seemed like the two of us were both holding our breath, and I shivered, my body burning up with desire which was only intensifying the more he let me take control. It was deeply empowering.

I was more than ready for him.

Wanting to tease him a bit, I lowered myself just far enough that my pussy brushed against the head of his cock. The tip slid against my wetness with ease, and his sharp intake of breath shot a bolt of pleasure straight through me. He tried to quiet the sound, but I'd heard it anyway, and my pussy clenched hard.

"Do you need my cock, princess?" he growled, his voice husky with his own desire.

"I need so much more than your cock," I answered slyly, unable to hide my smirk of victory as I finally allowed myself to mount him. The satisfying burn of his girth stretching me open took my breath away for a second, but I quickly found his gaze as I took more and more of him. With our eyes locked, I lowered myself all the way down his cock until I was sitting on top of it, my ass flush against his thighs.

My fingers dug into his shoulder, gripping him as I rolled my hips, eliciting another delicious groan from his lips.

Like a vice, my inner walls clutched around him, and he sucked in another sharp breath, which only spurred me on that much further. A bit more aggressively, I started to ride him, and he groaned, his fingers fluttering around my waist. The tip of his cock hit a place deep inside me that made me moan and his eyes lit up.

"Fuck, your pussy is so fucking tight, princess," he murmured, and I bucked my hips salaciously.

I threw my head back, slowing down my movements. Using my body to tease him, I drew out our pleasure, pushing both of us to the edge and then pulling back. Over and over again, I rolled my hips, and when he finally had enough, he growled and gripped my hips tighter and I stopped moving entirely.

I kissed his cheek, unable to stop myself from grinning with my victory. I'd teased him to the point of losing control, but I wasn't going to let this go any further.

This time, he was going to surrender to *me*.

"Ride me, princess, before I decide that you need my belt more than you need my cock," he growled, his frustration clear with every word.

I cleared my throat. Now was the time to put the rest of my plan into action.

"If you want me to ride you like your woman, you're going to have to do two things," I began.

He stiffened, pulling back just enough to meet my gaze. There was a glimmer of curiosity underneath his hazy veil of dominance, and I smiled wider. Cocking his head, his eyes narrowed as he tried to figure out what I might mean.

"What two things?" he murmured, finally giving in to me.

"First, stop stalling and give me that ring you bought me," I demanded softly.

He sucked in a breath through his teeth, almost like he was biting back his words. For a second, he looked almost relieved, but then his curiosity snapped back into place.

"And the second?" he asked.

"Second, you're going to let me handle the Secretary-General for you," I said, lifting my chin high.

His mouth opened like he was going to say something. I could tell that I'd caught him off guard and he didn't know what to do. For a second, silence reigned between us, and I tightened my inner walls around his cock just to grab his attention.

"I felt that, princess," he growled.

"Good," I replied, my tone sultry but confident.

He opened his mouth and then closed it again. Leaning over him, I brushed my lips against his cheek and then took his earlobe in between my teeth, biting just gently enough to get his attention, but not enough to anger him. He stiffened once more, and I cleared my throat.

"If I'm going to be your queen, then you need to trust me," I whispered. I allowed my hips to roll once more, slowly, purposefully, and maybe a bit greedily.

His hands tightened on my waist for a moment before sliding lower to my ass. My arms squeezed around his neck, and then suddenly he was standing up. With his cock still inside me, he turned around and then my back slammed against the bed.

Oh fuck.

Maybe I'd pushed him too far and now he was going to punish me with his cock. A whisper of nervousness roiled through me as he yanked one of my legs up high enough so he could smack my ass once really fucking *hard.*

I yelped, the unexpected sting taking me by surprise, but my body clenched around him anyway.

"I do trust you, princess," he growled.

Then he started to ride me himself. This time, there was nothing I could do other than take his cock as he plunged into me, over and over again until my body was on fire and every bit of me was sizzling with desire. With every thrust, my nerves spiraled higher, and my need intensified until I was mindless with it. As his cock sunk into me with increasing fervor, I lost track of my thoughts.

Then with terrifying ease, he flipped me over so that I was on top again.

"Now, you're going to ride me like you don't need my belt, little girl," he demanded, every syllable of his voice rolling through me like the tide. I sucked in a breath.

I knew what he was doing. He was fucking me into submission, and even though a part of me wanted to defy him, another much deeper part wanted him to do exactly that.

I loved when he forced my surrender.

His hands wound around my hips, and I bucked hard, enough to hear him groan in appreciation before I arched my back and really started to ride him.

Every movement made him sink deeper, made the head of his cock brush the place deep inside me that drove me wild, and I lost it.

All at once, something inside me snapped, and my need to come took over my every waking thought. My pleasure roared through me like a blazing fire, swallowing up everything I held dear and destroying it in a matter of seconds. White hot ecstasy burned through my every nerve, terrible and wonderful all wrapped up into one.

I threw my head back and bucked my hips wildly, going faster and faster as I came undone, shattering into pieces right there on top of his cock.

"That's it, ride my cock just like that. Fuck. You're such a good girl," he praised, and his words only spurred me on that much faster.

His thumb brushed against my clit, and my entire body bowed with intense sensation.

He was going to make me come again.

My heart raced, my breath quickened, and every sense felt heightened, attuned to his every response. The room around us seemed to fade into insignificance, leaving nothing but the electrifying connection that pulsed between us, a current of desire that was exhilarating and over-whelming and utterly consuming.

I relished his touch as his thumb slipped over my clit, teasing and taunting me with an orgasm, just like I had done to him.

Even as I fought him, I adored him for it.

"You're fucking perfect, princess," he murmured, and every-thing in me tightened up once again. I could feel myself hurtling towards the edge at a breakneck speed, and there was nothing that could stop it.

"Oh god," I breathed.

"Right now, princess, I am your god. Now ride me like it," he growled, and I broke right then and there.

With a shriek, my body did as he commanded, writhing on top of his cock like I had been made for it. I took every last inch of him and then some, coming apart at the seams as I moaned and screamed through another orgasm. I bit my lip, trying to keep it together, but it was useless.

His cock took full command of my body. There was no thought as I bucked and rolled my hips. Pleasure controlled my every move, sizzling through me like a fire to kindling. My inner walls clutched around him, and his cock throbbed inside of me.

"Faster, princess," he demanded, and I did. I rode him so fast that a sheen of sweat glimmered across my skin, but I didn't care.

My entire world stuttered.

I ground myself up and down, back and forth until my screams echoed off the walls all around us. I threw my head back as his cock jerked inside of me, and then a hot spurt of his seed was filling me up. I moaned, milking him for every last drop with my pussy. His thumb never left my clit as he forced my climax to the tipping point. With my head in the clouds, my eyes rolled back and I shattered.

Hard.

By the time my orgasm finally began to crest, I was shivering, one aftershock after the next quaking through me with wild abandon. I collapsed forward, and his arms wrapped around me.

Taking deep breaths, I settled against his chest, his heartbeat echoing soothingly in my ear. The aroma of his sweat intermingling with his cologne was intoxicating, and I breathed in deep, enjoying the way it surrounded me like a blanket. My fingertips brushed against the thick, coarse hair on his chest. His cock throbbed, still safely encased within my pussy, but neither of us rushed to move, simply enjoying the feeling of lying in each other's arms. My blood rushed through my veins, and then the pounding of my own heart took over my every sense.

"I do trust you," he murmured again.

I froze, wanting to believe him, and he rolled us to the side, pulling me against him.

"Do you really mean that?" I asked, not really knowing the answer, and he nodded.

"I do, Maci-girl," he whispered, his gaze locked with mine.

The way he held me, so securely yet so gently, spoke volumes. It felt as if every moment we had shared, every challenge we had faced, had led to this.

Being in his arms, feeling the steady beat of his heart against mine, I knew that this was where I was meant to be. Everything about it felt right, felt perfect—as if all the pieces of my life had finally fallen into place.

Eventually, he angled his hips back just far enough to pull his softening cock out of my body, and I sighed, missing the fullness of him, while also enjoying the feeling of his seed leaking from my body.

It made me feel owned.

"How did you know about the ring?" he finally asked, a note of curiosity in his voice.

I smiled, unable to hide the playful glint in my eye. "I have my sources," I teased. "Call them little birds, if you will."

"I'm going to start calling you Sansa from now on, Little Miss Game of Thrones," he said lightly.

"I don't hate that," I quipped, curling closer to him as my body temperature began to drop.

He chuckled, his smile widening. "And what about the Secretary-General? How will you handle him?"

Leaning closer, I nipped at his ear and reached down, gliding my fingers up and down the length of his cock, teasing him a bit more than I'd ever dared before. The velvet skin of his shaft was soft against my fingertips, and I did it again before I leaned in close and whispered, "As easily as I handle you."

He responded with a low growl, a mix of amusement and desire in his eyes. The sound of his low, seductive growl resonated deep within me, sending a thrilling shiver down my spine.

I felt the need to assert my own control once more, and I gripped his cock in my hand a bit more firmly. Slowly, it hardened against my palm and my pussy quivered nervously.

If I wasn't careful, I was going to get fucked again.

Not that I would mind...

My mind wandered back to the ring. I wanted to see it, but I wanted the grand gesture, the proclamation of love that you saw in the movies or read about in books, but in a way that was uniquely us.

"You know, I do expect a real proposal," I said, and his cock jerked underneath my hand.

Nikolaos' eyes twinkled with mischief. "Don't worry, I rented out the Parthenon," he replied, his voice rich with humor and affection.

"Did you really?" I asked with a soft giggle, the over-the-top ridiculousness of the idea amusing.

"Well now, Little Miss Game of Thrones, you'll just have to wait and see," he chided, and I blushed hard.

"I'll just have to talk to my little birds. I'll find out," I quipped, my cheeks aching a bit from smiling too hard.

"For now, though, naughty girl, I can see that you need much, much more of my cock," he rumbled as he rolled over me. Before I knew what was happening, his cock was inside me, fully erect and ready to go.

My inner walls spasmed around him.

I was ready too.

$\mathcal{M}$ aci

I did not, in fact, hear a single word about the proposal. No matter how much I dug, no one gave me anything. Not the cleaning staff. Not Andreas, so when I found a wrapped box on top of our bed one evening a few weeks later, my heart skipped a beat in anticipation.

Gently, I unwrapped the box, lifting the lid to reveal a sultry red dress inside. Its fabric was silky and luxurious and probably cost more than I had ever made in a year.

I wasted no time and slipped into the dress. With a deep breath, I turned to look in the mirror. It fit me perfectly, hugging my curves in all the right places. Its deep red color complemented my complexion, and the way it flowed gracefully with my every movement made me feel both powerful and feminine. The neckline was tastefully daring, revealing a bit of my cleavage and adding to the overall look. In that dress, I felt like a vision—confident, glamorous, and ready for whatever the evening had in store.

My mind tried to trick me and tell me that maybe this wasn't it, maybe he was taking me to another charity ball instead, but in my heart, I knew that this was it.

This was going to be the moment.

Nikolaos was going to ask me to marry him.

I needed to be ready.

I started with my hair, styling it into loose, elegant waves that framed my face, enhancing my features with a touch of sophistication. When I was done, each curl fell perfectly and added a touch of softness that contrasted with the boldness of the dress.

Next, I focused on my makeup, opting for a look that was both powerful and seductive. I chose a smoky eye shadow palette, blending the colors to create a sultry effect that accentuated my eyes. A stroke of eyeliner and a few coats of mascara added intensity to my gaze, making my eyes appear more alluring. For my lips, I selected a shade that matched the dress—a deep, rich red.

Bold yet classic.

Finally, I slipped my feet into a pair of black Louboutins.

I liked the fact that the color of my lips matched the bottoms of my shoes.

I'd look especially good when Nikolaos fucked me later. I smiled just thinking about it.

When I finally looked in the mirror, what I saw took my breath away. The combination of the dress, my styled hair, and the carefully applied makeup created an image of a woman who was both formidable and enchanting.

Now I was prepared for anything.

A knock on my door sounded, and I turned as it opened, only to see Nikolaos dressed in a tux.

The black fabric of the suit hugged his form perfectly, accentuating his broad shoulders and the lean strength of his frame. The crisp white shirt contrasted starkly against the dark material, and the black bow tie added a touch of classic charm.

The sight of him took my breath away; he was not just handsome—he was captivating. In that moment, as our eyes met, I felt an overwhelming desire to close the distance between us and lose myself in his arms, to feel his lips against mine, to feel his cock deep inside me, but now was not the time.

Tonight, I was going to become his fiancée.

Nikolaos gently took my arm, leading me downstairs and out the front door. There was a sleek limousine waiting outside, its polished exterior reflecting the soft lights of the evening. He opened the door like a gentleman and offered me his arm as I climbed inside. Then he climbed in beside me and took my hand in his as the limo pulled away from our home.

The drive felt smooth and almost dreamlike as the city lights blurred past us.

When the vehicle finally stopped, Nikolaus climbed out first, not letting go of my hand the entire time.

When I stepped out of the limousine, I was immediately struck by the grandeur before me. He'd brought me to the Museum of the Parthenon, and the sight of it was enough to take my breath away.

The museum, illuminated against the night sky, looked majestic. The modern glass and concrete structure, juxtaposed against the ancient backdrop of the Acropolis, created a scene of timeless elegance.

This is really it.

He led me towards the entrance, and I couldn't help but remark, "This is kind of like renting out the Parthenon." My voice was rife with amusement, but this had done more than take my breath away.

It was the type of grand gesture that a girl would dream of.

Nikolaos chuckled softly, and I looked at him, seeing a twinkle in his eye.

"Well, I thought you wouldn't want to make the climb all the way to the top in your pretty heels," he replied, his voice warm with amusement.

"True enough," I smiled, and he took my arm safely within his.

Nikolaos led me inside the museum, and I was immediately enveloped in a world of ancient beauty and modern architecture. The expansive glass walls offered a breathtaking view of the Acropolis, lit beautifully against the night sky.

Inside, the museum was a labyrinth of history and art, with displays of ancient sculptures and artifacts in every room.

"Look at this," he said, guiding me towards a particular exhibit. "This is part of the frieze of the Parthenon. Each sculpture tells a story from Greek mythology."

"What's this one say?" I asked.

"This panel here depicts a scene from the Panathenaic Festival, which was held in ancient Athens in honor of the goddess Athena. You can see the procession of citizens, the majestic horses, and the figures carrying ceremonial offerings right there," he explained.

I listened, fascinated as he pointed out various details. "And here," he continued, "the carvings show Athena and Poseidon. It's from the legendary contest where they competed to be the patron deity of Athens. Athena gifted the olive tree to the people, a symbol of peace and prosperity, and won their favor."

As we moved through the museum, I was fascinated by the artifacts and his explanations. There was a comforting rhythm in our conversation—my curiosity met with his insightful responses. It was clear that he not only wanted to share this experience with me, but he also wanted to nurture my interest and understanding, and I loved that about him.

Between the two of us, this was easy.

"The way these pieces have been preserved and displayed... it's like stepping back in time," I said, looking around in awe.

Nikolaos nodded. "That's why I love this place. It's a bridge between the past and the present. Every time I come here, I learn something new."

"It's incredible," I said softly, losing myself in the intricate carvings and incredible artifacts.

When we finally came to the end of the exhibits, there was a private room waiting for the two of us. One wall was comprised of floor-to-ceiling windows, offering a priceless view of the Parthenon from the top floor of the museum.

When my gaze finally settled on the table in the center of the room, I smiled. It was beautifully set under soft ambient lighting, covered with a pristine white tablecloth. On the table was a chilling bottle of champagne, along with two place settings fit for a king.

It felt like we were in our own secluded world, surrounded by the echoes of the past while creating a special moment that was uniquely ours.

It was so romantic that I didn't know what to say, so I said nothing at all and just beamed.

I think he knew what I was thinking.

Nikolaos gracefully pulled out a chair for me. As I took my seat, a waiter appeared, moving with quiet efficiency. He expertly popped the bottle of champagne, the sound echoing softly in the room, and poured us each a glass. The bubbles danced in the flute, adding to the magical ambiance of the whole thing, and I looked down, blushing a little at how special this all was.

As we settled into the dinner, the first course was presented: a delicate horiatiki, a classic Greek salad, vibrant with fresh tomatoes, cucumbers, olives, and a slab of feta cheese, drizzled with olive oil and sprinkled with oregano. It was so fresh and delicious that I moaned from the first bite to the last.

"This is quite the spread," I remarked playfully as we moved on to the second course, a creamy moussaka, its layers of eggplant, seasoned meat, and béchamel sauce perfectly baked. It was just as decadent as the first course.

Nikolaos smiled, watching me enjoy each bite. "For you, Maci, only the best. I wanted this night to be special."

By the time we finally reached the main course, a beautifully grilled sea bass, accompanied by lemon and herbs, the conversation flowed just as freely as the champagne.

"You really didn't hold back, did you?" I teased. "Renting out the entire museum, this exquisite dinner…"

He took my hand across the table, his gaze sincere. "You're worth every penny it cost to rent out this place. You're worth the world to me, princess."

His words made my heart swell with emotion. I couldn't help but compare the man I'd once thought him to be to the one that was here now.

To the rest of the world, he was a hard man, a figure of authority and strength, who seldom showed any softness. His business exterior was like armor, impenetrable and formidable. Yet, in the privacy of our moments together, he was a different person altogether. With me, he was a loving, caring man who wanted nothing more than to take care of me, to show me a tenderness that he guarded from everyone else, and that made my heart pound with emotion.

"I love you, Maci-girl," he declared. "From the moment you entered my life, you've transformed it in ways I never imagined. You've shown me a kind of love and understanding that I thought I'd never find. With you, I've found happiness. So with that, I have a question for you?"

"What's that? I breathed, playing along even as my heart seemingly leapt in my throat.

He stood up and fell to one knee in front of me, and I stopped breathing entirely.

The world seemed to pause as he reached into his pocket and pulled out a small, elegantly designed velvet box. The Greek name "Zolotas" was embossed on it. I didn't know the company offhand, but if that was the one Nikolaos had settled on, I knew it would be expensive and absolutely exquisite.

As he opened the box, the ring inside caught the light, sending a cascade of sparkles around the room. The princess-cut diamond was breathtakingly large, its brilliance unmatched. It was set in a simple yet elegant platinum band, the craftsmanship highlighting the stone's natural beauty.

Then he spoke and the beat of my heart nearly drowned out his words.

"Will you marry me, Maci-girl? Will you be my queen?"

Tears welled up in my eyes. The sheer joy that radiated through me felt like the warmth from the light of the sun.

I didn't have to think about my answer. I'd known what it had been from the first moment I'd heard about the ring.

"Yes," I replied, my voice filled with emotion. "Yes, I will marry you. There's nothing I want more than to stand by your side."

He slipped the ring on my finger, and then his hand was at the back of my neck, his lips on mine as he devoured me. The taste of champagne and herbs was fresh on his tongue as it tangled with mine.

"Fuck, princess. I was hoping you'd say that," he breathed, his own breathy disbelief apparent in his voice.

His kissed me again, and it was as if his lips were possessing me, claiming me and owning me all at the same time. His breath became mine, and I lost myself in that kiss.

His hand slid down the length of my torso and cupped my ass.

"You're mine now, Maci-girl," he growled, and then his fingers slid into the slit in my dress, brushing against the bare skin of my thigh, and my breath caught in my throat.

"Yours," I whispered, and then suddenly he lifted me up out of my chair. I wrapped my legs around his waist as he carried me to the window and pressed my back flush up against it, the sight of the Parthenon right behind me.

This was like a dream.

"From now on, this body is mine. These beautiful breasts are mine. Your tight little pussy belongs to me. Your perfect ass. Every bit of you is mine, and I intend to show you exactly what that means with my ring on your finger," he added. Without another word, he hiked up my dress.

He hadn't given me panties, so I wasn't wearing any.

And I loved that.

"I want to tell you something, princess," he murmured.

"What's that?" I breathed.

"I may have asked you to marry me, but regardless of your answer, you were always going to be my bride because you were meant to be mine."

My entire body quivered with desire, and my pussy clenched hard. His hard cock pressed against my center, and I drew my lip in between my teeth.

What he said should have pissed me off. I should have been angry that he had decided this for me, that the whole proposal was a sham to give me the illusion of choice, but I didn't care.

Instead, his raw possessiveness made me tremble with spiraling heat.

"Bastard," I whispered, wanting to show at least some element of strength while reeling from the desire rampaging through me like a sea monster on the prowl. His gaze remained locked with mine, ravenous and devilishly certain.

He rocked his pelvis against me, teasing me with his erection, and my body sang. It was almost impossible not to roll my hips and go along with him, but I remained strong, at least until he palmed my breast and pinched my nipple through the fabric of my dress.

"You can protest all you like, *little girl,* but you love being mine. You love it when I break you on my cock," he purred, and my core squeezed tight. I bit my lip again, and he leaned forward, nipping it with his teeth, right before he drew me into a soul-crushing kiss.

His lips moved against mine with a fervor that left no room for doubt, each motion asserting his claim over me. In this kiss, I felt his deep longing, his undeniable ownership, and a passion that seemed to consume us both.

Using one leg, he hoisted me up against the window, then reached between us and freed his cock. In one smooth motion, he lined himself up with my entrance and slammed himself inside me.

It was a punishing stroke that took my breath away. Every muscle in my body tightened all at once, the pain from his thrust burning through me with a savagery only he was capable of.

"I don't," I lied, toying with him simply because I could and because I knew it would only make him take me that much harder.

"You do, my little bride. That's exactly why your sweet little pussy is clenching my cock right now," he growled, and I couldn't help but tighten around him as he punctuated every word with a hard thrust. He chuckled knowingly, and my face burned red hot, shameful arousal spiraling through me in spades.

I didn't have any snappy retort. In fact, he plunged into me so deeply that he stole my breath away, and I moaned instead.

"That's right, princess. You're taking my cock so well," he praised, and I threw my head back, losing myself in every stroke.

The image of what we were doing flashed before my mind. Him holding me up against the window with the Parthenon in the background, lit up under the night lights where anyone could see if they knew where to look.

It was salacious.

It was incredible.

I wrapped my arms around his neck, holding on as he started to pound into me. Wildfire danced through my veins. Blood rushed to my head, and all at once, everything snapped into place.

"Oh! Please," I begged.

"Fuck, you're so tight. Come for me, baby," he snarled, and my body tightened around him. He groaned out loud, and I immediately decided that it was the sexiest sound I'd ever heard.

My body listened.

My passion imploded into a fiery display of pleasure, pain, and raw bliss. In an instant, my head was in the clouds and my body was singing. Exquisite ecstasy burned through my veins, so much that it took over my every waking thought.

It was consuming.

It was terrifying.

And it was utterly incredible.

Nikolaos didn't slow down with that first orgasm, but I didn't expect him to. In that moment, I knew what he was doing.

He was fucking me into submission.

His cock surged in and out of my channel, pounding into me like he owned every inch of my body. I teetered close to the edge of orgasm once again, and just when I thought my fucking couldn't get any rougher, it did.

With savage thrusts, he consumed my body with his. I screamed, but then he plunged in deeper, *harder*.

I was going to be sore long after this was over.

"Come for me again, my queen. Let me feel this sweet pussy squeeze my cock while I fill it with my seed."

His words were enough to send me over the precipice. A storm of desire raged through me, quickly spiraling out of control. Wave after wave of heated bliss burned through me as he growled so low that I nearly vibrated right there, impaled on top of his cock.

With several brutally hard strokes, he finally plunged all the way inside of me, and then his seed spurted deep in my belly. Each surge of his come was like a branding iron, hot and sordid and entirely taboo.

I loved every second of it.

For a long moment, he just held me there against that window, our ragged breaths echoing around us. I could feel his cock softening inside of me, but he didn't rush to pull out of me. With our bodies flush against each other, I enjoyed the feel of him all around me.

I was captivated by the intensity in his eyes. I could hear his steady, rhythmic breathing, intermingling with mine. The scent of his cologne, a rich and inviting aroma, filled my senses. The taste of his lips lingered, a mix of sweetness and something uniquely him.

I was blissfully happy.

"I love you, Maci-girl. You're mine. Forever," he declared, his voice hoarse.

"I love you too, Nikolaos," I relied, my voice soft.

And I meant it.

Slowly, he pulled his cock free of me and let me down to my feet. I stood on shaky legs, but he didn't let go. Instead, his arm wound around my waist as he led me back to the table and pulled out my chair. It was only after I was in my seat that he let me go, albeit reluctantly.

"You look radiant. Freshly fucked and still dripping with my seed," he purred, and my shameful arousal sizzled through me like a hot knife through butter.

"Thank you, sir," I stammered, my cheeks flushed.

My face burned hot when the doors opened, and our waiter rolled in a tray covered with desserts. He placed several on the table, and my eyes opened as wide as saucers as I took in the sheer decadence of every dish.

There was a rich, velvety chocolate mousse topped with gold leaf, its texture promising to be as smooth as silk. Beside it, a traditional Greek custard-filled phyllo pastry glistened under the light, its syrupy coating shimmering enticingly. And then there a delicate baklava, layers upon layers of phyllo dough, nuts, and honey, arranged to create a perfect balance of crunch and sweetness.

I couldn't resist any longer, so I took a bite of the chocolate mousse. The moment it touched my tongue, a moan of delight escaped my lips. The mousse was as smooth and rich as it looked, melting in my mouth and flooding my senses with its decadent chocolate flavor.

I swallowed and my eyes flicked up to meet his.

"I've thought of something," I began. I needed to make certain of something else, before things went any further.

"What is it, princess?"

"You won't be able to hide me when I'm your wife. A marriage like ours deserves to be seen," I said, a hint of playfulness in my tone despite the serious undertone.

Nikolaos looked at me intently. "I needed to hide you at first, but I don't need to anymore. But I want you tell me why. Why *did* I need to hide you Maci-girl?" he prompted, his expression curious.

I thought for a moment before responding. "Well, I guess initially I was kind of a liability. It wasn't safe to parade me in front of your enemies, plus I was outside your normal circle."

"What else," he pressed.

My mind raced, going over our every interaction until I finally settled on something else.

"As more time goes on, it seems like my presence might have led you to make some seemingly bold, some might call them rash decisions, specifically the bombing of the Stefanidis fleet, the fight at the charity ball, and what happened in the meeting with the Secretary-General."

He nodded, acknowledging the truth in my words. I expected him to be angry at my blatant observation, but he wasn't surprised, almost as if he had come to the same conclusion himself.

"But if you married me and kept it quiet, it would make us look weak," I continued, and he looked at me, his expression thoughtful.

"What needs to happen next?" he pressed.

"We need to announce it to the world. A big wedding. A luxurious honeymoon that happens to be documented by several purposefully placed paparazzi."

"That's right," he smiled, cocking his head, his pride radiating from him in waves.

"Owning this, owning us, it shows your strength. It won't just be a marriage; it will be a statement of power, that you can have whatever you want and make it yours. It's a power move all of its own."

Nikolaos's eyes gleamed with admiration. "Exactly, Little Miss Game of Thrones."

I smiled, a sense of empowerment filling me.

"Then let us turn heads," I said confidently.

"That we will," he confirmed.

CHAPTER 25

 ne week later
Nikolaos

Maci was going to be my bride.

She belonged to me, and I to her. With her by my side, it suddenly seemed possible to have a sliver of happiness, a chance at a life that wasn't just about power and control, but also included love.

The thought took me by surprise. If you had asked me if I would feel this way six months ago, I would have told you that you lost your mind.

But here I was, soon to be a married man, and my heart swelled with pride and joy.

Maci wasn't just going to be my wife; she was going to be my queen. The thought of her, my beautiful, strong, and intelligent woman, standing with me against whatever challenges we might face, gave me a sense of completeness I hadn't known I was missing, and I would treasure her forever because of it.

I knew she was going to be strong and that she had every capability of leading by my side as a figure just as powerful as me.

I couldn't wait to go home, put her over my knee, and remind her who was in charge. Then I'd tie her to the bed and make her come with my tongue until she begged for mercy, and then I'd force her to come for me some more.

My cock throbbed to life with need.

She was going to get fucked long and hard after I finished eating out that sweet little pussy.

A loud clatter broke me from my internal reverie, and I finally looked around the warehouse. Someone had dropped a box on their foot, but from the looks of things, they appeared to be alright.

Everything appeared to be functioning as normal.

The buzz of machinery mixed with the muffled conversations of my workers echoed throughout the vast space. My eyes scanned the rows of shelving, each filled with neatly arranged goods, ensuring everything was organized and in working order.

The smooth concrete floor under my polished shoes and the occasional cool draft that swept through the large space brought a sense of calmness to me, and I allowed myself the luxury of letting myself relax.

As I walked, I ran my hand along the fabric of my suit, adjusting the fit unconsciously, a habit borne from years in the business world where appearances were as important as actions.

Suddenly, the sound of sirens pierced the air, drawing closer and closer until they were right outside the warehouse. Then a group of uniformed police officers burst in, their presence both unexpected and overwhelming all at once.

My workers all stopped in their tracks, looking back and forth between themselves and then back to me.

A stern-faced cop approached me, and I lifted my chin expectantly. I'd been raided by the cops before, and I'd survived. I would do it again.

"Mr. Kaligaris, we've received reports of illegal merchandise being moved through your warehouse. We are here to search the premises," he stated firmly.

I was taken aback, but I didn't let it show. I maintained my composure, putting my business mask into place.

"My operations are completely legitimate, but you will have my full cooperation for the search," I responded, hiding my growing unease as much as possible.

"Here's the warrant authorizing this search, Mr. Kaligaris. We must follow due process."

Taking the document, I scanned it briefly. "I see. Well, as I said, you have my full cooperation. I believe in the rule of law."

The officer nodded. "Thank you for your understanding. We aim to be thorough but efficient."

"Of course," I replied. "I trust this will be conducted fairly. I assure you, my operations are lawful."

He looked at me squarely, his jawline set with resolve. "Of course, Mr. Kaligaris. Let's proceed."

As the police combed through the warehouse, I watched, confident yet anxious. The warehouse was large, storing various goods, and I was certain nothing incriminating was housed there. However, my confidence was shattered when one of the officers discovered something with a shout.

"Sir, you need to see this," another officer called out. A lieutenant walked over to him and knelt down. I moved just far enough to keep them in view.

Behind a stack of crates, a collection of firearms was neatly arranged in a thick cardboard box. My heart sank at the sight. I had no knowledge of these weapons being in my warehouse. They'd been moved here without my approval. It was clear this was a setup, but there was nothing to be said for the moment.

I'd let my team of lawyers handle it from here on out.

As I watched the police continue their search, I knew this was just the beginning of a much larger battle. This incident wasn't just an attack on my business; it was a direct challenge to my authority and position.

This was a declaration of war, and I was ready to defend my empire, my future with Maci, and everything I had worked so hard to build. The game was on, and I was not one to back down from a fight.

I needed to get back home.

Immediately.

* * *

As soon as I walked through the doors of my mansion, Andreas and Maci were waiting for me. I beckoned them to follow me into the sitting room, where there was a glass of bourbon already waiting for me.

I glanced at Maci knowingly and she smiled back at me.

Such a *fucking* good girl.

I grabbed it and swallowed it down, needing to settle my mind. One drink would do the trick. Maci moved to fill it again for me, but I waved her away, knowing I needed to keep a level head.

"The warehouse was raided by the police today," I began.

Maci's eyes widened in shock and the image of her on her knees sucking my cock flashed before my eyes.

"Raided? But why?" she asked, her curiosity sexy as fuck.

"They found a stockpile of weapons," I continued, the words tasting bitter. "Weapons I knew nothing about. Weapons I didn't authorize to be in my warehouse."

Andreas' expression turned grim. "Do you think this is connected to the Secretary-General?"

"It has to be," I replied. "It's too coincidental. This is his move against me."

Maci stepped closer, her concern evident. "What are you going to do?"

I looked at them, determination settling in. "We fight back. We need to find out who's behind this and clear my name. This is not just an attack on my business; it's an attack on us."

Andreas nodded, "I'll start digging, see what I can uncover. We won't let them get away with this."

Maci cleared her throat. "You promised you'd let me handle the Secretary-General," she said, her voice steady but resolute.

I glanced at her, my hesitation written all over my face. This was dangerous territory and letting her do so would be thrusting her right into the middle of it. The risks to her safety were real. Truthfully, the stakes had never been higher.

Yet, as I deliberated, I couldn't ignore the confidence in her voice, the resolute way she stood her ground. She had already proven herself adept at navigating my world, showing both a shrewd judgement and tact in situations I'd never expected she could handle. How could I deny her this? Her strengths, her insights, they weren't just supporting my operations anymore; they had become integral.

I need her.

It was a gamble, but one that might pay off. Trusting her was not just about believing in her abilities; it was about respecting her as my equal.

In that moment, I realized that my role wasn't to shield her from danger, but to support her as she faced it. Maci was no mere spectator in my world; she was a player in her own right.

With a deep breath, I finally made my decision.

"You're right, I did. What do you have in mind?" I asked, locking her gaze with mine.

Maci's eyes held a determined glint, and it made my cock rock hard. I wanted to fuck her right then and there, but instead, I lifted my chin and waited for what she said next.

"I want you to set up a meeting. Just me and the Secretary-General. I need to confront him, face-to-face."

The idea was bold, even risky, but Maci had proven herself more than capable. If anyone could navigate this treacherous situation, it was her. As wary as I was of her taking the lead, I needed to let her. I needed to trust her.

I needed to let her be *my queen*.

"Alright, I'll arrange it. But be careful, princess. We don't know what he's capable of."

She nodded, a fierce look of determination on her face. "I know. But it's a risk we need to take. I have a plan."

"Tell me everything," I replied.

The smile that lit up her face made it all worth it.

CHAPTER 26

 *wo weeks later*

Maci

I took a deep breath, trying to prepare myself for the night. Not only was I going to be the face of the Kaligaris family all on my own, but I was going to go against the Secretary-General head-to-head.

He was going to listen to everything I had to say. I was going to make him.

It was time to put my plan into motion.

In just under an hour, I was to attend a charity gala event for "The Smile of the Child," a renowned Greek organization dedicated to supporting orphans and vulnerable children. Every elite member of Greek society was going to be there, including the Secretary-General. We'd made certain of it.

All it had taken were a few bribes in the right places to secure the guest list and ensure he was coming.

Nikolaos, who had made arrangements to appear out of town, had in fact discreetly stayed to oversee the evening's developments. He had made a substantial donation to the charity in my name, a gesture that would significantly bolster our standing among the elite.

We'd let our engagement leak to the media. Immediately, our phones were ringing with requests for interviews, but Nikolaos and I had made certain that neither of us had been seen in public, not until tonight at the charity ball anyway.

My presence alone would draw attention. We were counting on it.

My strategy was clear: utilize charm and tact to subtly win over the crowd. Every interaction needed to be a calculated step, leaving behind a trail of favorable impressions in my wake. Tonight, I would play my part to perfection, helping to garner support and turn opinions in our favor.

In addition, it was my job to get the Secretary-General all alone so the two of us could have a frank conversation about what the future was going to hold for him and my future husband.

I took a deep breath. I knew I could do this.

With a bit of self-assurance, I stood in front of the mirror and looked at my reflection. I'd chosen a beautiful sage green dress with a matching clutch that complemented my complexion and the color of my eyes. The dress was both elegant and commanding, perfect for the role I was about to play. I'd styled my hair in loose, sophisticated waves, framing my face quite elegantly, or so I thought. My makeup was impeccable, a balance of bold and classic, enhancing my features perfectly. I exuded confidence from every pore.

My fingers tightened around the clutch. It was heavier than usual. Nikolaos had insisted that I carry a gun for my safety. He'd even taken the time to teach me how to use it.

I thought it was a bit much, but truthfully having it made both of us feel better.

As I gave myself a final once over in the mirror, I felt ready.

Ready to represent the Kaligaris family, ready to stand up to the Secretary-General, and ready to shape the future for myself and Nikolaos.

With a final, determined glance in the mirror, I turned and made my way downstairs and out the front door. Stepping into the waiting limo, I took a deep, calming breath, steadying myself for the night ahead.

When the limo pulled up to the venue of the charity ball, I pulled my shoulders back and made myself the perfect picture of bold confidence. Stepping onto the red carpet, I was immediately engulfed in the bright lights and the loud clammer of the crowd. I could feel the eyes of all the attendees on me, curious and speculative. Honestly, it was a little daunting, but I didn't let it show.

Immediately, a throng of paparazzi swarmed around me, their cameras flashing.

"Maci! Over here! Can we see the ring?" one of them called out.

I smiled and held up my hand, allowing the cameras to capture the sparkling glint of the diamond. "It's quite something, isn't it?" I said, my voice tinged with excitement.

"Is there a wedding date set?" another shouted.

I replied coyly, "Let's just say it will be a grand affair. You'll have to wait and see." We hadn't exactly begun planning anything, but they didn't need to know that.

As I moved to walk inside, their questions followed me.

"Will it be in Greece? A big Greek wedding?" one of them yelled.

"Who's designing your dress, Maci?" another shouted.

"Any hints on the honeymoon destination?"

Their voices became a blur as I stepped into the venue, leaving the flashing lights and shouted questions behind.

As I entered the grand ballroom, the venue's elegance hit me smack in the face. Crystal chandeliers cast a warm, inviting glow over the room, while the ornate decorations and luxurious furnishings spoke of refined elegance. It was beautiful. Whoever had done the decorations should get a raise.

The guests, a blend of high society and business elite, were dressed in their finest. Among them, I recognized a well-known Greek shipping magnate, his suit tailored to perfection, conversing with a group that included a famous local actress in a stunning scarlet sequined gown.

Before I could take it all in, an elegantly dressed woman in a beaded blue gown approached me and smiled warmly. "Congratulations on your engagement! The ring is stunning."

I didn't recognize her, but I could tell from the size of the ring on her own hand that she was someone important.

"Thank you so much," I replied, my smile matching hers. "We're both incredibly excited."

Another guest, a distinguished gentleman, joined in at her side. "I heard about the proposal. Nikolaos is a lucky man. Any ideas on where the wedding will be?"

"We're still considering a few places. It will definitely be something memorable," I answered. As we spoke, the sound of a string quartet filled the background, adding a serene melody to the buzz of conversations around the room.

Politely, I excused myself and took my leave. As I moved through the crowd, a waiter dressed in a fine black suit approached me with a tray full of drinks.

"Champagne, Miss?" he offered, presenting a flute filled with the sparkling liquid.

"Yes, thank you," I replied with a smile, taking a glass.

I turned to scan the crowd, the glass of champagne in hand. My eyes searched the room until they finally landed on my target, Secretary-General Christos Georgiou. He stood out with his dignified posture, his suit perfectly tailored, exuding a sense of power and authority. His hair was neatly combed, and his face bore an expression of cool confidence and sharp calculation.

My heart leapt into my throat.

His gaze met mine across the room, a silent acknowledgment passing between us. With a composed demeanor, I made my way to the bar, the murmur of the crowd blending into the background. Shortly after, he joined me, his approach calm and deliberate.

"Good evening, Miss Williams. Wait. I'm sorry," he paused, "soon to be Mrs. Kaligaris," he corrected with a polite nod, his voice smooth as he sipped a glass of whiskey.

"Secretary-General Georgiou," I replied with equal poise, "It's an honor to meet you."

For a moment, the two of us were silent as we casually sized each other up. His gaze was contemplative, and then he cleared his throat.

"Your presence here, it's not just for the charity, is it?"

I met his gaze boldly, not backing down in the slightest. "You're right. There's more at play here, and I think we both know it's time to address it."

"I have to say, I underestimated you," Christos remarked quietly, though the tension between us could have been sliced with a knife.

"It's not the first time I've heard that," I replied with a small, confident smile, meeting his gaze head-on. I needed him to know that I wasn't just some damsel in distress. I was a powerhouse in my own right.

"You must be something special for him to not only marry you, but send you here all alone," he said. "Either very clever or very stupid, and I know it's not the latter."

I returned his statement with a calculated smile. "You're wise, Secretary-General," I responded, holding his gaze steady with mine.

On the inside, I was dancing with glee. This was going exactly how it needed it to go.

Then he cleared his throat and the tension between us grew thicker.

"If you want to do business with me, I expect the answer to this next question to be the truth," Christos said, his tone low and semi-menacing. "Why did he send you here instead of coming himself?"

"What makes you think *he* sent me?" I countered, maintaining a composed front as I took a sip of champagne, my eyes firmly locked with his.

Christos seemed caught off guard, his sharp gaze searching mine for answers, but I gave him none. "Surely he knows you're talking to me."

"He's the kind of man that knows things, yes," I replied, cryptically yet truthfully. Christos needed to know that my name meant something too, and that I wasn't the type to back down. Not now, not ever.

"What do you want then?" Christos asked. His brow furrowed with curiosity, but his gaze remained cautious, and I sipped my champagne, drawing out the tension between us a bit further.

I took a deep breath before responding, "My husband is normally a very calm, calculated man, but when it comes to me, he can be very aggressive. You must understand."

"Make me understand," he said, his eyes narrowing formidably.

"You see, some people tried to hurt me, and he got very angry. He did some things to ensure that I was kept safe... And while he does not regret them, he understands that he put you in a difficult spot."

My words were carefully chosen, conveying both a confession and an olive branch, an acknowledgement of the difficult situation we both found ourselves entangled in, and I waited with bated breath to see how he would respond.

Christos leaned in, his interest piqued. "You bring up a good point. Let's talk about those things, shall we?"

"If you insist," I replied carefully.

"Let's start with the charity ball incident with Alexios," he probed.

I waved my hand dismissively. "A minor scuffle. You and I both know that it was blown out of proportion. Nikolaos can be protective, and emotions ran high that night. It's of no real consequence to either of us."

"True enough," he nodded slightly, considering my words.

"What else?" I pressed.

His brow furrowed, and a flash of anger flittered across his features. "And what about the incident where Nikolaos insulted me? That was a direct affront, and I must say, I didn't take kindly to it," he said next.

I met his gaze evenly. "That was a mistake, driven by emotion rather than logic. He understands the implications and respects your position. I apologize on his behalf. It won't happen again."

"It probably didn't help when I insulted you either," Christos said, a note of realization in his voice.

I nodded, acknowledging his point. "That certainly added fuel to the fire. Emotions were already running high... and it escalated things unnecessarily."

Christos seemed to consider this, the weight of the situation apparent in his expression. "I see. It was a heated moment on both sides."

"Indeed," I replied, taking another sip of champagne.

Christos nodded. "The charity event and the... misunderstanding between us were unfortunate. But let's focus on the future, shall we?"

He took a sip of his whiskey, and I narrowed my eyes, assessing him. I knew what he was doing.

He was skirting around the real issue. Neither Nikolaos' insult, nor the charity ball was the problem here, and we both knew it. Maybe he was testing me, seeing if I knew what Nikolaos had done against the Stefanidis family. Maybe he wasn't. Knowing I needed to take the lead, I cleared my throat and addressed the elephant in the room.

"The incident with the Stefanidis' ships—that's what all of this is really about, isn't it?" I said directly, cutting through the diplomatic dance right to the source.

He paused for a moment, as if weighing his words before he responded. "It's a significant part of the current... situation," he admitted cautiously. His gaze searched mine, and I lifted my chin, holding my ground.

"I understand it was a drastic measure," I continued, "but it was a response to a direct threat. That's all it was."

Christos sighed, a hint of frustration in his expression. "It's a complex issue. It's created a lot of red tape for me."

"I understand it's been difficult for you, but we're seeking a resolution between you two, not ongoing conflict," I asserted. "There's room for negotiation. We can find a middle ground."

Christos nodded slowly, seemingly considering my words. "Negotiation might be possible. But it won't be simple."

"I didn't expect it to be," I said firmly. "But it's necessary. For all parties involved."

"Someone needs to answer for it," Christos asserted, his tone indicating that the matter was far from settled.

I paused, then confidently said, "I have an idea."

Christos cleared his throat, his expression shifting to one of blatant surprise. Raising an eyebrow, he asked, "And what might that be?"

"The Pappas family has been causing problems for you, haven't they?" I began, leaning into the conversation. "Their encroachment on your business territories, undercutting your contracts, and spreading rumors, not to mention your work on the underground trafficking ring the Ministry has been working to uncover for nearly a decade."

Christos' eyes opened wide in disbelief before he nodded, a grim acknowledgment in his gaze. "They've been a persistent thorn in my side for a long time."

"Maybe we can use this situation to our advantage. What if we could shift the blame for the Stefanidis' ships incident onto the Pappas family? It would certainly tie up a number of things for you, wouldn't it?" I continued.

His eyes narrowed as he considered the suggestion. "That's a bold move."

"It would require pooling our resources, a bit of... creative strategizing," I said, careful to gauge his reaction.

He didn't seem to hate the idea. In fact, he looked like he was taking to it like a fish to water.

Christos leaned back, a slow smile spreading across his face. "That could solve quite a few of my problems for me..." His eyes flashed to mine. "But how would we do it?"

"We can start by fabricating some documents and communications that imply the Pappas family's involvement in the shipping incident," I continued. "These would need to be convincing but untraceable back to us. Maybe some forged emails or financial records that suggest they funded the operation."

Christos nodded in agreement. "I have contacts who can create such documents. We'll need to ensure they're leaked at the right moment, ideally when the Pappas family is vulnerable."

"Exactly," I said. "And we should also have a few well-placed rumors in the media. Nothing too direct, just subtle hints that lead to suspicion. Once the authorities start investigating, the planted evidence will do the rest."

Christos looked thoughtful, "This requires precise timing and execution."

"We'll need to coordinate our efforts closely," I concluded. "It's a risky play, but with the right moves, we can turn this situation to our advantage."

"I must admit, I'm impressed."

Sipping the rest of my champagne, I placed the empty glass on the bar and Christos quickly flagged down the bartender to get me another.

"A play like this would certainly take the Pappas family out of the picture," he mused, circling his glass of whiskey in his hand. I watched the amber liquid climb the sides closely before I locked my gaze with his once more.

"That it would," I replied casually.

For a long moment, he was quiet, but then he shifted his gaze back to me. He didn't look like he underestimated me anymore. In fact, he was eyeing me with the same sort of respect he would a man.

"Do you have any other advice for me?" he asked, and I cleared my throat.

"Yeah. Get a girl like me," I whispered with a wink, and he threw his head back with a laugh.

"I'll keep that in mind," he chuckled.

CHAPTER 27

$\mathcal{M}$*aci*

I'd done it.

I'd executed every facet of our plan perfectly and now it was time to go home to Nikolaos.

Standing at the edge of the crowd, I felt a strange cocktail of relief and something else as the charity ball drew to a close. I didn't know why, but I couldn't shake off a sense of something unfinished, like a sentence left hanging in the air or like a fall that never quite made it to the ground.

I shook my head. I didn't know what was wrong with me. I should be happy. I'd done it. I'd brokered a deal and settled the dispute between Nikolaos and the Secretary-General.

I *should* be celebrating.

Instead, I watched the room slowly empty, the once lively space quieting down. The staff moved silently, clearing tables draped in snow-white linen, their efficiency a stark contrast to the night's earlier chaos. With my clutch in hand, I set my empty champagne glass on a passing tray.

I took a deep breath and walked through the room, nodding in greeting to the staff as I passed them by. Their faces were friendly, but they all looked relieved that the night was over and that they could go home soon too.

I felt the same.

The soft silk of my dress brushed against my skin as I adjusted the skirt a bit higher so that I could walk more freely. My feet ached from hours of standing and dancing, and I couldn't wait to sit down and tell Nikolaos all about the night.

He was going to be so proud of me.

Stepping towards the grand entrance, the click of my heels on the marble floor seemed to echo in the emptying space. I walked outside, the crisp night air hitting me and the doors closing behind me with a soft, final sound.

As I stepped out into the cool night, a shiver ran through me, but it wasn't just from the cool breeze. The moon bathed the deserted red carpet in its pale light, creating long, eerie shadows that seemed to circle around me like a wolf on the prowl. The paparazzi and the reporters had long since left, as had the security staff manning the doors.

It was eerily quiet.

I swallowed hard, the sound of my heart pounding loud in my ears.

Something still felt off, and as I hesitated, scanning the area for any sign of life, I realized how alone I was.

Suddenly, I felt a firm grip on my shoulder, pulling me back, and then there was a hand roughly clamping over my mouth from behind. A wave of panic washed over me as my heart pounded in my ears. I struggled, but the grip only tightened, an iron band of restraint that refused to let me go no matter how hard I fought.

Fuck. What was happening?

Then, a familiar voice hissed in my ear, a voice that haunted my nightmares, "Hello again, Maci."

I knew that voice.

It was Alexander Pappas.

My body went rigid with fear, memories of the kidnapping flooding back in a terrifying rush. His presence, so close and menacing, sent a chill down my spine. I remembered this feeling of helplessness, the dread that filled me when he had taken me before.

I'd vowed that I'd never be so helpless again.

"Shh," he whispered menacingly, as if reading my panic. "No one can hear you. No one will come."

I tried to speak, to scream, but his hand muffled any sound I could make. My mind raced, searching for a way out, but I was trapped in his grasp. I struggled hard for a minute, but he was so much bigger and stronger than me.

Fuck. This is bad.

His other hand tightened around my arm, and he started to drag me away from the light of the red carpet and into the shadows.

As we moved further into the darkness, I prepared myself for the struggle I knew was coming. Alexander Pappas might have caught me off guard, but I was not the same person he had kidnapped before.

This time, I was ready to *fight*.

I snarled, twisting my body hard and almost breaking his grasp.

Then footsteps approached, and two other figures materialized from the darkness, their forms cloaked in the night, and I stilled. The two men were huge. He must have brought them along as his muscle, and I snarled again, unwilling to go down without a struggle.

I was outnumbered now. I might have had a chance fighting against Alexander on his own, but now that it was three to one, my chances were growing slimmer by the second.

"Need a hand, Alex?" one of them jeered, a smirk evident in his tone. His voice grated on my nerves. He leered at me as he grew closer, his gaze settling on my breasts as they heaved up and down from the exertion of fighting Alexander off.

I wanted to rip his eyes straight out of his skull.

"Just keep a lookout," Alexander growled in response, his attention still firmly on me.

"Where are you taking me, Alexander?" I asked, my voice trembling slightly but loud enough for all of them to hear.

"To a place where we can talk without interruptions," he replied, his voice cold and devoid of emotion.

I hated him.

The second man chuckled. "Yeah, a nice, quiet *chat*. That's all."

I didn't like the insinuation in his tone.

"I just want to understand why you're doing this," I said, stalling for time as my fingers fumbled with the clasp of my clutch bag.

Their malignant laughter filled the air, a sound that made my skin crawl, but it provided the perfect cover for me. With a quick movement, I opened my clutch and wrapped my fingers around the small gun that Nikolaos had insisted I take to protect myself tonight. I had thought it was a bit over the top, but I couldn't be more thankful for it now.

Before they could react, I pulled the gun out and pressed it directly to Alexander' skull. The laughter died abruptly, replaced by a tense silence.

"Let go of me, Alexander," I said firmly, the gun unwavering in my hand. "I'm not going anywhere with you."

For a moment, the two of us were at a standoff, the night air thick with tension. Then, slowly, he released his grip on me, raising his hands in a gesture of surrender. The two men stepped back, their eyes fixed on the gun in my hand.

"Seems like our little bird has talons," the first man said, a note of respect in his voice.

"Maybe we need to clip her wings," the other one snarled.

"Don't take one step farther. I'm not afraid to use this," I threatened.

They didn't listen.

Like they were invincible, the two men lunged at me simultaneously, their movements too swift and far too desperate. As they moved closer, I recognized them as the two men that had kept me captive. They had underestimated me once; I wasn't going to let them do it again.

Reacting instinctively, I squeezed the trigger.

The sound of the gunshots shattered the night, two sharp reports that echoed off the surrounding buildings.

In an instant, their whole world changed.

The first man staggered back, a look of shock and pain crossing his face as he fell to the ground, clutching at the blood pouring from the gunshot to his throat. The second, hit square between the eyes, stood there looking forlorn for a long moment before he collapsed with a loud thud.

For a few seconds, everything stood still.

Alexander sprang into action. He was on me in an instant, his hand seizing my wrist with a vice-like grip. He twisted hard, and the pain was immediate and intense, shooting all the way up my arm and making me cry out. I couldn't hold onto the gun, and it clattered to the ground, slipping out of my reach.

Fuck.

"You shouldn't have done that, Maci," Alexander hissed, his face inches from mine, his grip unrelenting. "Now I'm going to have to make you pay for that."

Pain coursed through my wrist, but I refused to show him any semblance of fear. "You shouldn't have underestimated me," I retorted, meeting his gaze with open rebelliousness.

I would stand my ground, no matter what.

Alexander's grip on my wrist was unyielding as he dragged me into a nearby alley, away from the street and any potential witnesses. The darkness of the alley felt suffocating, the cold night air closing in around me. Unmercifully, he pushed me against the cold, rough wall of the venue, his body an immovable barrier between me and any hope of escape.

"You're going to regret killing my men," he snarled, his face inches from mine, his breath hot against my skin.

I tried to push back against his chest, but his strength was overwhelming. "Let me go and I won't tell anyone about this," I spat back, trying to mask my fear with defiance.

Alexander's eyes narrowed, a cruel smile playing on his lips. "Oh, Maci, you still don't understand, do you? This isn't just about you. This is about the men that your fiancé killed, my men. The guns we planted didn't really have our intended effect, but what happens next is going to be a message, special just for *him.*"

"And what message is that?" I demanded, struggling to keep my voice steady.

"That no one defies the Pappas family. That anyone who tries will be dealt with... harshly. That nothing he owns is safe from us, even you," he replied, his grip tightening.

I could feel the cold wall pressing against my back, the hard reality of the situation setting in. Fear twisted in my stomach, but I refused to let it consume me. I needed to keep a level head, and that was exactly what I was going to do.

"So, what now? You're going to kill me?" I challenged, trying to find a crack in his resolve.

Alexander leaned in closer, his voice a menacing whisper. "Killing you would be too easy, Maci. No, I have something else in mind for you."

His words sent a chill down my spine, but I refused to cower. "You won't get away with this, Alexander. Nikolaos knows that I'm here. He'll come looking for me."

He chuckled darkly. "By the time he starts looking, it will be too late."

He suddenly spun me around, pushing me against the wall with a force that knocked the breath from my lungs. His hand pressed against my back, pinning my breasts firmly against the cold, unyielding surface. The rough texture of the brick wall scraped against my skin through the fabric of my dress.

Fuck.

He planted his other hand next to my head, effectively caging me in. I could feel his breath on the back of my neck, and I had to force myself to swallow back the bile in the back of my throat.

I tried to push back against him, to find some leverage, but it was futile. His strength was overwhelming, and in that moment, I felt the full weight of my vulnerability.

I'm not going to fight my way out of this.

His hand reached down, fumbling with the fabric of my dress as he dragged it up, revealing the backs of my calves, then my knees, and then my thighs, all the way up until the chill air of the night caressed my bare ass. His hand gripped my right bottom cheek, and I shrieked.

He's going to rape me.

The sound of another man clearing his throat in the alley broke through the quiet, and I turned my head. In an instant, a wave of relief crashed over me.

He came for me.

"Nikolaos," I breathed.

In an instant, I knew I was safe.

"No one lays a hand on my wife and gets away with it," Nikolaos stated, his voice low and dangerous. He stepped forward, an unspoken threat in his every move. "Now I have no choice but to kill you."

Alexander's face fell, and he turned his head, momentarily caught off guard.

It was as if the entire world had gone still in that single moment.

Without hesitation, Nikolaos drew his gun with a swift, practiced motion. The sound of the gunshot shattered the silence of the alley, resounding like a harsh verdict in the middle of a courtroom. His bullet hit its mark with deadly precision, right in between Alexander's eyes, and in an instant, blood splashed across the cold alleyway, some droplets splattering against my cheek and down the length of my dress.

Alexander's body jerked from the impact. Then, as if in slow motion, he collapsed to the ground behind me in a heap. I finally pulled in a breath and stepped away from the wall, pressing my hand to my chest.

Nikolaos turned to me, his expression softening slightly. "Are you alright?" he asked, his voice now laced with concern.

I straightened up, lifting my chin and adjusting my dress back into place, a mixture of relief and lingering adrenaline coursing through me. "When you play the game of thrones, you win or you die," I replied, my voice tinged with a mix of sarcasm and gratitude.

"There's my queen," he smirked.

CHAPTER 28

 *ight weeks later*
Maci

The wedding had been a day to remember.

As I walked down the aisle, adorned in an exquisite Elie Saab gown with its delicate lacework and elegantly trailing train, I felt impossibly regal, transcending from mere princess to queen with every step.

The venue bloomed with vibrant golden yellows and rich oranges, adorned with sunflowers and marigolds that radiated warmth and joy. The atmosphere was inviting and lively, a perfect backdrop for our special day.

Our reception had been like stepping into a fairytale, surpassing even the grandest charity balls I had attended. Held in a hall that was the epitome of elegance and class, the setting was nothing short of magical.

The culinary offerings, prepared by a renowned Michelin-starred chef, were an absolute delight. We indulged in luxurious lobster thermidor, risotto tinged with the subtle earthiness of truffles, and a dessert spread that was a feast for the senses. The highlight was a towering chocolate fountain, surrounded by an irresistible array of macarons and petit fours.

Adding to the enchantment had been the live orchestra, their melodies weaving a spellbinding aura throughout the evening. The climax was a spectacular firework display, illuminating the night sky in a kaleidoscope of colors, marking our wedding not just as an event, but as an extraordinary, once-in-a-lifetime event.

It was hard to imagine that it had only been yesterday. With a lazy smile, I leaned against the railing of the balcony and looked out, the soft waves of the ocean breaking on the sand only about a dozen feet away. The morning sun glistened on the water, creating a shimmering pathway that seemed to lead to the horizon. The coastline was adorned with a mix of rugged cliffs and gentle slopes, dotted with lush greenery that added vibrant splashes of color to the landscape.

The sound of the television in the background broke the tranquility, and I turned around, listening to the sounds of a newscaster trailing off details about one news story after another until one in particular caught my attention.

"In breaking news, the Pappas family, a prominent name in Greek business circles, has been arrested on charges of human trafficking, ties to organized crime, as well as the act of terrorism in the bombing of the Stefanidis shipping fleet. This major crackdown follows the recent shocking discovery of Alexander Pappas' body,

further intensifying the investigation. His father, Ioannis Pappas, is among those arrested. The family, influential in various sectors, now face a series of grave allegations. The arrest and the link to Alexander's death have sent shockwaves through the business community. Questions are being raised about their alleged criminal activities. Stay with us for more updates on this developing story."

Nikolaos strode out to the balcony and wound his hands around my waist, pulling me against him.

"It would seem *our* plan worked," he murmured.

"That it would seem," I agreed, leaning back against him. "Though, I must say, it was mostly my brilliant strategy that made it happen."

He chuckled, a low sound that vibrated through me. "Oh, really? I seem to recall it being more of a joint effort, my queen."

I turned in his arms, facing him with a playful smirk. "Well, maybe a tiny bit, but you have to admit, I was the mastermind."

Nikolaos raised an eyebrow, amusement in his eyes. "Is that so? I guess I should just leave all our future plans to you then."

"Maybe you should," I teased.

Nikolaos leaned in closer, his breath warm against my ear. "The Secretary-General mentioned you claimed it was all your idea," he whispered with a hint of playfulness and intrigue in his voice. "But let's not forget who's in charge here."

A shiver raced down my spine.

"It's me, isn't it?" I taunted, my voice breathy and soft, knowing full well what I was doing.

With a growl, he pulled me in for a kiss. It started off gently at first, but I could sense the underlying intensity in the way his lips sought out mine. His hand found the back of my scalp, gripping my hair just firmly enough to send a shiver of delight down my spine.

The kiss deepened, our tongues intertwining and spiraling together. He stole my breath, and I stole his, both of us trying to assert dominance over the other even though I knew who was going to eventually win.

Even though I know it isn't going to be me.

Then he lightly nipped my lip hard enough to hurt, a teasing yet assertive gesture that left no doubt in my mind that this was simply the start of something much more intense.

"I think, naughty girl, that you haven't been over my knee in quite some time," he purred, and my legs nearly gave out beneath me.

I grinned, knowing my teasing would eventually instigate something exactly like this.

His hands drew down the length of my body until they eventually settled on the tie around my waist. I was wearing only a robe, so it was easy for him to yank it open and strip me bare right there on the balcony.

My cheeks burned red hot, knowing anyone could walk by on the beach and they'd see me naked. I knew the possibility was slim because Nikolaos had booked out the entire hotel for the length of our stay. He told me it was simply because he wanted the waitstaff focused solely on us, but I knew it was because he planned to fuck me whenever and wherever he pleased, and he didn't want anyone else to see what belonged to him.

I didn't hate the idea... In fact, my pussy quite liked it.

Without another word, he grasped my wrist and pulled me into the extravagant suite. The large, plush bed was draped in sumptuous linens and decorative pillows. Floor-to-ceiling windows offered a breathtaking view of the sea, adding to the suite's grandeur. The sight of it still took my breath away, but I was quickly distracted as he led me towards the bed. With a definitive push, he bent me over it and then his hands were all over me.

"You make such a beautiful queen, my sweet girl. I'm so proud of you," he murmured, and a rush of joy flitted through me like a rolling wave. His hand ran up and down my back, soft and fluttering, until he reached up, gripped my hair, and wrenched me off the bed.

"But every queen needs her king, doesn't she?"

"Yes, sir," I breathed, pain splintering across the back of my skull as liquid arousal pooled between my thighs. Instinctively, I pressed my thighs together, trying to hide my nakedness, but in an instant, his hand was between them, stroking my wet slit and very lightly teasing my clit.

"You need this reminder, don't you?"

His fingers danced over my needy bundle of nerves, and words escaped me, but they weren't needed.

He knew what my answer was before he even asked the question.

I shuddered with desire as he pulled his hand away, my body inadvertently moving as if I was seeking out his touch. My hips rolled and my back arched, only for him to smack the right side of my ass hard enough to sting.

The unexpectedness of it took my breath away far more than the pain. He slapped my left side, then the right, falling into a steady cadence that soon had me kicking and squirming beneath him.

His palm bit into my upper thighs, and I cried out, only for his hand to press down in the center of my back, pinning me to the bed just as I pushed my hands down against it.

I fought.

He won.

I *liked* it when he overpowered me. It made my pussy even wetter.

So, I fought harder. With incredible ease, he captured my wrists behind my back and used his feet to spread my legs open wide, exposing me completely to his view. His hand reached down between my thighs, and then he slapped my pussy hard enough to make me cry out.

"Naughty, naughty girl," he growled.

The sound rolled down my spine like a drop of water. My breath hitched in the back of my throat, and my pussy clenched hard as I imagined what he might do and realizing I didn't know, which only made my arousal spin that much higher.

Nikolaos had a way of always keeping me on my toes.

He spanked my pussy again, and a delicious stinging volley of pain barreled through me like a stampede of wild horses. I cried out, but he only rewarded me with another firm slap between my thighs before he leaned over me and kissed along the line of my shoulder.

He bit down and I keened, overwhelmed by the deep burn, but impossibly turned on at the same time. I squeezed my eyes shut, struggling to take it at the same time that I wanted more.

With a firm hold on the back of my neck, he dragged his lips down the length of my spine until he bit down on my bottom cheek much harder than he had my shoulder.

For a moment, panic spiraled through me, and my legs began to tremble, but then he let go and a glorious wave of pleasure followed. I thought it might just be a fluke, but when he did it again, the wave was much stronger this time.

If his hands had been between my thighs, I would have come.

"Please," I begged.

"What do you need?" he murmured, his voice soft and seductive.

"I need you," I whined.

"You're going to need to be much more specific than that, my beautiful queen," he chided, and I rose up on my tiptoes as he slid the flats of his fingers over my pussy. He slapped it lightly enough to make me flinch, but I was too turned on to really feel the sting at all.

When I didn't reply right away, he bit me again, once more on each cheek and much more firmly than he had the first time. I gasped for breath, the agony overwhelming until he let go at long last. My clit pulsed so hard that I would have fallen had I been standing up.

"I need your cock," I finally wailed, and he made a soft grunt of approval.

"That's my good girl," he praised, and a shiver of desire raced down my spine straight to my pussy. Molten passion simmered between my thighs, and I wanted nothing more than to come with all of him inside me.

"Please," I pleaded.

"Not yet, my queen," he murmured, and my hackles raised with suspicion.

What was he up to? Hadn't he teased me enough already?

It turned out, the answer was *no*.

His fingers flitted between my thighs, teasing me endlessly to the edge of orgasm and then back again. Time after time, he drove me straight to the precipice and pulled back, causing a piercing cut of denial to ricochet throughout my body, and I cried out. Before long, the teasing and the denial became far more painful than either the spanking or his bites.

Soon my legs were trembling, and I was on the edge of tears.

I began to *beg*.

"Please. I can't stand it. Oh please. I can't take it, sir," I pleaded. My voice quivered with the passionate need coursing through me. I pushed up onto my tiptoes, trying to show him how impossibly needy I felt, and I whimpered with my aroused shame as a droplet of my wetness rolled down my inner thigh all the way to my knee.

I wondered if he'd seen it. I hoped he had.

"I'm going to give you my cock, my needy little queen, but you're not going to come for me until you beg me for something else," he began, and a shiver of fear raced through me.

"Sir?"

What could he possibly have planned for me?

I hummed with nervousness as he circled my clit, making my eyes roll back in my head as I suffered for him.

"If you want to come for me, you're going to beg me to fuck this pretty little ass."

I started. He'd teased my bottom hole before, and I'd fought against him, making it hurt more than I knew it should. In response, my muscles clenched tight just as he sunk his fingers inside my pussy. I tried to fight back as those same digits slid up the cleft of my ass, but he held me firmly in place, and his fingers settled over my very reluctant hole. I tried to squeeze my bottom cheeks together, but he kicked my legs apart a bit wider and it soon became impossible.

"I've looked at this pretty little hole many times, my queen, imagining just how it's going to feel when I slide my cock inside it," he said darkly, and then he pushed one finger inside me. I yelped, the burning stretch almost more than I could bear. My muscles spasmed hard, and I was there at the edge of orgasm once again before I realized what was happening.

No.

I couldn't be getting off on this.

It would be too shameful, too wicked, too taboo...

Too fucking good.

Before I could react, he'd pressed another finger into my asshole, using my own copious arousal as lubricant. Slowly, he slid them in and out of my bottom before he released his hold on my wrist and unbuckled his belt. I looked over my shoulder as he pulled it free with a flourish, flinching at the swishing sound it made as the image of it cracking across my bare cheeks flashed before my eyes.

The foreign feeling of his fingers fucking my bottom was almost too much to bear, but then the head of his cock brushed against my entrance, and my whole world suddenly centered on what was happening between my thighs.

Just as he added a third finger, he plunged his cock inside my pussy with a single, savage thrust. He sank in all the way to the hilt. I expected him to start fucking me, but he remained still as my body struggled to accept both his cock in my pussy and his thick digits inside my ass.

My fingers gripped the luxurious linen duvet beneath me, and I arched up, suffering through every moment of blazing hot agony as my body rushed to accommodate being so full.

Maybe I could trick him into just fucking me like this. I clenched my pussy around his cock, and he growled in appreciation, but he didn't start moving yet. Instead, he just held his hips flush against mine and continued to pump his fingers in and out of my asshole.

My body burned. My asshole ached.

"If you want to come for me, my queen, you're going to do it with your king's cock in your tight little ass," he reminded me, and I wailed.

Slowly, he pulled his cock free and slid it back home. Over and over again, he drew it out, teasing and taunting me with pleasure just beyond reach as he fucked my ass with his thick fingers.

When the pain finally faded, it started to feel good.

Really fucking good.

Like so good that I wanted to come.

He didn't let me.

Instead, he just teased me with it, drawing me just to the edge and then pulling back until my every nerve was quivering with it, ready to fire at any given moment.

"*Please*," I begged.

"You know what needs to happen, my needy little queen," he purred, and the wickedness of his words shot straight to my clit.

"Not there," I pleaded.

"The longer you wait, the less gentle I'm going to be with that tight virgin hole," he warned, and just to prove his point, he thrust his fingers inside me roughly enough for a sharp stab of pain to radiate through me. I drew my lip in between my teeth, nibbling at it as I struggled with both my need and my shame.

"Sir," I breathed.

"Every inch of this beautiful body is mine, my queen, including this beautiful little hole. Mine to take. Mine to punish. Mine to fuck," he said, his voice husky, and my inner walls tightened around him.

"Please sir," I tried one last time, and he cleared his throat, the sound menacing to my ears as he pulled his fingers free from my asshole. Using his hand, he spread my cheeks open wide, exposing me to his view in the most salacious and vulnerable way I could have ever imagined.

He slowly thrust inside my pussy, and I whimpered, my need growing far too intense to push aside any longer.

"Be a good girl and beg me to fuck this tight little ass before I decide I'm just going to take it with nothing more than your own arousal slickening my cock."

Oh my god. Even though I'd never been fucked that way, I knew instinctively that would hurt far more. I didn't want that. I just wanted to come. *Hard.*

"Please fuck my ass," I finally whispered, hardly even aware the words were slipping free from my lips before I could stop them.

"Good girl," he growled, and then suddenly he pulled his cock free from my pussy. He reached over me and grabbed something off the nightstand, and I only just realized it was lubricant before it was squirting on top of my poor little hole. I blushed as he stroked his own cock, knowing exactly where it was going very, very soon.

When the slickened tip pressed against my asshole, I tensed. He didn't let that stop him, though, as his hands wound around my hips and he pushed forward, stretching my tight hole around the wide girth of his cock without mercy.

Pain billowed through me as I cried out and tried to crawl away from him, but he held me in place as he slowly sunk one inch and then two inside me. When his hips finally pressed flush against my ass, a deep, delicious agony was sizzling through me with savage abandon. As much as I tried to relax, that was easier said than done. Wave after wave of burning pain radiated around my asshole, but eventually each wave began to lessen.

Soon the only thing left was rampant desire.

"You're my queen, aren't you?"

"Yes, sir," I breathed.

"But it's your king that fucks this pretty little bottom, isn't it?"

"Yes, sir," I whimpered. This was too much, but still, it wasn't enough. I needed more and he knew it.

"Are you ready to come for me?"

"Oh god, please," I begged, my voice shaking with my need.

His fingers dug into my hips as he pulled his cock out and slammed it back inside. A fresh wave of pain washed over me, and I cried out, but he didn't slow down.

He *fucked* my ass, and he fucked it *hard.*

Before I knew what was happening, my muscles were seizing, and then I was coming apart at the seams. White hot bliss burned through me, taking me prisoner, and not letting go. Wildfire sizzled down the length of my limbs.

Breathless, I clutched at the duvet, holding on for dear life as he took my virgin hole as hard as he *wanted* and as hard as I *needed.*

I shattered so hard that my head flew up into the stars.

Wave after wave of sizzling ecstasy burned through my limbs. My toes curled and my back arched as I took him deeper in my ass before I knew what I was doing.

"That's it, my queen. Come hard for your king," he demanded.

I did. I came so hard that I screamed.

His cock plunged into me, over and over again as he fucked me. Without warning, he jerked my hips backwards and slid his hand underneath me, finding my needy little clit in an instant.

"You're going to break for me while I fuck this virgin ass. I'm not going to stop until there's pretty little tears trailing down your cheeks, because those are mine too," he demanded.

I clawed at the bed, but that didn't save me.

With every thrust, my asshole ached, but with his fingers between my thighs, I was already coming again before I could even think to stop it.

Blazing fire rolled through me, wave after wave of it, until my entire body was quivering. Pain and pleasure began to intermingle, and then my climax took me by storm.

I screamed as I lost control, again and again until my eyes watered, and then I was sobbing, giving him exactly what he wanted without even meaning to. He took my surrender by force, and even as tears trailed down my cheeks, I couldn't stop coming.

"Who do you belong to?" he demanded.

"You," I wailed.

"And this beautiful little body?"

"You," I cried.

"And this tight little asshole?"

"You, my king!"

"Then come for me, one last time, my very good girl," he demanded.

I did. I came so hard that I broke into a million little pieces.

Just like I was supposed to.

Because as much as I wanted to be his queen, I wanted something more.

I wanted him to be *my king.*

Don't want it to be over? Need more?

Join my newsletter for an exclusive scene where Nikolaos surprises Maci with a trip to Santorini where the wine flows freely and he reminds her what it means to belong to him with a tasting of another kind...

https://BookHip.com/JZLLSQG

AFTERWORD

Stormy Night Publications would like to thank you for your interest in our books.

If you liked this book (or even if you didn't), we would really appreciate you leaving a review on the site where you purchased it. Reviews provide useful feedback for us and our authors, and this feedback (both positive comments and constructive criticism) allows us to work even harder to make sure we provide the content our customers want to read.

If you would like to check out more books from Stormy Night Publications, if you want to learn more about our company, or if you would like to join our mailing list, please visit our website at:

http://www.stormynightpublications.com

ABOUT SARA FIELDS

Do you want to read a FREE book?

Sign up for Sara's newsletter and get a FREE copy of Sold to the Enemy!

https://www.sarafieldsromance.com/newsletter

About Sara Fields

Sara is a USA Today bestselling romance author with a proclivity for dirty things, especially those centered in DARK, FANTASY, and ROMANCE. If you like science fiction, fantasy, reverse harem, menage, pet play and other kinky filthy things, all complete with happily-ever-afters, then you will enjoy her books.

Email: otkdesire@gmail.com

Break Me, Daddy

When Shane Kavanagh waltzed into the Murphy pub as if he owned the place, what set my heart racing wasn't his brash arrogance, his obnoxiously gorgeous eyes, or his scoldy yet sexy tone. It wasn't even him promising to spank me and then ravage me the way no man has ever dared.

It was how he made me feel like a naughty little girl and a blushing virgin when I'm neither.

I'm the daughter of a powerful Irish mafia family and he's the boss of a rival organization, but when he rides me with his belt tight around my throat it doesn't make me want to call a hitman.

It makes me want to call him daddy.

Watch Me, Daddy

When I threw Irina Morozov over my shoulder and carried her off, it was to rescue her from a brutal bastard who didn't deserve her... but I could smell her arousal as she kicked and fought.

She would have been wet and ready for me that night, but I didn't take her. I made her wait.

I made her beg.

When I pin her to the bed, rip her panties off, and claim her virgin body the way it was always meant to be claimed, she won't just be screaming my name with every desperate climax.

She'll be calling me daddy.

Share Me, Daddy

Connor Murphy was the perfect husband for a bratva kingpin's daughter. An Irish mafia boss I could marry to secure an alliance between our families. It was all supposed to be so simple...

But then our wedding was attacked and I ended up on the run with his brother Caden.

Now I'm caught between two men, and I can't tell which way is what.

Not when Caden takes me over his knee, and definitely not when Connor bends me over and bares my bright red ass with his brother watching before making me come so hard I pass out.

But the most shameful part isn't them spanking me, or sharing me, or even them making me beg before they claim me both at once, filling me completely while I writhe and scream and climax.

It's calling them both daddy while they do all of that.

BOOKS OF THE KEPT AS HIS SERIES

Mine to Keep

I can still remember the moment I first heard Cyrus Holt's deep, commanding voice.

I didn't know who he was or about the life he'd left behind. I was just a trembling orphan on the run from a monster, and he was the man offering me shelter and not giving me a choice about it.

This boss of bosses didn't assign someone else to watch over me. He slept on the floor next to my bed when I woke up scared, then spanked me like a naughty little girl when I lied to him.

He could have claimed me that night, ravaging me without mercy or remorse.

But he didn't.

He made me beg for it first.

Because he didn't just want me as his for a night. He wanted me as his to keep.

Mine to Hold

Baby girl.

The man whispering those words in my ear isn't just a powerful mob boss. He's the brute who stripped me bare, whipped me with his belt, and claimed my virgin body roughly and shamefully in front of his men as I screamed and begged and came for him until I collapsed in his arms.

I should hate it when he calls me that.

But all I do is blush as I wait for him to make me his all over again.

Because I'm his to hold.

Forever.

Mine to Take

After escaping both my father's plans to marry me off and the Russian mafia, I woke up this morning thinking I was a free woman... until I saw the man sipping coffee in my hotel room.

He's a billionaire as powerful as any mob boss, yet even as he spanks me into soaking wet, shameful surrender I can't help begging him to ravage my virgin body right then and there.

I can run, but I know soon I'll be kneeling at his feet, bare, blushing, and ready to be claimed.

Because I'm his to take.

MAFIA AND BILLIONAIRE ROMANCES
BY SARA FIELDS

Fear

She wasn't supposed to be there tonight. I took her because I had no other choice, but as I carried her from her home dripping wet and wearing nothing but a towel, I knew I would be keeping her.

I'm going to make her tell me everything I need to know. Then I'm going to make her mine.

She'll sob as my belt lashes her bottom and she'll scream as climax after savage climax is forced from her naked, quivering body, but there will be no mercy no matter how shamefully she begs.

She's not just going to learn to obey me. She's going to learn to fear me.

On Her Knees

Blaire Conrad isn't just the most popular girl at Stonewall Academy. She's a queen who reigns over her subjects with an iron fist. But she's made me an enemy, and I don't play by her rules.

I make the rules, and I punish my enemies.

She'll scream and beg as I strip her, spank her, and force one brutal climax after another from her beautiful little body, but before I'm done with her she'll beg me shamefully for so much more.

It's time for the king to teach his queen her place.

Boss

The moment Brooke Mikaels walked into my office, I knew she was mine. She needed my help and thought she could use her sweet little body to get it, but she learned a hard lesson instead.

I don't make deals with silly little girls. I spank them.

She'll get what she needs, but first she'll moan and beg and scream with each brutal climax as she takes everything I give her. She belongs to me now, and soon she'll know what that means.

His Majesty

Maximo Giovanni Santaro is a king. A real king, like in the old days. The kind I didn't know still existed. The kind who commands obedience and punishes any hint of defiance from his subjects.

His Majesty doesn't take no for an answer, and refusing his royal command has earned me not just a spanking that will leave me sobbing, but a lesson so utterly shameful that it will serve as an example for anyone else who might dare to disobey him. I will beg and plead as one brutal, screaming climax after another ravages my quivering body, but there will be no mercy for me.

He's not going to stop until he's taught me that my rightful place is at his feet, blushing and sore.

Pet

Even before Chloe Banks threw a drink in my face in front of a room full of powerful men who know better than to cross me, her fate was sealed. I had already decided to make her my pet.

I would have taught her to obey in the privacy of my penthouse, but her little stunt changed that.

My pet learned her place in public instead, blushing as she was bared, sobbing as she was spanked, and screaming as she was brought to one brutal, humiliating climax after another.

But she has so many more lessons to learn. Lessons more shameful than she can imagine.

She will plead for mercy as she is broken, but before long she will purr like a kitten.

Blush for Daddy

"Please spank me, Daddy. Please make it hurt."

Only a ruthless bastard would make an innocent virgin say those words when she came to him desperate for help, then savor every quiver of her voice as she begs for something so shameful.

I didn't even hesitate.

I made Keri Esposito's problems go away. Then I made her call me daddy.

The image of that little bottom bare over my lap was more than I could resist, and the thought of her kneeling naked at my feet to thank me properly afterwards left me as hard as I've ever been.

Maybe I'm a monster, but I saw the wet spot on her panties before I pulled them down.

She didn't come to my door just for the kind of help only a powerful billionaire could offer.

She came because she needed me to make her blush for daddy.

Reckoning

Dean Waterhouse was supposed to be a job. Get in. Get married. Take his money and get out.

But he came after me.

Now I'm bound to his bed, about to learn what happens to naughty girls who play games.

The man who put his ring on my finger was gentle. The man who tracked me down is not.

He's going to make me blush, beg, and scream for him.

Then he's going to make me call him daddy.

Bride

This morning I was a businesswoman with no plans to marry, but that didn't matter to him. He decided tonight was my wedding night, so it was. All he let me choose was the dress he would tear off me later.

When I told him I wanted him to be gentle, he laughed at me, then ripped off my panties.

I shouldn't have been wet. I shouldn't have moaned. But I was, and I did.

When he threw me on the bed, I told him I'd never be his no matter how he made me scream.

He just smiled. The kind of smile that said this was going to hurt and he was going to enjoy every moment of it. Then he bent down and whispered something in my ear that shook me to my core.

"You're already mine. You always have been."

Daddy's Property

As Cami Davis stands in front of me in her nightgown, cheeks blushing and voice quavering, I know what she's come to ask me even before she can muster the courage to speak the words.

Did I really mean what I said to her earlier tonight?

Would I really take her over my knee and spank her like a naughty little girl?

She's a nineteen-year-old orphan and I'm a billionaire with plans to run for mayor. I shouldn't even be thinking about pulling down her panties and turning that cute little bottom bright red, let alone bending her over the dining room table and claiming her roughly right then and there.

But the moment I found her squatting in my newly purchased estate I knew what I needed.

Her.

Calling me daddy.

The Count

Jasmina Harker is an innocent virgin, but it doesn't matter.

I want her.

No, I need her.

From the very first moment I laid eyes on her, I knew she was the one. I craved nothing more than to tear the clothes right off her and force one screaming climax after the next from her quivering body until she admits that she needs me too.

I may be the worst kind of monster, but she will still be mine.

Stolen Vows

The moment I saw Natasha Page standing at the altar, waiting for a fiancé whose lies had already cost him his life and put hers in danger, I knew she would be speaking her vows today after all.

To me.

I could have claimed her that night, ravaging her quivering virgin body as brutally as my lust demanded. But I made her beg before I tore off that beautiful dress and took what belongs to me.

Because I don't just want her vows. I want her heart.

BOOKS OF THE BONDED MATES SERIES

BY SARA FIELDS AND KOREY MAE JOHNSON

Mate

When the primal force that drives wolves to claim a mate takes hold, there is no fighting it.

The moment we felt the mate bond, Kaci had only one choice to make. Surrender to instinct and bear our pups like a good girl, or force us to chase her down, belt her ass, and breed her hard.

She chose hard, and she got it. Over and over again.

But the truth is she was ours long before we marked her.

BOOKS OF THE DRAGONBORNE KINGS SERIES

Dragon King

For centuries, every woman in my family has vanished on the night of her twenty-first birthday, then returned telling tales of being shamefully ravaged by a man who could turn into a dragon.

Tonight he came for me.

I fought, but he just tore off my clothes and spanked me until I was wet and ready for him.

The brute didn't take me right then and there. He made me beg for it first. But even before he marked me as his, I knew he wasn't going to send me home after he mounted and claimed me.

The dragon king is never going to let me go.

Because I'm his mate.

Ice King

When I snuck out of the house on my twenty-first birthday, I didn't expect to be struck by a bolt of lightning… or to wake up in a strange land and be saved from freezing to death by a dragon.

Then the beast shifted before my eyes into a man more regal than any king and hotter than dragon fire. A man who didn't hesitate to bare and spank me for daring to resist his rescue.

I knew in that moment not just that I would be his one day, but that I was his already.

The way he held me in his lap and caressed my burning bottom while my arousal soaked his massive thighs told me he knew it too, and that it was all he could do not to claim me right then.

But pain has left his heart as frozen as his realm, and it will take more than pure lust to melt it.

It will take the touch of his mate.

Feral King

When the king of this realm saw me bathing in a stream, he did his best to warn me. Keep my distance or the curse upon him would set his blood on fire and he would ravage me brutally.

I didn't, and he did.

But he did more than just pin me to the forest floor and mount me like a feral beast.

He made me his, and no matter how savagely he ruts me or how thoroughly he blisters my bare backside while trying to scare me away, I'll never stop being what I was always destined to be.

His mate.

BOOKS OF THE ALPHA BROTHERHOOD SERIES

Savage

I thought no alpha could tame me. I was wrong.

Many men have tried to master me, but never one like Aric. He is not just an alpha, he is a fearsome beast, and he means to take for himself what warriors and kings could not conquer.

I thought I could fight him, but his mere presence forced overwhelming, unimaginable need upon me and now it is too late. I'm about to go into heat, and what comes next will be truly shameful.

He's going to ravage me, ruthlessly laying claim to every single inch of me, and it's going to hurt. But no matter how desperately I plead as he wrenches one screaming climax after another from my helplessly willing body, he will not stop until I'm sore, spent, and marked as his.

It will be nothing short of savage.

Primal

I escaped the chains of a king. Now a far more fearsome brute has claimed me.

The Brotherhood gave him the right to breed me, but that is not why I am naked, wet, and sore.

My bottom bears the marks of his hard, punishing hand because I defied my alpha.

My body is slick with his seed and my own arousal because he took me anyway.

He didn't use me like a king enjoying a subject. He took me the way a beast claims his mate.

It was long, hard, and painfully intense, but it was much more than that.

It was primal.

Rough

I came here as a spy. I ended up as the king's property.

I was captured and locked in a dungeon, but it was only when I saw Magnar that I felt real fear.

He is a warrior and a king, but that is not why my virgin body quivers as I stand bare before him.

He is not merely an alpha. He is my alpha.

The one who will punish and master me.

The one who will claim and ravage me.

The one who will break me, but only after he's made me beg for it.

Wild

She's going to scream for me and I don't care who hears it.

I traveled to this city to disrupt the plans of the Brotherhood's enemies, not tame a defiant omega, but the moment Revna challenged me I knew punishing her would not be enough.

Despite her blushing protests, I'm going to bare her beautiful body and mark her quivering bottom with my belt, but she won't be truly put in her place until I put her flat on her back.

I'm her alpha and I will use her as I please.

Enigma

An alpha could not tame her. Now she will kneel before a god.

For endless ages I've kept this world in balance, and over the centuries countless women have writhed and screamed and climaxed beneath me. But I've never felt the need for a mate.

Until today. Until her.

When I touch her, she trembles.

When I mark her defiant little bottom with my belt, her bare thighs glisten with helpless arousal.

When she lies next to me blushing, sore, and spent, my lust for her only grows stronger.

The world be damned. I'm going to claim her for myself.

BOOKS OF THE OMEGABORN TRILOGY

Frenzy

Inside the walls I was a respected scientist. Out here I'm vulnerable, desperate, and soon to be at the mercy of the beasts and barbarians who rule these harsh lands. But that is not the worst of it.

When the suppressants that keep my shameful secret wear off, overwhelming, unimaginable need will take hold of me completely. I'm about to go into heat, and I know what comes next…

But I'm not the only one with instincts far beyond my control. Savage men roam this wilderness, driven by their very nature to claim a female like me more fiercely than I can imagine, paying no heed to my screams as one brutal climax after another is ripped from my helplessly willing body.

It won't be long now, and when the mating starts, it will be nothing short of a frenzy.

Frantic

Naked, bound, and helplessly on display, my arousal drips down my bare thighs and pools at my feet as the entire city watches, waiting for the inevitable. I'm going into heat, and they know it.

When the feral beasts who live outside the walls find me, they will show my virgin body no mercy. With my need growing more desperate by the second, I'm not sure I'll want them to…

By the time the brutes arrive to claim and ravage me, I'm going to be absolutely frantic.

Fever

I've led the Omegaborn for years, but the moment these brutes arrived from beyond the wall I knew everything was about to change. These beasts aren't here to take orders from me, they're here to take me the way I was meant to be taken, no matter how desperately I resist what I need.

Naked, punished, and sore, all I can do is scream out one savage, shameful climax after another as my body is claimed, used, and mastered. I'm about to learn what it means to be an omega...

BOOKS OF THE WOLF KINGS SERIES

Alpha King

I thought I could defy the most powerful mafia boss in the city, but as Lawson Clearwater rips off my nightgown and pins me to the bed I'm certain he can smell more than just my fear.

This beast isn't just here to punish me. He's here to mount me, rut me, and mark me as his.

Forever.

Alpha Boss

She came here to find her sister. Her mate found her instead.

When she blew off my offer to help rescue her sister, Natalia Kotova learned the hard way that defying an alpha shifter will get you spanked until you are sobbing, then mounted and rutted.

But she's not bound to my bed with her dress and panties in shreds and every hole sore just because she needed a shameful lesson in manners from the most powerful mob boss in the city.

She's here because she's my mate.

Alpha Brute

I knew Elijah Baumann was a brute before he ripped off my clothes and blistered my bare backside with his belt. I knew it even before he mounted and rutted me with that same belt pulled tight around my throat to hold me helplessly in place for every desperate, shattering climax.

It was the way he looked at me.

Not like he hoped he might have me one day. Like I already belonged to him.

Like I was his mate.

BOOKS OF THE VAKARRAN CAPTIVES SERIES

Conquered

I've lived in hiding since the Vakarrans arrived, helping my band of human survivors evade the aliens who now rule our world with an iron fist. But my luck ran out.

Captured by four of their fiercest warriors, I know what comes next. They'll make an example of me, to show how even the most defiant human can be broken, trained, and mastered.

I promise myself that I'll prove them wrong, that I'll never yield, even when I'm stripped bare, publicly shamed, and used in the most humiliating way possible.

But my body betrays me.

My will to resist falters as these brutes share me between the four of them and I can't help but wonder if soon, they will conquer my heart...

Mastered

First the Vakarrans took my home. Then they took my sister. Now, they have taken me.

As a prisoner of four of their fiercest warriors, I know what fate awaits me. Humans who dare to fight back the way I did are not just punished, they are taught their place in ways so shameful I shudder to think about them.

The four huge, intimidating alien brutes who took me captive are going to claim me in every way possible, using me more thoroughly than I can imagine. I despise them, yet as they force one savage, shattering climax after another from my naked, quivering body, I cannot help but wonder if soon I will beg for them to master me completely.

Ravaged

Though the aliens were the ones I always feared, it was my own kind who hurt me. Men took me captive, and it was four Vakarran warriors who saved me. But they don't plan to set me free...

I belong to them now, and they intend to make me theirs more thoroughly than I can imagine.

They are the enemy, and first I try to fight, then I try to run. But as they punish me, claim me, and share me between them, it isn't long before I am begging them to ravage me completely.

Subdued

The resistance sent them, but that's not really why these four battle-hardened Vakarrans are here.

They came for me. To conquer me. To master me. To ravage me. To strip me bare, punish me for the slightest hint of defiance, and use my quivering virgin body in ways far beyond anything in even the very darkest of my dreams, until I've been utterly, completely, and shamefully subdued.

I vow never to beg for mercy, but I can't help wondering how long it will be until I beg for more.

Abducted

When I left Earth behind to become a Celestial Mate, I was promised a perfect match. But four Vakarrans decided they wanted me, and Vakarrans don't ask for what they want, they take it.

These fearsome, savagely sexy alien warriors don't care what some computer program thinks would be best for me. They've claimed me as their mate, and soon they will claim my body.

I planned to resist, but after I was stripped bare and shamefully punished, they teased me until at last I pleaded for the climax I'd been so cruelly denied. When I broke, I broke completely. Now they are going to do absolutely anything they please with me, and I'm going to beg for all of it.

SCI-FI AND PARANORMAL ROMANCES
BY SARA FIELDS

Feral

He told me to stay away from him, that if I got too close he would not be able to stop himself. He would pin me down and take me so fiercely my throat would be sore from screaming before he finished wringing one savage, desperate climax after another from my helpless, quivering body.

Part of me was terrified, but another part needed to know if he would truly throw me to the ground, mount me, and rut me like a wild animal, longer and harder than any human ever could.

Now, as the feral beast flips me over to claim me even more shamefully when I've already been used more thoroughly than I imagined possible, I wonder if I should have listened to him…

Inferno

I thought I knew how to handle a man like him, but there are no men like him. Though he is a billionaire, when he desired me he did not try to buy me, and when he wanted me bared and bound he didn't call his bodyguards. He did it himself, even as I fought him, because he could.

He told me soon I would beg him to ravage me… and I did. But it wasn't the pain of his belt searing my naked backside that drove me to plead with him to use me so shamefully I might never stop blushing. I begged because my body knew its master, and it didn't give me a choice.

But my body is not all he plans to claim. He wants my mind and my soul too, and he will have them. He's going to take so much of me there will be nothing left. He's going to consume me.

Manhandled

Two hours ago, my ship reached the docks at Dryac.

An hour ago, a slaver tried to drag me into an alley.

Fifty-nine minutes ago, a beast of a man knocked him out cold.

Fifty-eight minutes ago, I told my rescuer to screw off, I could take care of myself.

Fifty-five minutes ago, I felt a thick leather belt on my bare backside for the first time.

Forty-five minutes ago, I started begging.

Thirty minutes ago, he bent me over a crate and claimed me in the most shameful way possible.

Twenty-nine minutes ago, I started screaming.

Twenty-five minutes ago, I climaxed with a crowd watching and my bottom sore inside and out.

Twenty-four minutes ago, I realized he was nowhere near done with me.

One minute ago, he finally decided I'd learned my lesson, for the moment at least.

As he leads me away, naked, well-punished, and very thoroughly used, he tells me I work for him now, I'll have to earn the privilege of clothing, and I'm his to enjoy as often as he pleases.

Marked

I know how to handle men who won't take no for an answer, but Silas isn't a man. He's a beast who takes what he wants, as long and hard and savagely as he pleases, and tonight he wants me.

He's not even pretending he's going to be gentle. He's going to ravage me, and it's going to hurt.

I'll be spanked into quivering submission and used thoroughly and shamefully, but even when the endless series of helpless, screaming climaxes is finally over, I won't just be sore and spent.

I will be marked.

My body will no longer be mine. It will be his to use, his to enjoy, and his to breed, and no matter how desperate my need might grow in his absence, it will respond to his touch alone.

Forever.

Prize

Exiled from Earth by a tyrannical government, I was meant to be sold for use on a distant world. But Vane doesn't buy things. When he wants something, he takes it, and I was no different.

This alien brute didn't just strip me, punish me, and claim me with his whole crew watching. He broke me, making me beg for mercy and then for far more shameful things. Perhaps he would've been gentle if I hadn't defied him in front of his men, but I doubt it. He's not the gentle type.

When he carried me aboard his ship naked, blushing, and sore, I thought I would be no more than a trophy to be shown off or a plaything to amuse him until he tired of me, but I was wrong.

He took me as a prize, but he's keeping me as his mate.

Alpha

I used to believe beasts like him were nothing but legends and folklore. Then he came for me.

He is no mere alpha wolf. He is the fearsome expression of the virility of the Earth itself, come into the world for the first time in centuries to claim a human female fated to be his mate.

That human female is me.

When I ran, he caught me. When I fought him, he punished me.

I begged for mercy, but mercy isn't what he has in mind for me.

He's going to force one brutal climax after another from my naked, quivering body until my throat is sore from screaming and he's not going to stop until he is certain I know I am his.

Then he's going to breed me.

Thirst

Cain came for me today. Even before he spoke his name his power all but drove me to my knees.

Power that can pin me against a wall with just a thought and hold me there as he slowly cuts my clothes from my quivering body, making sure I know he is enjoying every blushing moment.

Power that will punish me until I plead for mercy, tease and torment me until I beg for release, and then ravage me brutally over and over again until I'm utterly spent and shamefully broken.

Power that will claim me as his forever.

Alien Conqueror

He's going to take me the same way they took our planet. Without gentleness or remorse.

I dared to defy him, but as this alien brute rips my clothes off and mounts me with my bottom still burning from his punishing hand it is clear what is in store for me isn't mere vengeance.

It is conquest.

Soon I will know what it means to be utterly and shamefully broken, my helpless body ravaged and plundered in every way imaginable, and when he is done I won't just be sore and spent.

I will be his.

Guardian

After watching over this world for millennia, a girl wandering in the woods should have been of no interest to me. But the moment

I saw her bathing in a stream, I knew Emma was mine.

I kept myself from throwing her over a fallen tree and ravaging her… but only for a few hours.

If she had been obedient, I might have held instinct at bay a little longer. It was the scent of her helpless arousal as I reddened her bare bottom that tore away the last vestiges of my self-control.

But it would have made no difference in the end.

Sooner or later, she was always going to scream my name as I mounted and rutted her.

A beast must claim his mate.

Dark Beast

Many a blushing lass has screamed my name in bed over the long years I've walked this land, watching over humanity even after they turned their backs on me. But I've never claimed a mate.

Until Layna.

When I first set eyes on this beautiful creature she was fighting for her life against more men than I could count, and at that very moment I vowed to protect her… and to make her mine.

That is a promise I plan to keep, even if it means stripping her bare, marking her bottom with my belt, and forcing her to one heart-stopping climax after another until she surrenders completely.

I'm not just going to keep her safe. I'm going to keep her forever.

Blushing Bride

No man had taken a woman as his and his alone for centuries… and he hadn't even asked.

He'd just told her she was to be his bride, watched her blush at the shameful term, then fisted her hair and pulled her in for a brutal, possessive kiss the moment she opened her mouth to protest.

A kiss that made clear this wasn't up to her, and that even if it were they both knew she would choose to wear his ring, share his bed, and one day bear his children. A kiss that said she was his already, and there was so much more to come as he taught her what that meant in every way.

She climaxed then and there as his tongue claimed her mouth.

She didn't say yes, because she didn't need to. Her body said it for her.

Dragon King

For centuries, every woman in my family has vanished on the night of her twenty-first birthday, then returned telling tales of being shamefully ravaged by a man who could turn into a dragon.

Tonight he came for me.

I fought, but he just tore off my clothes and spanked me until I was wet and ready for him.

The brute didn't take me right then and there. He made me beg for it first. But even before he marked me as his, I knew he wasn't going to send me home after he mounted and claimed me.

The dragon king is never going to let me go.

Because I'm his mate.

The Wolf

I used to believe werewolves were no more than scary stories to be told around a campfire. Then one of them ripped off my clothes, marked me with his teeth, and claimed me like a wild beast.

I didn't just come for him. I came until I blacked out, screaming my surrender into the dark Las Vegas night, and when I woke up sore and spent I knew for certain what I'd only feared before.

Kane Lockhart is a monster. And I'm his mate.

BOOKS OF THE CAPTIVE BRIDES SERIES

Wedded to the Warriors

As an unauthorized third child, nineteen-year-old Aimee Harrington has spent her life avoiding discovery by government authorities, but her world comes crashing down around her after she is caught stealing a vehicle in an act of petulant rebellion. Within hours of her arrest, she is escorted onto a ship bound for a detention center in the far reaches of the solar system.

This facility is no ordinary prison, however. It is a training center for future brides, and once Aimee has been properly prepared, she will be intimately, shamefully examined and then sold to an alien male in need of a mate. Worse still, Aimee's defiant attitude quickly earns her the wrath of the strict warden, and to make an example of her, Aimee is offered as a wife not to a sophisticated gentleman but to three huge, fiercely dominant warriors of the planet Ollorin.

Though Ollorin males are considered savages on Earth, Aimee soon realizes that while her new mates will demand her obedience and will not hesitate to spank her soundly if her behavior warrants it, they will also cherish and protect her in a way she has never experienced before. But when the time comes for her men to master her completely, will she find herself begging for more as her beautiful body is claimed hard and thoroughly by all three of them at once?

Her Alien Doctors

After nineteen-year-old Jenny Monroe is caught stealing from the home of a powerful politician, she is sent to a special prison in deep space to be trained for her future role as an alien's bride.

Despite the public bare-bottom spanking she receives upon her arrival at the detention center, Jenny remains defiant, and before long she earns herself a trip to the notorious medical wing of the facility. Once there, Jenny quickly discovers that a sore bottom will now be the least of her worries, and soon enough she is naked, restrained, and shamefully on display as three stern, handsome alien doctors examine and correct her in the most humiliating ways imaginable.

The doctors are experts in the treatment of naughty young women, and as Jenny is brought ever closer to the edge of a shattering climax only to be denied again and again, she finds herself begging to be taken in any way they please. But will her captors be content to give Jenny up once her punishment is over, or will they decide to make her their own and master her completely?

Taming Their Pet

When the scheming of her father's political enemies makes it impossible to continue hiding the fact that she is an unauthorized third child, twenty-year-old Isabella Bedard is sent to a detainment facility in deep space where she will be prepared for her new life as an alien's bride.

Her situation is made far worse after some ill-advised mischief forces the strict warden to ensure that she is sold as quickly as possible, and before she knows it, Isabella is standing naked before two huge, roughly handsome alien men, helpless and utterly on display for their inspection. More disturbing still, the men make it clear that they are buying her not as a bride, but as a pet.

Zack and Noah have made a career of taming even the most headstrong of females, and they waste no time in teaching their new pet that her absolute obedience will be expected and even the slightest defiance will earn her a painful, embarrassing bare-bottom spanking, along with far more humiliating punishments if her behavior makes it necessary.

Over the coming weeks, Isabella is trained as a pony and as a kitten, and she learns what it means to fully surrender her body to the bold dominance of two men who will not hesitate to claim her in any way they please. But though she cannot deny her helpless arousal at being so thoroughly mastered, can she truly allow herself to fall in love with men who keep her as a pet?

Sold to the Beasts

As an unauthorized third child with parents who were more interested in their various criminal enterprises than they were in her, Michelle Carter is used to feeling unloved, but it still hurts when she is brought to another world as a bride for two men who turn out not to even want one.

After Roan and Dane lost the woman they loved, they swore there would never be anyone else, and when their closest friend purchases a beautiful human he hopes will become their wife, they reject the match. Though they are cursed to live as outcasts who shift into terrible beasts, they are not heartless, so they offer Michelle a place in their home alongside the other servants. She will have food, shelter, and all she needs, but discipline will be strict and their word will be law.

Michelle soon puts Roan and Dane to the test, and when she disobeys them her bottom is bared for a deeply humiliating public spanking. Despite her situation, the punishment leaves her shamefully aroused and longing for her new masters to make her theirs, and as the days pass they find that she has claimed a place in their hearts as well. But when the same enemy who took their first love threatens to tear Roan and Dane away from her, will Michele risk her life to intervene?

Mated to the Dragons

After she uncovers evidence of a treasonous conspiracy by the most powerful man on Earth, Jada Rivers ends up framed for a terrible crime, shipped off to a detention facility in deep space, and kept in solitary confinement until she can be sold as a bride. But the men who purchase her are no ordinary aliens. They are dragons, the kings of Draegira, and she will be their shared mate.

Bruddis and Draego are captivated by Jada, but before she can become their queen the beautiful, feisty little human will need to be publicly claimed, thoroughly trained, and put to the test in the most shameful manner imaginable. If she will not yield her body and her heart to them completely, the fire in their blood will burn out of control until it destroys the brotherly bond between them, putting their entire world at risk of a cataclysmic war.

Though Jada is shocked by the demands of her dragon kings, she is left helplessly aroused by their stern dominance. With her virgin body quivering with need, she cannot bring herself to resist as they take her hard and savagely in any way they please. But can she endure the trials before her and claim her place at their side, or will her stubborn defiance bring Draegira to ruin?

BOOKS OF THE TERRANOVUM BRIDES SERIES

A Gift for the King

For an ordinary twenty-two-year-old college student like Lana, the idea of being kidnapped from Earth by aliens would have sounded absurd… until the day it happened. As Lana quickly discovers, however, her abduction is not even the most alarming part of her situation. To her shock, she soon learns that she is to be stripped naked and sold as a slave to the highest bidder.

When she resists the intimate, deeply humiliating procedures necessary to prepare her for the auction, Lana merely earns herself a long, hard, bare-bottom spanking, but her passionate defiance catches the attention of her captor and results in a change in his plans. Instead of being sold, Lana will be given as a gift to Dante, the region's powerful king.

Dante makes it abundantly clear that he will expect absolute obedience and that any misbehavior will be dealt with sternly, yet in spite of everything Lana cannot help feeling safe and cared for in the handsome ruler's arms. Even when Dante's punishments leave her with flaming cheeks and a bottom sore from more than just a spanking, it only sets her desire for him burning hotter.

But though Dante's dominant lovemaking brings her pleasure beyond anything she ever imagined, Lana fears she may never be more than a plaything to him, and her fears soon lead to rebellion. When an escape attempt goes awry and she is captured by Dante's most dangerous enemy, she is left to wonder if her master cares for her enough to come to her rescue. Will the king risk everything to reclaim what is his, and if he does bring his human girl home safe and sound, can he find a way to teach Lana once and for all that she belongs to him completely?

A Gift for the Doctor

After allowing herself to be taken captive in order to save her friends, Morgana awakens to find herself naked, bound, and at the mercy of a handsome doctor named Kade. She cannot hide her helpless arousal as her captor takes his time thoroughly examining her bare body, but when she disobeys him she quickly discovers that defiance will earn her a sound spanking.

His stern chastisement and bold dominance awaken desires within her that she never knew existed, but Morgana is shocked when she learns the truth about Kade. As a powerful shifter and the alpha of his pack, he has been ordered by the evil lord who took Morgana prisoner to claim her and sire children with her in order to combine the strength of their two bloodlines.

Kade's true loyalties lie with the rebels seeking to overthrow the tyrant, however, and he has his own reasons for desiring Morgana as his mate. Though submitting to a dominant alpha does not come easily to a woman who was once her kingdom's most powerful sorceress, Kade's masterful lovemaking is unlike anything she has experienced before, and soon enough she is aching for his touch. But with civil war on the verge of engulfing the capital, will Morgana be torn from the arms of the man she loves or will she stand and fight at his side no matter the cost?

A Gift for the Commander

After she is rescued from a cruel tyrant and brought to the planet Terranovum, Olivia soon discovers that she is to be auctioned to the highest bidder. But before she can be sold, she must be trained, and the man who will train her is none other than the commander of the king's army.

Wes has tamed many human females, and when Olivia resists his efforts to bathe her in preparation for her initial inspection, he strips the beautiful, feisty girl bare and spanks her soundly. His stern chastisement leaves Olivia tearful and repentant yet undeniably aroused, and after the punishment she cannot resist begging for her new master's touch.

Once she has been examined Olivia's training begins in earnest, and Wes takes her to his bed to teach her what it means to belong to a dominant man. But try as he might, he cannot bring himself to see Olivia as just another slave. She touches his heart in a way he thought nothing could, and with each passing day he grows more certain that he must claim her as his own. But with war breaking out across Terranovum, can Wes protect both his world and his woman?

Claimed by the General

When Ayala intervenes to protect a fellow slave-girl from a cruel man's unwanted attentions, she catches the eye of the powerful general Lord Eiotan. Impressed with both her boldness and her beauty, the handsome warrior takes Ayala into his home and makes her his personal servant.

Though Eiotan promises that Ayala will be treated well, he makes it clear that he expects his orders to be followed and he warns her that any disobedience will be sternly punished. Lord Eiotan is a man of his word, and when Ayala misbehaves she quickly finds herself over his knee for a long, hard spanking on her bare bottom. Being punished in such a humiliating manner leaves her blushing, but it is her body's response to his chastisement which truly shames her.

Ayala does her best to ignore the intense desire his firm-handed dominance kindles within her, but when her new master takes her in his arms she cannot help longing for him to claim her, and when he makes her his own at last, his masterful lovemaking introduces her to heights of pleasure she never thought possible.

But as news of the arrival of an invader from across the sea reaches the city and a ruthless conqueror sets his eyes on Ayala, her entire world is thrown into turmoil. Will she be torn from Lord Eiotan's loving arms, or will the general do whatever it takes to keep her as his own?

Kept for Christmas

After Raina LeBlanc shows up for a meeting unprepared because she was watching naughty videos late at night instead of working, she finds herself in trouble with Dr. Eliot Knight, her stern, handsome boss. He makes it clear that she is in need of strict discipline, and soon she is lying over his knee for a painful, embarrassing bare-bottom spanking.

Though her helpless display of arousal during the punishment fills Raina with shame, she is both excited and comforted when Eliot takes her in his arms after it is over, and when he invites her to spend the upcoming Christmas holiday with him she happily agrees. But is she prepared to offer him the complete submission he demands?

The Warrior's Little Princess

Irena cannot remember who she is, where she came from, or how she ended up alone in a dark forest wearing only a nightgown, but none of that matters as much as the fact that the vile creatures holding her captive seem intent on having her for dinner. Fate intervenes, however, when a mysterious, handsome warrior arrives in the nick of time to save her.

Darrius has always known that one day he would be forced by the power within him to claim a woman, and after he rescues the beautiful, innocent Irena he decides to make her his own. But the feisty girl will require more than just the protection Darrius can offer. She will need both his gentle, loving care and his firm hand applied to her bare bottom whenever she is naughty.

Irena soon finds herself quivering with desire as Darrius masters her virgin body completely, and she delights in her new life as his little girl. But Darrius is much more than an ordinary sellsword, and being his wife will mean belonging to him utterly, to be taken hard and often in even the most shameful of ways. When the truth of her own identity is revealed at last, will she still choose to remain by his side?

Made in United States
Troutdale, OR
04/17/2024